WAIT TILL I TELL YOU

CANDIA McWILLIAM was born in Edinburgh. She is the author of *A Case of Knives* (1988), which won a Betty Trask Prize, *A Little Stranger* (1989), *Debatable Land* (1994), which was awarded the *Guardian* Fiction Prize and its Italian translation the Premio Grinzane Cavour for the best foreign novel of the year, and a collection of stories *Wait Till I Tell You* (1997). In 2006 she began to suffer from the effects of blepharospasm and became functionally blind as a result. In 2009 she underwent surgery that cut off her eyelids and harvested tendons from her leg to hold up what remained. Her most recent book is her critically-acclaimed memoir, *What to Look for in Winter: A Memoir in Blindness.*

BY THE SAME AUTHOR

A Case of Knives
A Little Stranger
Debatable Land
What to Look for in Winter: A Memoir in Blindness

WAIT TILL I TELL YOU

CANDIA McWILLIAM

B L O O M S B U R Y
LONDON • BERLIN • NEW YORK • SYDNEY

First published in Great Britain 1997
This paperback edition published 2011

Bloomsbury Publishing, London, Berlin, New York and Sydney

49–51 Bedford Square, London WC1B 3DP

A CIP catalogue record of this book is available from the British Library

ISBN 978 1 4088 2295 1
10 9 8 7 6 5 4 3 2 1

Typeset by Hewer Text UK Ltd, Edinburgh

Printed by Clays Limited, St Ives plc

www.bloomsbury.com/candiamcwilliam

To Rosa Beddington
and
Robin Denniston

CONTENTS

NORTH

Shredding the Icebergs

The hot days when the wasps came and trudged all over the scallops with their legs and feelers and the Fantas sold faster than the teas at the seafood stall; on such days I used to see these *types* congregating and I would ask myself where will the human race end? Looks like a contest between in the gutter singing glory and so neat you'd need to wear a headsquare to procreate.

I would think: where did these different kinds of souls get born and how do they hatch? Do they take one another in as they dither about, or do they walk right the way through each other like ghosts? It was my job to hand out the sustenance to these tribes, so that meant I was implicated, just like a keeper in the zoo handing over the bucket of sprats or peelings. It was my doing these folk got the energy to stand up, stick around, walk about the town, pull out their wallets in exchange for a few more items to lose, and struggle on to the boats without fainting from hunger on account of not having had a snack between after lunch coffee and early afternoon tea, or between that one last drink and the first of the evening.

These hot days were when the body paid for carrying on as if your skin could be forever hidden under wool. In this context, Scottish people come off particularly poorly. Unpeeled, we have a selection of looks, unless there's been a genetic accident and the body's holding up against the punishment. We're spare and sandy, or red and beety, or sweaty and soft with burning cheeks and meeting eyebrows, or blue-skinned blondes with the junkie posture who go old overnight at twenty-eight or the second baby. The men are redhaired or blackhaired and mostly wronghaired, sprouting at the shoulder blade or tailend or inner arm. I'm not complaining though. Duncan is a freak of nature and the kids take after him. They've all got his sweatless skin and black eyes, his white teeth and tidy form. They look like kids in a film made for childless adults. I look like a mother. What people have aye said about me is, 'It's a mercy she's nice eyes. Her eyes are nice.'

They're nothing like me at all, to look at, the kids. The wonder is that he took me and the answer is the usual one. He was tired of the success and the freedom. He never understood why he had been given them, did not know how to use them, and was relieved when they weren't there any more and I was there instead, keeping them off, success, freedom and the women, all the three.

We run the stall together and Joanne and Ian and Dougie help in the school holidays. Joanne's gone veg so she does not do cockles or whelks but she is neater at garnish than the boys and she washes up the crocks with the water out the tea urn faster than any of us.

In the cold, we keep a brazier outside the stall, and we've a plastic tent with stripes like a seaside one, where we get a bit of shelter from the wind. We tried selling the snacks right indoors, but it slumped. There was no spirit of adventure for the customers eating prawns in Marie Rose sauce off a clamshell in a shelter.

It's more of a sport, more of a holiday, to do it outside in the biting wind or salty rain. And on the hot days, though there are fewer of those, they swarm around the stall, but they won't go inside for fish, only drinks and ices, and even then they prefer to walk around with those. When they've finished, they leave their tins and cartons and implements right there, with less thought than a dog shitting. It's as if the wrappers and cans and wee wooden forks are as natural as leaves.

I'd go round, or Duncan would, with a big bin lined with a black liner, like someone collecting pennies after a Punch and Judy show. They'd all look baffled and turn to their friends or family in order to avoid our eyes. I never approached them till they were finished the tub of mussels or the ocean stix, and you'd think they'd welcome a place to put the rubbish, but they seem to need it to talk with, like a beast marking a place before feeling at home.

Occasionally you'd get one who was considerate. They'd pick a piece of debris off the ground, carry it carefully to the bin, drop it in with a little twitch of distaste, repeat the operation and then keep this up with ever smaller specks of rubbish till you looked up and thanked them, which was what they wanted, because then they could explain to you how much better it would be if you packed the whole operation up in cabbage leaves, or offered a fully automated rubbish chuting device such as they know a man who makes fine examples of not far out of town, it's a starter enterprise on a wee grant from the Board and he's heard we're not doing so bad how about a partnership with his friend, OK he won't be modest, it's the man himself standing right here on this spot my word but those shrimps were good and that pink sauce was unusual.

On the hot days the smells from the kitchens of the steamers that go out to the islands hang around this pier and the gulls don't bother to move off further than three feet away from the stall. Then we cut the lettuce into ribbons round the back and I sort it into clamshells ready for the fish when the orders come. We don't reckon to sell the sample dishes we put out the front under cling, so they're what the gulls get. In the sun the shellfish turns. It goes a grey pink and smells of primary school pants.

The sunset comes so late sometimes I'm counting shellfish into lettuce at eleven at night. The wasps are gone by then, but the cats come and lie right on your feet, buzzing with the assumption that all fish is theirs by law. Ian and Dougie shoogle them off their trainers, but Joanne and her dad slip them soused herring over the sell-by and the remains of milk crushes. In the stall it smells of vinegar and commercial strawberry and smoked fish. If there's shredded lettuce over, I bag it up and put it in the fridge for tomorrow, and any fish that won't stretch another day, I take it over to the bench on the esplanade where there's always someone been slowed down on their evening struggle home from the hotels. I can usually offer them a roll or two as well. They sit there shouting out intimate comments to the closed-up faces of Woolworths and the Royal Bank, standing up to attack the night from time to time till it beats them down to sleep.

We start at five in the morning, even after a hot day. In summer it's blue and you can hear the day beginning on the islands close-in, the doors opening, the outboards coming to life. Later the tractors start up, bringing the children down to the jetty to come over to school here on the mainland. The fishing boats are coming in after the night, their men making coffee. I watch the boats come in off the edge of the sea. There are mornings the water's flat and silver over beyond Lismore and the boats seem to tug the skyline in with them as they come, tight behind each boat in a V, till it's pulled so thin it melts away when the boat's alongside. I used to watch Duncan fretting these mornings and I'd fetch his tea and quiz him about it, is it sweet enough, would he be wanting more and so on.

This annoyed him but it kept him off the thoughts he'd been having. His brothers Tam and Gordon go out on the boats. They've part ownership of the *Hera*, out of Islay, and they make a living that can be good depending on the catch. They've a deal over the clams and crabs with a man runs a restaurant for rich tourists up at Port Appin. They would pour scorn on Duncan's and my booth and our prices to fit the pocket. Their wives shop in Glasgow for their clothes. Tam has a woman as well down by Dunstaffnage he'd buy the coats for and take out for meals while Moira bides in and gets her pound of flesh in the form of a car. At family occasions, their kids wouldn't mix with ours. They'd ask them the odd question so's it'd look normal, but the questions would be phrased like geography questions to remote tribespeople. It's like they'd never met kids before that didn't have the things they had. They couldn't rightly see people that weren't dressed the way they thought was right.

Duncan's and my kids carried on the rivalry, if you could call it that with only the one side competing, by looking like their father. Their cousins are all decked out in their loose, grubby-coloured gear with the words on it and the slobbering trainers with the tongues out, but the spots and tufts and bulges aren't away just because your shirt says Quiksilver Surfwear and cost three lobster dinners and a half of Smirnoff. And they scratch. They scratch in under these clothes and pull out from their body's crevices small finds they sook out from their nails with a sleepy look, or rind off on bits of paper, or ball up and flick without looking where they're going.

I anticipated no change but heaviness, no new life, in these young cousins of my children. These are the ones, I would think, will live as they do till they burst from heart or get shrunk by the cancer. It's a tussle which thing they take's going to get them first. Suffocation from the cigs, gagging from the takeouts, blootering into extinction from the drink, or the shove out into the morgue from one small pill or a final poison smoke. At least with our kids, I'd say to Duncan, there's the option of a climbing accident. Don't mind me, I just used to say these things.

The kids swore the other things are out of the question, though I would never be sure they'd played safe till I could see them certified pure on the autopsy table aged seventy-five, like all mothers of my sort, the anxious kind, the ones can't believe their luck.

In the snow, that comes more rarely to us here beside the sea than intheways a few miles and up by the Ben, the snacks we sell go in the deep frier Duncan and I bought for our twelfth anniversary from the mail order. It's a lid goes on over the squiggling fish pieces inside, you scoop it all out with a slotted spoon; dish it out on greaseproof and shake over the vinegar. Hand it out fast as you can fry it up and the hot smell moves along the pier with the wind.

Strangers talk to one another eating hot food in the snow. They don't eating the cold snacks in the heat. It's to do with my theory that folk don't enjoy things that come too comfortable. Standing in the snow, with the white islands on one side and the raw hill on the other, the sea actually under their feet that slip about on the pier, these people behave as though they've made their way over twenty miles of ice to make it to our wee booth; even though there's the hotels over the way, the railway cafeteria and the Chinese up the alley behind Chalmers and MacTavish's selling the twenty different carryout potato fillings.

The best day in snow we've had at the booth was this January, right after the New Year. It was that chilly I'd invested in the gloves with the cut-off fingertips and a wee flap goes over likc a mitten, so you've got the movement of the fingers and the recovery period for them after inside the top bit that goes over like an egg cosy.

There was one of these groups of folk around that isn't any shape, just humans not seeing each other, the tall ones with guncases letting dogs in and out of cars, the other ones not wearing enough clothes and shouting at one another from close up and telling jokes without listening. There was some call for the soup I keep on the go, it was kidney bean and lamb skirt, Duncan was busy at the frier, and Joanne was cutting monk tail for the mixed seafood medley. The boys were preparing the two coatings in the back, batter and breadcumbs. It offers a choice to the mouth. Men take crumb and the women batter, I find. But I can be wrong. After all, it's a crude division, sorting people into sexes.

Then up the pier comes a wee thing on high bootee heels, with an umbrella covered with yellow flowers. Her feet leave treads small as marks in pastry in the snow. She's giggling like a bird. The seagull next to her looks as if it could pick her up by its beak with the one orange dot on its hook. She's Japanese, come to see this other wee country that's made such a success out of the whisky.

Her man is reversing down the pier away from her but towards us, his black loafer shoes going blacker with the snow, and the turn-ups in his trousers collecting it. He's snapping her of course, and she's posing with a soft handful of snow, her face up squint to it like a bunch of flowers, breathing in the crystals, and blowing them off the snow in her hands out to him and to us. It's the kind of snow takes its time about landing. It twirls and rests in any light it can get.

We're watching her as she leaves these little steps as small as the gulls' triangular plods, but pointing the other way, the way she's coming. The light is the snowlight of glary grey though the mountain is all white, and the islands are blue and yellow in the folds of their whiteness. The brazier is black and blue and red and the frier fills the air with a bottled-up hissing. I notice that the characters around our family booth have become a group. They have been woken up for a while from themselves.

Down the pier she comes with her snow posy and we watch her yellow-flowered umbrella come closer behind her, her bit of private weather.

Just as the Japanese man's about to catch his raincoat on the brazier, two men budge and pick it up to move it, taking care to adjust it between the relative heights of their grips, so the coals on the top stay level. Nothing disturbs the glow of the brazier. The heat between the coals is like red mortar. Only the ash shifts and falls, leaving a grey trail in the snow.

The Japanese man turns round, perhaps feeling the heat moving back and away from him in the cold Western air, and seems to be taking it all in, the plastic striped tent, the fried food in paper, the red-faced people of differing largeness, the brown dog with a tuna-coloured nose, the black one whose tail has drawn a fan in the snow, and he includes us all in his greeting, 'Good evening.'

By the time the girl has arrived and shaken the snow off her woolly gloves, he is halfway round the individuals who now compose a group around the brazier outside the tent where I hoped to keep my family safe from the world outside. I flip back the knitted snoods of my mitts, and begin to use my fingers, until I am almost enjoying the sensations they are prey to, bitter cold, a stinging where the vinegar gets into the cuts I'm never without, the chill glittery ribbons of iceberg, the hot stubbled shell of the fritters made with crumb, the light deflatable sheen of the battered fish. I enjoy the dexterity the exposure has given me.

Ian and Dougie and Joanne are posing for the camera in the snow outside our small striped plastic tent. The couple take several more snapshots of the group. More snacks are ordered. I thin the soup to make it go round, it's so thick after its day reducing in the stockpot.

In Japan, someone will almost certainly think that the booth is where we live, up here among the snows and floating islands of the West Coast. They will see our brazier and the people around it and in their minds will arise some idea of the tribes within which we live, huddled together for warmth, waiting for boats to take us away to islands in warmer waters, accompanied by dogs and protected by taller men with guns.

You can take it any way you need to.

Since round about then, I've been letting the children out and about that bit more. Duncan has gone shares with a man sets creels not far out beyond Kerrera. We'll sell the lobster here from the tent on the pier, when we get some.

The year is outwith my control, as it always was. I am letting the days come in with what they carry and leave with what we can give them. When I cut the icebergs into these light shreds, the thing that was the size of a head is spun out and the gaps between its smithereens filled in with a thousand layers of air so you get a basin of stuff airier than lawnmowings and sparkling like fibreglass. And so the days go on, chopped into finer and finer shreds of lightness that I think at last I can feel, each one, just before it goes.

Carla's Face

An undertone overlaid the proceedings, escaping through the small crevices between what people said and what they meant. The whole day had taken its toll, from the first unfair bright promise after dawn, until now, when they all sat around with nothing to do after the funeral itself but to drink, or not to. Either option demanded a dedication Carla considered she was short of. She'd come to the island right the way over from Stirling where she'd built up a loyal clientele who appreciated her and the facilities offered by her discreet salon opposite the steakhouse. You'd not get women on an island coming to a person known to be a hairdresser/beautician, not regular enough at any rate to make it worth Carla's while. Twenty-two women on the island, each one prepared to visit a hairdresser maybe the twice in her life – for her own wedding and a daughter's. At the outside, if there were more daughters, up to five times, including baptisms and other people's funerals. So that made a maximum of, say, sixty visits to the hairdresser by each generation. Supposing Carla could expect her working life to last forty years, that averaged out at one-point-five clients per annum, not overwhelming. Topped up, she'd to admit, by doing the hair of the dead. But that was quiet, too; vital, but quiet.

They died at two peaks, the islanders; too young, or very old. The old ones looked prettier, more silvery, less troubled, than the young ones, who as a rule died violently, by drowning or in drink. They got very green as to the complexion when they'd lingered below the water for a good while. The drink made them blue or purple. These were colours you could not massage back to a natural shade unless you caught the body fresh, with the blood vessels suggestible. Carla loved soothing the skin of the dead, it was like putting a quarrel straight for good and all, but the business was slow in a place where there lived no more than a hundred souls, all known to her so well that they seemed like part of herself. As they were. The old ones were the cousins of her grandparents, the middle-aged ones cousins of her parents and the young ones her own cousins, some of them by now parents. On the mainland they fell pregnant as young but were not always as young when they carried a baby the whole way up to the birth. There was no hiding a baby on a piece of land the size of a hill dropped into the sea, dwelt on by more gulls than sheep, more sheep than people and as many herons as children, as many eagles as professional men, and those two eagles soberer.

The doctor was speaking just now, in the front room after the funeral, looking out through the window at the waves that pushed closer as the day advanced. The graveyard was in sight, stones leaning away from the sea and few enough in number to look sociable not military. If rain came suddenly, a family could picnic among the stones for shelter, passing around the salt for the hardboiled eggs. On the stones grew lichens like dried lace and damp velvet. The grave that was newest, around which the men had all stood at the funeral today and thrown earth down on to the coffin in quantities that did nothing to cover its nakedness, that new grave was bright and freshly made now, with a puffy quilt of mainland-grown flowers high upon it. The flowers would be taken by the rain and the wind even before the rabbits could get them.

Between the two commitments, to take drink or not to, the doctor had taken the high road to heaven and was not drinking. From time to time he went out to his car to remedy this position he had assumed as a man deserving of respect, by taking a nip from the quarter bottle in his glovebox. There were further quarter bottles, to the total of two and a quarter bottles, in places known to the doctor. When it sank below the two bottles in reserve, he became edgy and was a less effective physician. Since there was but the one shop, it was known well what dosage of liquor the doctor prescribed for himself.

So, today, he was not drinking, in contrast to the minister, who held it only right that he, in his position of confidant and comforter of the mourners, should share with them in the loosening and rinsing out of their grief.

'He was a fine specimen,' said the doctor.

'Rare,' said the minister, thinking of the broken heap of flesh and breath that Andrew had been in life. He'd had arms like the sides of feeding sows, loose and pendulous below the one defined strip of lean.

'Rare? That he was. No one like him at all, at all.' The doctor's stern sobriety was catching up with him quicker than the minister's dutiful boozing.

'All God's creatures,' said the minister, seeing an opening to an area where no one could gainsay his superior rights of access, 'are differently wonderful.'

'Differently wonderful,' said the doctor, who, truly sober, would have been turned away by the soap in the words.

'Are you telling me,' asked wee Ian, who had been drinking all the way since Glasgow, which made a train's worth followed by the ferry's worth followed by the welcome from the island followed by last night followed by the freshener before the funeral, the stiffener in the kirkyard and now the serious drinking, 'are you telling me that you came over all the way, Carla MacDougall, just to do Andrew's make-up for his coffin?' If, in life, a man had worn make-up in sight of wee Ian, his voice suggested, he'd've laid him out cold. 'Make-up,' he said. Indeed the word did sound unseemly and dishonest in his mouth. He said it so's you heard what make-up was, thought Carla; a made-up thing, a lie. She didn't think lies were so bad. You might need the odd small one. Wee Ian was too big for the front room, though it was his wife's; he worked on the mainland and came home for a long weekend once a month. He was in quarrying and wanted to get into stone reconstitution. The only work on the island was old-fashioned work, with no future. From time to time wee Ian stretched out his hand for a pork pie and popped it on the end of his tongue like a pill. The acids in his saliva made short work of it before even he reeled it in to the shelter of his teeth. Gratefully his stomach took the liquefied food and dismissed it, needing more soon after.

'Andrew, now; did he look good, according to your estimation, when you'd finished with him?' Ian seemed to be, thought Carla, quite interested in the technicalities, for a man who'd never taken her profession that seriously before. She sipped her wee drink, couldn't mind what it was, she drank that rarely. Anyhow, it warmed her in the head, and she thought kindly of Ian as she spoke to him. He'd been a handsome boy for one summer, and beautiful light on his feet. She'd never had the luck. Now no woman would call him luck if he came her way; all the veins in his face had risen and flowered red under his big hide. Whereas she, who had been a mouse, was, say it herself though she did, transformed since a girl. Getting away from the island had started that. No one in Stirling knew what she had started out with, or why exactly she had each feature, like the people on the island did, on account of knowing every exact last detail of her ma's pregnancy and labour. In a place as small as this everything was explained because there was nothing to do but talk and little but one another to talk about.

'Jesus, Carla, you're different fi how ye was,' said wee Ian. She could not deny it. She'd been a plain kid with legs like pudding pushed in tight to its bag. Her hair had been a mat of turfy brown, and her teeth all over the shop. She'd known nothing of presentation and the art of making the best of herself. Her skin had freckled up like a blotched bird's egg then and she'd no clothes to speak of. And absolutely no poise.

She recrossed her legs and tugged at the jacket of the ensemble she'd ironed this morning on the same kitchen table where the night before she'd worked on the scunnered dead face of Andrew. She ironed at the table on an old yellow blanket so stiff it squeaked under the iron. It had been nice working at that table because of the view down to the churchyard and the flickering advances of the sea, lifting the small blue creel boat that was tied to an iron loop under all the yellow seaweed. She curled a sleek loop of red hair behind her right ear; it was a semi-permanent tint called Unfair Advantage. In her ears shivered silvery sections of what looked like chainmail for fish. These were cool against her neck, calming her when she made herself take another sip, for the conviviality. Her legs began to get the tense feeling they had when she'd held a pose for too long for the Stirling Amateur Photographic Club. She could feel all the tendons twanging for release. But, even though it was just Wee Ian, she decided to give him the full toe-balanced, calves-tensed treatment. As a matter of fact, she could do her exercises at such snatched moments, she'd found, and men never noticed, though women could deliver funny looks. It was pure envy.

Carla had evened out her skin tone for years now by the use of the sunbed in her salon. Honestly, she did not know how other women did without. Her whole skin'd a gorgeous tan, a deep colour, more rose-brown than holiday-brown, she liked to think. She tanned in her undies from modesty, not for health reasons. You did not know when a client might require an impromptu appointment, and readiness was Carla's watchword.

Wee Ian was as uncouth as most of these men, thought Carla; she could not have borne it if she'd lived here to this day. Not the way she was now, used to the gracious things of life and a certain style.

Carla'd done nail extensions on herself after fixing Andrew's make-up for his coffin. She did not want his family to feel she'd taken no care with her own grooming, like an operative, when they were all family if you thought about it.

'Yes, I will, thanks,' she called to Jessie, who was passing with a plate of ham sandwiches and a bottle, although with her back to Carla. Jessie looked at her in a startled way, and extended and poured. Picking up the sandwich wasn't easy as it was the sort with a big edge on it, crust was it? Nail extensions meet more peaceably around a thinner sandwich. To eat the sandwich at all required two hands, of which only the thumb and forefinger could be used. The nail extensions perforated the bread otherwise, and collected butter and ham in their long copper-coloured arcs. The copper was an echo of the Unfair Advantage. It had been a wee treat to herself on turning forty, the colour change. A shift to the mellower register as a sign she'd no quarrel with anything life might send her way.

Ian was watching her in several directions like a man watching a tank of fish. It was a sign of the way he could not hold his drink, Carla thought. His eyes strayed over her face and body and he looked as if he might cry or be sick.

'Jessie,' he called, 'ye mind Carla?' Ian had only married Jessie from necessity as Carla recalled it. He'd broken all the other hearts his one brief summer of flower, and Jessie was the sensible one of all the girls. Except that she'd married Ian, reflected Carla.

'I do that,' said Jessie. She was slight and had more grey than black hair and a plain old suit in navy wool with sheepdog hairs on it. Not one to set a living room alight, Carla could see.

'Will I get yous a nice cup of tea?' Jessie asked Carla, looking into her painted eyes with clean blue ones.

'How *did* you *guess*?' said Carla, socially, in a great swoop before she finished the rest of her glass, against waste.

As Jessie left, Carla saw how Ian rubbed his wife with his shoulder, quite hard, as though he'd an itch, as she went past with her tray and her dishcloths and her used plates. Flat shoes, Jessie wore, and her face was weathered like spring petals late in the season. Jessie dropped a kiss on to the head of her husband. It was like going unclothed in public, thought Carla. How could a married woman do that?

The doctor came in from outdoors, a healthy flush on him. It was colder than ever out now the stars were starting. Some people with children had taken them home. There was music, the sound of a fiddle from the upstairs room and something on the telly or the radio from elsewhere in the front room. No, it was worse. It was the minister, singing, quite a few of them singing. It was worse even than that. It was religious music, sung quite ordinary-style, as though it had any place in folks' houses. 'Be ye lift up ye everlasting doors, so that the king of glory shall come in. Who is the King of Glory?' They asked the question of each other with their big drunken faces hanging down off their eyebrows. Then they answered the question, nodding, looking pleased as though they had just recalled a name they'd earlier forgotten from an important story. 'The Lord of Hosts and none but He the King of Glory is!' They looked very pleased about that. No one seemed embarrassed at this inappropriate moment to bring God up, when he'd had his way already in the graveyard and at the funeral with the tears being blown off their faces by the wind. Indeed, they were giving this singing their all. It is the way with drunk men, thought Carla.

She took a glass from behind a photoframe with a snap of Ian and Jessie's Rhona holding up a lamb with a face looked like it'd been drinking ink and the black had seeped all into the whirls of wool. The glass was half full; she took the stuff in it down in one and returned the glass carefully behind the now less interesting photo, tucking it thoughtfully in under the support at the back of the frame, so's it wouldn't disrupt Jessie's decor. Such as *that* was. There was another glass needed tidying in this manner, Carla happened to see, just in behind the curtain that had not been drawn. The sea showed only as a crisping pale blur the size it seemed of a hand mirror under the white simple moon. Otherwise the water might have been sky, fallen down to meet the land. She replaced the glass behind the curtain. The creel boat bobbed on the lifted water or floated in the sky, whichever was which. No sound went on as long as the sound of the sea, that was always there. Two hundred yards from Ian and Jessie's house, the graveyard had gone blue and then grey and was now silver.

'If you give her the tea, Jessie,' said the clearly drunken doctor advancing before the brown pot that loomed behind him, 'I'll try to help with the other wee bit problem.'

It was the usual way for Carla. She was just looking about to see who 'her' might be, when she realized it was her own self they were on about. People never let up talking about her. It was why she'd left the island in the first place. No privacy. No time to yourself. No life of your own. No respect, for you surely could not have that in a place where you were too well known.

'Milk, Carla?' asked Jessie, 'or straight?'

'You go on and laugh at me,' said Carla. 'Laugh. I'm soberer than the lot of them. And prettier.' The fat ugly drunken men in the corner looked at her and resumed their indecent singing of the psalms of David in metre.

She felt the familiar powerful helplessness when she gave in to the instinct to do something wrong. As a rule, she did this late at night in the salon, and she would run around talking to her now absent clientele as she did within her head when they were present, answering with her truth instead of their own, anatomizing their faults and explaining why they were right to fear death. Another great advantage of loneliness was the freedom it gave you to meet yourself. And often the self you met was different from the one you'd met before.

'You're tired, Carol dear,' said the doctor.

'You look exhausted yourself, doctor,' said Carla. 'By the same token, if I may so say. And it's Carla. I live in Stirling now.'

'Is that right?' asked the doctor, getting busy with a glass of water and rattling a glittery sheet of what she could have sworn were jumping beans. 'You don't have to change your name when you move house,' he continued. 'I know people who've emigrated down under and they're still called what they were always called.'

'What's that?' asked Carla. She wanted to know the name of someone who had gone all that way, down to Australia. If she'd've done that it wouldn't have been anything as ordinary as Carla she'd've selected.

'The name they were always called. Their first name. The name they had first. I don't know. There are too many to think.'

'You either know no one who has been to Australia, or you are a very drunk man,' said Carla, and she fell to the carpet in a shining heap of orange limbs and pleated aubergine wool, thus avoiding the gelatine-and-insult placebos the doctor had been about to offer her. Her mixed hair, the mauve-red of neepskins and beetroots, lay more successful than the rest of her assembled self, in a rich fan on the carpet. Her poor disgraced faceful of paint had melted under the onslaught of the day.

Jessie began to pour tea for the thirty or so people left in the room. Each time she went back to the kitchen to fill the pot again, she gave Wee Ian a new thing to do. While she poured and milked and sugared the first few teas, Ian carried Carla to the kitchen table, and laid her along it, rolling the tablecloth up against her so that she wouldn't flop on to the plates of biscuits or curl up around the two big trifles Jessie had done in crystal-type bowls for when the last drinkers began to cry and need their pudding, around five in the morning that would be.

While Jessie dished out the second wave of teas, Ian did as she'd told him and went to get cotton wool and glycerine from the bathroom. Carla had that horrible orange skin, he thought, skin that needs watering, it's so parched, dried out to the colour of the sand in Bible lands. She was the colour of certain stones you got in quarries down in England, terrible thirsty stones that lasted less than eight hundred years.

Mind you, he thought, Carla herself must've been thirsty. She was out like a light. As he remembered it, she'd not done this to herself as a girl, when she'd been nothing to look at and never been anywhere but the island. He shook the glycerine in its bottle. It sparkled and shattered like crazy jelly and then pulled itself together till it was back to looking like water.

He was behaving sober but knew as he watched his careful actions from his brain that felt as though it was up on the dresser with the diesel receipts that he was not. He got very good at exacting tasks about a day into a blinder. But, God, he could take it. He was four times the size of the wee orange creature passed out on the kitchen table.

'Undress her,' said Jessie, pouring hot water into the shiny brown teapot that seemed to be spelling letters out of its spout in steam. 'Not right the way down. And fold her suit.'

The aubergine ensemble came away in three pieces. Each time he lifted Carla, he tried not to look at her body. This meant looking at her face, at the unpeeling animal-like false lashes growing off her eyelids, at the runs of mauve and fibrous black that had rained down her cheeks, at the awful shredded moustache of colour that had crept up from her mouth to her nose through the cracks in the orange mask that was like a dry riverbed. When he'd got down to her underthings, he saw she was orange all over except inside the plain flesh-coloured undies that were not the colour of her flesh. Inside them she seemed white as candles. The tiny white hairs grew out of her hard skin the way a pig's did out of a ham. The bottoms of her feet looked nice and soft and ordinary. He covered her with the tablecloth.

'Here's your tea,' said Jessie. 'Now go upstairs and fetch me one of Rhona's magazines. Nothing too way out. I want one with a make-up page. You know, Ian, a step-by-step to teach the wee girls how to put on the war paint.'

Ian had been about to start. He enjoyed the topic of his own daughter and make-up, especially if he'd had a dram. 'Ye'll not leave the house like a hoor!' and so on. He had all the words ready in his head and had heard them said to his sister by his own father. 'What d'ye want to paint your face for, to show it to laddies who've known you unpainted all your life? Eh? Wee hoor? Laddies that're mostly your own folk? Speak out will ye? And don't be insolent!' He knew what to say.

'Say *nothing* Ian,' said his wife. 'And don't wake Rhona. She keeps the magazines on the chair by the bed.'

He came down the stair with a pile of the slippery scented coloured rubbish falling out down between his belly and his forearms. When he got back, Jessie had shut the door from the kitchen into the front room, so he closed it too. On the table under the cloth lay stiff, thin Carla, her face cleaned off by Jessie, who was just wiping it around the forehead with a swab of cotton wool. The white fibre was like snow next to the red-brown skin whose colour was cooked deep in.

'Find me the clearest chart you can. You know the kind of thing. "Getting ready to go out on a date." Something like that. Don't say it's disgusting. It doesn't mean the kids are doing anything. It's practice.'

'Eh?'

'For courting.'

'Rhona?'

'Rhona's fourteen. One day you'll fall off the boat and find she's a big girl. Let her learn. She's safe here, at least. All she does is try out faces. Now, you hold that guide up for me and I'll have a try with the stuff out of Carol's handbag. She'll feel better that way.' Carla's bag contained many pots and sticks and wands, all of them with complicated names that gave no sign of where on the face they were intended for. Jessie worked slowly, without confidence but with the care of a good cakemaker following a new recipe. Layer by layer, as the light for applying colour to a human canvas grew clearer with the rising of the sun, Jessie remade the face of an older Carol into that of a younger, easier, Carla. Ian sat beside the kitchen table and spooned trifle into his mouth, sops of sponge and sweet sherry and custard and dream topping with a delicate adornment of coloured sugar strands falling to his acidic stomach to lie there and counteract with soft bulk the headache that was forming in his head, a not wholly unwelcome reminder that he was alive, that it was a new day, that his brother lay quiet in the earth beyond the house and before the sea, and that two women he had known all his life were close to him in the morning's light, one absorbed in kindness and the other returning to herself.

In the living room beyond the door, those mourners who had not yet left slept in the places where they had at last succumbed. The doctor and minister were away. A familial intimacy carried from body to body. Nothing was ugly. In the creek below the kirkyard the boat lay up on the hard brown sand. The sea was only a white rumour beyond the rocks.

The Only Only

The first ferry for a week was fast to the quay, the thick rope springs holding it to, looped fore and aft over iron cleats the height of children. The weather had been so hard and high that there was seaweed all over the island, brought in by the wind, and the east wall of each house was drifted up to the roof. The children dug in to these drifts and made blue caves to sit in, smoothing till the cave's inner ice melted and set to a clear lucent veneer.

Seven children lived on the island and attended the school together. Sandy was the only only among them; the rest had brothers or sisters. She was a girl of eight born to the teacher Euphemia and her husband Davie, who set and lifted lobster-pots for his main living, though the ferry company kept him on a retainer to attend the arrival and departure of the ferry, three times a week when the sea would let it through. Davie'd to hook up and untie the boat, watch for the embarkation of livestock and the safe operation of the davits on the quay. He had an eye to the secure delivery of post and to the setting in place of the gangplank so that it would hold in a swell.

He liked his job. It involved him with everyone who lived on the island and he was careful to respect this. If he knew that the father of a child off just now inside its mother on the ferry to be born on the mainland was not the man with his arm around the woman as the ship parted from the land, he did not say. Davie was not an islander born, although Euphemia was; she could remember her grandmother skinning fulmars to salt them for the winter and she herself could feel if the egg of a gull might be taken for food or if it was fertilised and packed with affronted life. Davie had boiled up a clutch of eggs once and they had sat down to them with a salad and pink potatoes from outdoors; the tapping and the faint window of membrane had seemed right enough, but when he'd got through to the boiled halfmade chick with its eggtooth sticking out like a sail needle's hook, he'd got sick. He still looked away when a seal heaved up the rocks to die after a gashing; the thickness of the blubber inside gave him a lurch, like seeing the legs above an old woman's stocking tops. In death a seal keeps its enthusiastic expression; the human face falls to neutral peace, but the seal appears to trust even death.

Because there had been no boat for some time, everyone was on the pier today. It was a social occasion although it was so cold. Something seemed to have slowed the sea, its salt particles surrendering to the grip ice has on water. On the Atlantic coast of the island, rockpools were freezing over, the crabs moving in under sea lettuce to escape seizure by the ice. Among the blue-brown mussels that clustered around the stanchions of the pier hung icicles at low tide. The sea was unusually quiet, hushed by the cold from lapping or thrashing the shingle or the harbour walls. Only the hardiest boats were still down in the water, fishing boats and a clam skiff that had been neglected and had taken in water that was now a hard slope of grey ice halfway up to the gunwales.

On the slip where the smaller boats came alongside there was a tangle of nets and a pile of polythene fishboxes. Yellow, orange, mauve and electric blue, the nets were neatly trimmed with a white buzz of rime. The impression of a deserted, frozen harlequinade was emphasised by a pair of red heavy-duty gloves lying on the weed next to a single yellow seaboot.

Sandy stood with Euphemia in a group of women. People asked the teacher about their children; in such a community there was no chance of going unnoticed. Talk was the pastime, talk and work the currency. Euphemia was pleased to be among women, with her daughter. When, as now, she was irked at her man she did not tell, or it would have been round the place before tea.

She wanted him to give up the boat and come into teaching at the school with her. She could not see the future in working on the pier. It took up a good day three times a week, when the following up had been done, the cargo counted, the letters sorted and settled in the red Land Rover to be taken round the only road by the post; and by the time drink had been taken, with the purser maybe, or with whoever came off the boat or was in the bar off a fishing boat.

He was a good man, but where did these boat days go? Whereas, should he come in with her at the teaching, they would see their work as it grew day by day. And he could still do the lobsters, if there were any left in the sea. With the French and the Russians and the warm-water breeders at it, the sea was full of mostly red herrings, forget the silver darlings.

Sandy now, she would see more of her father if he came in with the teaching, and then Euphemia maybe, when it was all settled, would get down to having another baby.

The purple line at the horizon lay over the slow grey sea. The air smelt of weed, cigarettes and diesel; the post office van was idling and the men gathered around it in their oilskins, smoking for the warmth. The children of the island were standing against the rail at the end of the pier, their feet kicking against the robust wire barrier with a bright harsh chiming. Six of them red-headed, in shades of red from orangeade to a bracken mixed with rough briar brown, and one of them with the crow-black hair that does not shine and goes with blue eyes. The children were waiting to wave, even those who were waving no one off; it was the boat, which was the presiding event of their lives, that they wished to acknowledge.

Against the folding evening clouds, and frosted by their departing rims of hard light, the shining ruby-juice red of Sandy's straight hair and the drained white of her face seemed to

Euphemia to be stamped like a royal seal set to important words. It was not easy to think of Sandy with a brother or a sister. But Euphemia did not approve of only children; especially not here, where circumstances were already isolated in the world's eyes. It was not possible to imagine loving Sandy any less or loving any child more than Sandy was loved; it was hard to imagine the love that Davie and she bore for their child stretching to accommodate more, but Euphemia was convinced that this would occur naturally, without pain, like passing through a door into a new room with open windows.

The ferry was loaded. The gangplank was lifted on its ropes and let down to the pier for rolling and storage in the metal waiting room at the end where the children hung and bobbed and cuffed one another's bright heads. A long plaintive blast warned that the boat must soon go and the children hollered back to it through cupped hands. Lights were coming on in the boat; soon the dark would land over them all, steaming across the water from the purple edge of the sea.

Davie was checking that goods had been properly exchanged, the gangmower sent to the mainland for fixing by June time, the cowcake fetched up out of the hold, the canned goods and frozen gear stowed ready for the shop, the box of specially requested medicaments boxed up for the doctor, the beer rolled into the pub's Bedford van; detail was what mattered in this job, and he took a pride in it.

In the restful numbed cold silence, people began to prepare themselves to make farewell and to depart for their homes. The moment the children loved was coming, when they could wave to the boat as it pulled out and away from the island, seagulls over the wake like bridesmaids. They stood and waited at the pier end, looking out to sea.

There was a creak, a sodden tugging groaning. The seagulls gathered. The eighty people on the pier experienced the shared illusion that it was they and not the boat who moved. The rudder of the ship was churning deep under the water which, astern, showed silvery green below its surface and white above. The air was still enough for a hundred separate lifted voices to reach the ears intended as the twenty souls on the boat looked down to the crowd on the pier. The children waited.

The stern spring of the boat cracked free of the cleat from which Davie had forgotten to lift it. After the first tearing report of the bust rope came the whipping weight of sixty yards of corded hemp and steel, swinging out through its hard blind arc at the height of a good-sized child.

'Lie down, get down, for God's sake,' yelled a man. The women fell to the ground. Unless they were mothers, when they ran for their little ones to the end of the pier as the thick murderous rope lashed out, rigid and determined as a scythe to cut down all that stood in its way.

Sandy lay under her mother's heart, hearing it in the coat that covered them both. The concrete of the pier seemed to tremble with the hard commotion of the rope's passing over them.

Snapped out of her dreams, Euphemia held her only child.

The boat continued to move away, its briefly lethal rope trailing behind it, a lone seaman at the winch above, coiling it in to usefulness. The black ferrous patina on the big cleat had burned off under the seething tension of the rope; its stem was polished by force through to a pale refined metal blue. The children from the end of the pier comforted their mothers, who stared out to the disappearing ship seeing, abob in the water, the heads of children cut off at the neck, their frozen sweetness of face under the streaming curtailed hair; red, red, red, red, red, red or black, and to grow no more.

Those American Thoughts

'There's places over there you'd not thank me if I took you right enough when all's said and done. The people are different, not like here. They're different. They'd cross the road before they would talk to you on the public street. And it's five highways wide.' Craig soaked up a good bit of his lager.

'The street?' Elise fiddled with the kirby in her hair. It was chosen from a selection at Boots to be the shade closest to the colour of her hair. Her bobcut was dark brown with a halo where the pearlised restaurant lamp over their table was reflected.

'The road.'

'Is the street not the road then?'

'No the way it is here. And no way is the road the street. They use roads for getting places, not for living in. If you're walking along the cars'll give you a wide berth because anyone walking along must be mad. Or not have a car, which is the same as mad right enough. There it's. There's your food. Looks warm any road.'

Craig was having a bad evening. He'd come all the way North back home to Aberdeen to let Elise know he wanted out from their engagement and he was giving a talk about attitudes to vehicles in the United States, where, he'd given it out, he'd been these last two months. On an engineering job, another lie. They couldn't get enough bridges, he'd said. Over water; inland waterways. Great demand for Scottish know-how. The Scots had a name for bridges.

In actual fact, he'd been washing up in a tourist hotel on Loch Lomondside, with occasional bar work after the last bus took away the nonresident staff. There'd been a large number of Americans at the Girning Stramlach Inn, right enough. And he must stop saying right enough. His mouth was operating against his brain. It did that around the women. Then again, he'd been with Elise seven years, since she was fourteen, so he owed her the gentle letdown.

They were in the Edwardian Bar at Lillie Langtry's. She was having a mince masala pitta surprise and Craig had stuck with what he knew and gone for a mixed grill, not noticing until too late that it'd come under 'Vegetarian'. So his plate looked like what the papers showed found in old burial sites to prove that Caledonian man had once been a grain eater or what have you. He'd catch up on his meat intake with a poke of scratchings after he'd fetched Elise off his conscience.

The lights were low, the music soupy. In the corner a group of big men emptied pints of Murphy's. Outside in the main road the Mercedes-Benzes of these men waited to be re-entered. On the curled coatstand in the corner their full-length Antartex sheepskin coats hung. They wore square rings of gold and bracelets whose links looked as if they might be useful in a fight. Hard shrewd faces crested their big bodies. They were off the rigs, in Lillie Langtry's to get in the mood before a night onshore with the dalls and the drink. They had the stilted gentleness of athletes. It made them the nearest thing to heroes the evening could offer, in a place making so high a bid for atmosphere as Langtry's, with its purple plush and brass lamps and oldness slapped on over the same new underneath as anywhere else.

Elise looked at the burned sweetcorn, not even took off the husk, that Craig had ordered. He'd changed in America, right enough. Perhaps there were a lot of things new about him now. Loving someone was like that. New things happened to them and it was a new thing for you too. Bringing you together, in a sense. She wondered, even if she did go to America, if she could ever fancy a whole green pepper scared out of its wits like that, looking like a frog's got stepped on.

Her Diet Lilt came in a tall glass with a line at the top to control spurts of generosity on the part of the bar staff. The line came off if you scratched it with a knife, not if you did so with a fingernail. She didn't want to find these things out but Craig was making all this silence, and she had to do something. In their own home there'd be things to do if he took silent, but out like this, now, it was harder. Plus, she was shy of the pitta bread. Would you eat it like a carry-out or, being here, use the knife and fork provided since the two of them were sitting down not walking along or snogging in between mouthfuls?

She preferred a reunion by the sea or at the chippy, always had. It took them back to their beginning. She never had to bother then with the people they'd become on top of the ones they recognised at once in each other, efficient Elise who remembered her calculator and Craig who'd not and needed one for his maths exam so he'd took it off her and brought her for a cod-roe fry with pineapple fritters to follow after school. They ate walking along the sea edge, the food and, it seemed, the air hot and crisp and sweet and salt in their mouths and hair, with the smell of iron and fish and ships coming down damp with the night.

'It's a calculator works by the sun's rays,' said Elise, for something to say, because Craig was that old, sixteen, and she thought it might be greedy to pass comment on the fritters. Her fingers were grease to the bone, and there was salt in her papercuts and sugar in her bunches. It was brilliant, but she'd no idea what to say to her mother when she got in late that night.

'Just tell her you've been to America,' said Craig, but he took her home good as gold and explained about the calculator and the examination and the obligation he'd felt to give Elise a wee something to say thanks. After that he was in her house most days. Her parents bought him a calculator for his seventeenth birthday. She began to worry they'd put him off by being keen. He showed no sign of this however and seemed to like being asked to do the things a son does, but for her parents, not his own, who were busy with their garden pond and fixture concession. They travelled sometimes, for the sculptures, that arrived twice a year in a big lorry, wrapped in blankets, looking like a grey extended family arriving at hospital, complete with pets.

Craig cleaned her parents' old lawnmower, even though his own mum and dad had a Hayter Hovercut, on summer sabbaths, easing its tired blades and joints with 1001 oil, before pouring the bin of fine clippings into the compost tip. Before going home on a Wednesday night, if he'd been over to her house, he'd save her mother and put out the dustbin, a drum of hefty pale shineless metal, ribbed like something military. She'd kiss him after that and be at once interested and bored by the possibilities that lay in so adult a routine so early in her life. It seemed dignified and glamorous to be kissing someone who knew that her mother disinfected and dried the bin on a Thursday, someone who now smelled of the peelings and papers in that bin. It was exciting to imagine being with Craig so long that she knew everything about him. The feeling that they were both old and young was good. The being old was a fantasy like being beautiful or dying, things that could never happen.

Never did she feel that she had leapfrogged something she might miss, for she saw her friends who went from boy to boy looking old and messed, like babies too late for bed.

Positioned about Lillie Langtry's at certain points where no real, weighty human might rest were life-size rag dolls dressed in Edwardian clothes. Lillie herself sat on top of the Liqueurs section, legs crossed and diamanté-buckled shoes hanging too loosely to be coquettish in front of the yellow and blue and green drinks in their mad scientist's bottles. At the back of the bottles was a mirror, so you saw double the drink. The rag figures were stuffed with kapok, soft lumpy stuff that they very slowly shed through their loose lock-knit bodies, so that there lay about each floppy figure, after a time in the one pose, a faint sheepish shadow. The faces of these big dolls were stiff, flat and starchy. Nostrils, lashes, dimples and brows were achieved by stitching. The hands of the dolls were like seal's flippers, the fingers inseparable.

As time passed at Lillie Langtry's each evening, the dolls, that had begun the evening seeming to have little to do with the actual appearance and bearing of humans, seemed to grow more real, as the drinkers and diners, courting couples and spouses, sacrificed their individuality to the softening forces available at the bar or in one another's company, or bestowed by the advance of night. The dolls remained unchanged, slumped, inward-looking, but not so inhuman as they had appeared, simply preoccupied.

By the morning they had become empty again. It was part of the interest of going to Lillie Langtry's to see where the staff would reposition the dolls next. Although to move the dolls was the prerogative of the staff at the restaurant, Craig had a friend Murdo who'd been sacked from his position on the garnish and maintenance side for posing two of the dolls in a way that was felt not to be tasteful or even historically accurate. It was true the dolls had a reserved look about them that made it hard to think of them taking anything like the kind of initiative Murdo had in mind.

Elise forked the mince out of her pitta, mashed it around in a swarfy tangle of raw carrot and swallowed it with a go of the Lilt. There were women arriving for the riggers now, great-looking girls on heels, carrying backwards off a few casual fingers short jackets with fur on at the neck. Drinks arrived, ice, and small bottles of tonic. Coral nails flashed as the women palmed their nylons smooth over their insteps and up over ankle bracelets. Only a woman couldn't groom herself like these ones would put the ankle bracelet on over the stockings, Elise had noticed. These women wore the bracelets like wedding rings, seriously, to say something about themselves.

Although it seemed that the women who had just arrived hardly spoke, the noise from the group of riggers grew. The men seemed to fill out, their voices too, in the presence of the women. The women looked in small mirrors at parts of themselves, eye-teeth, frownlines, upper lips, glimpses of throat. When they had put their mirrors away with snappings and zippings and wary lumbar movements of roosting, they started to try to get a view of parts of themselves harder to see, shoulder blades and elbows, knee-backs and the inner surfaces of nail ends; some looked at the tips of their high heels as though checking that nothing had been impaled there since the last look. One or two of the women spoke to one another to enlist help in checking some part of the construction that was hard to see by even the utmost craning, the hang of a dress over a buttock, the alignment of a belt with a hem at the back. It all looked private, but public, as though the women knew what gestures pleased the men, suggesting to them things about which they had been thinking for weeks out in the North Sea but could not name here or now.

Lillie Langtry watched with unsighted approval. Elise looked on and wondered where you learned those things. Was it from men or from other women, or was it born in you like knowing how to walk in heels and never telling people you'd heard their story before, and being unpopular with dogs?

Craig had returned to their table with his next lager. He'd filled out in America. He'd been that busy he probably had no time to eat right, just grab strange things. He'd not even had the time to be in touch with her, though he'd thought of her, he said, and here was the woollen jacket to prove it. A nice cut, with room for growth, she noticed; a jacket for the future, for when she'd a trout in her well. She thought of the old words he'd always used for the time when they would start a family, and knew herself lucky to be so young and with an unbroken past, shared with a man she knew so well she knew his way of using words. Right enough.

She smiled to herself in a way of which he had always been fond. It irked him now because it was the smile that told him she was happy. A trout in the well, Elise was thinking. Then after it's born, it's let loose in the stream.

Craig's gift to Elise was some kind of jacket for playing sports in, very American. It was made in China, she'd seen on the label that said 'ALL AMERICAN DIENAMIC SPOTSGEAR'. It was a nice shade of grey, with big numbers on it in purple. It'd be good for walking Bonnie, her Airedale cross, before anyone got up and before Elise changed for work at the library.

No one noticed what you wore at the library, Craig said, which made Elise take more care than ever. There were people came in there saw no one but the library staff from year's end to year's end. Why should they think the whole world lived in stained flannel and clotted wool?

Craig had been watching the women with the riggers, while he stood at the bar looking as though he was deciding what vintage of Tennant's to ask for. If you were with someone from sixteen it was natural to look at women, thought Elise, and these women were for looking at. He'd've been half the man if he'd not keeked.

Nonetheless, Craig returned to their table looking as though he expected her to start in on him about it. Had he not noticed she never did?

Craig was fidgety. One of the women in the group was getting under his skin. It was a bother that she kept looking at him. How was he supposed to jilt Elise with that slatch looking on? She was a redhead with the skin of a brunette and a suit all bobbles in lilac, chained over the bosoms. It was her drink told Craig why she bothered him. She was drinking a schooner of something that was lilac too. It was Parfait Amour, that looks like meths but moves slower out the bottle, held back by the sugar. There'd been a fuss at the Lonnachs and Creel bar of the inn on Loch Lomondside when that liquor had been called for by a handsome woman with a high-spending oilman fresh in from Texas to Glasgow. Craig'd had to cycle over to the stores at Ardlui and there was no Perfect Armour there. They tracked it down at the minister's house; the bottle had been a gift from his son-in-law who worked for human rights somewhere they didn't have them and got queer gear duty free. It had been this very redhead had wanted that purple drink he'd cycled for, Craig was sure. It stood to reason. She'd a right nerve to be here too, that one.

Elise watched Craig scrape the black off of a courgette on his dish. He hated the skin, so he just ate the part of the veg that remained between the charred part and the skin. It was mostly seeds, that he picked out of his teeth with one of the cardboard Lillie Langtry's matches that got soggy very quick. There was a little pain behind her heart as she thought that he wasn't enjoying his food this evening. She felt for him like that, in the anxious everyday way. When they were married, she'd help him with everything so he needn't end up an evening out full of charcoal and compost even if ate off of an oval plate with dishwasher-proof lilies painted on. They could choose things together then.

'I'll just off and get myself a poke of scratchings,' she said, and walked over to the bar. Closer to the group of laughing men and preening women, she smelt the burst and fallen smell of big flowers that was the mixed perfumes of the women, and saw that the men were having floppy steaks, from which the women were cutting wee ribbons that they ate off forks as if the meat were pasta.

The redheaded woman in her suit that was like bunched lilacs saw Elise and envied her, independent, neat, fresh, and able to buy herself a pack of snacks any time and eat it. She raised her half-full purple glass to Elise and smiled with her cheeks at her over it. Her smile said, '*Men.*'

Elise smiled back. Her smile had no words behind it because she had no answer to the comment in the plural.

'You're very free with your foolish grins,' said Craig, as she opened the scratchings, did not take one and put them in front of him.

'She's nice. She smiled. Nice to see a person smile here at a stranger.'

'You'll be getting plenty smiling in the library, no?'

'It's quieter.'

'Smiles don't make sound do they, Elise? Eh?'

'There are no ladies in purple raising their glasses to me in Reference, Craig.'

Here they were using their names against each other on this night when she wanted to please him and he wanted to hurt her in the least noticeable way.

It was she who unfroze first.

'Will we have a sweet? You'll've had great sweets in the States.' The moment she had spoken she heard her foolish eagerness.

'Aye, the usual things.' He finished the most recent lager. 'There was Mississippi Mud Pie, Key Lime Pie, your Banana Toffee Pie. The usual things. Pies.'

Elise said nothing. She looked down at the Lillie Langtry's menu, where these very puddings, described in shocking detail, were listed. She decided to pursue her curiosity. If he was this bored, or that out of it, he wouldn't notice.

'There'll've been lovely women over there.'

'Och, gorgeous,' said Craig, bitterly. 'Gorgeous.' He might just have received a bill for the gas. In his mind there paraded the beauties of the kitchen on Loch Lomondside, three married women and a wee wanting girl who peeled potatoes all to the same size and said she ate the peelings at home at the hostel in the evenings.

This was dreadful. He was wanting to tell Elise the truth.

He looked over to the purple woman. She was starting on another of her drinks. She gave him a very familiar look, not flirtatious, but reproving. The cheeky besom, who was she to give him a ticking off? He finished the scratchings, and told the waitress he'd have an Irish Coffee with the sweet, and another lager just for now.

A pretty woman sitting for some reason above the racks of bottles looked kindly at Craig. She understood him.

Then he realised his mistake, and looked away from the Lillie Langtry doll as though it'd seen through to his own stuffing.

Elise asked for a cup of tea, which was moody of her, he thought. For relief from her familiarity and from her clean parting and nice teeth, he looked at the purple lady, who had put down her drink now and was smoking. Through the smoke he saw her face, and it knew him and knew what was in his mind. This painted woman was judging him through her filthy smoke.

He'd a good mind right enough to go over to her and tell her what a troublemaker she was wherever she went with her Parfait Amour and legs and eyes. No, first he must be cruel to be kind and make Elise see there was no big day ahead, just the usual small ones.

'Elise, while I was in eh America I did em a lorra thinking. I thought a lot. Know what I mean?'

'Uh huh,' said Elise, looking forward to her tea and wondering how she could get Craig to let her drive without upsetting him. When he used to say 'Lorra' he was either drunk or trying to impress someone. But now it was maybe an American accent.

This American thinking had been effortful, she saw. And, that tired with the trip over from the States, he wasn't sober, either.

'Thinking, aye, right enough. In America.' He saw himself, thinking in America, in his mind. Since they were taking place in America these thoughts were unusually pure and free and big, with enormous cactuses and skyscrapers surrounding them.

Everything was important in America. Those American thoughts of his were very important.

'I'm just away to the toilet for a moment,' said Elise. 'I'll not be long. It's magic to see you again. You've not been looking after yourself though.'

Craig's American thoughts receded. The cactuses disappeared behind the rainy hills of Loch Lomond, the skyscrapers fell like settling smoke. He thought of the deadly afternoon in the coach travelling back up, the video history of the clans playing on the screen at the front and the way the old people didn't emerge from the chemical toilet for half an hour at a time.

He'd have one more try, before his habits closed around him and the old familiar things had won over the shiny new stuff he just knew must be waiting somewhere for him.

'It's just we were that young when we started, Ella. I just need a space.' Aye, that was it, space was the word he'd been guddling for. 'The space, Ella, I need it. To myself. See, you crowd me. I'm crowded. Stop crowding me.' Will I never stop saying that, he thought. Let's try another angle.

'Just give me space,' he concluded. Though all he could think of was a locked box without windows being took round corners he couldn't see at a terrible rate while he listened to the past going round and round on a tape and his own dirt swilled around below him. 'It's a bit of space that I need. Just so's I can see where I'm going. God, Ella, I don't even know where I've been.' In warming to his subject, he was blowing it away.

She'd seen at once what he was saying. It was lucky she was on the way to the washroom, any road.

The Ladies had a woman in a picture hat in silhouette on the door. Inside was a wee sofa with another of those daft dolls sitting on it. From the safety of the cubicle Elise let herself go and talked to it loudly to keep herself from crying.

'Space. He needs space. It's space he needs right enough. I crowd him out. See that, I crowd him out. We were that young when we began we need to go into *space*.'

Elise felt better as she came out. The lilac woman was waiting on the sofa beside the doll, looking unsurprised.

'Whoever spouted all that blash at you must've been in America, my wee peat,' she said. 'It'll pass over, right enough. Water under the bridge, I'd call it.'

Ring If You Want Something

'The way we stop my mother coming around the whole time is we're really friendly with my stepmother,' said Alice. She held Fergus on her knee, sitting up in front of her like a delegate of her personality. He was in a towelling suit that left only his hands and face free but he still glowed more than anything in the room. He was just over the five months.

'Why do you have to stop your mother coming round?' Catriona had no children yet. She turned her tea-coloured hair over in her fingers as she spoke. Her high shoes were in front of the sofa where she lay; they were made of suede the pink of sugar roses. She tossed her car keys between her hands.

Fergus was not remotely taken, even with the keys. He could perhaps sense Catriona's indifference to his appeal, his enormous eyes, the forehead full of ideas, his stalk of a neck, the feet that could curl like ferns.

'When you've a baby your mother remembers having you and wants to make the same mistakes she did with you only on your baby this time.'

'How come you know that?'

'I guessed it and I'm taking no chances.'

'Where does your stepmother improve on your mother?'

'Because she's not,' said Alice, 'and she's generous with everything but advice. I want to make my own mistakes.'

'Why make any?' Catriona could see that a baby was just a person, that was all. No problems there, just treat it like a person, but smaller. She reached for her coffee.

Within Catriona's bag, the telephone rang.

Fergus turned his righteous gaze on the bag. From his shining mouth bulged a bubble like another lip, made of sheer milk.

'Oh, no,' said Catriona, though she was relieved to hear the summons of the phone in the bag.

'Don't worry about us,' said Alice.

'I won't.'

'Catriona MacAllister,' said Alice's old friend, shaking her hair and hanging her head back in a way that told Alice there was a man on the line and that Catriona was thinking of him watching her while she spoke.

Alice remembered when she herself had behaved in this way. Now she could not think of a time before now, when Fergus's gaze was all in all, even his father Fraser's less important.

In the garden beyond the cottage windows, Fraser was tying up the daffodil leaves into knots now that the flowers had died back. Under the trees the knotted leaves stuck out like topknots in the grass. The sea beyond the parapet sparkled. The cannon on the castle ramparts were green with salt, the wooden guncarriages splitting and sinking under the weight of the green guns.

'That'll be just fine with me,' said Catriona into her wafer of telephone that was like a mirror to her, telling her she was desirable, 'but I'm over in Ayrshire at present so I'll maybe not be with you till quite late in the day. Oh. Well, that's fine too, as long as you know I'll not be able for more than a quick meal and then straight home to my own place. Yes, I can eat meat. I carry low sodium salt. Uh huh, it's beautiful here. The daffs are out, yellow everywhere. There are birds in the trees too. I'll be miserable to get back to Glasgow.'

Dougan the Muscovy duck tapped at the window with his red beak that looked like it had barnacles and cold sores. The branches of the trees over the knotted, finished daffodils were on the verge of more than budding. They were empty of birds.

Dougan tapped again. His feathers were mottled, black and white, spatters of pigment not as artful as that of many birds, nor as reassuring as the markings of a cow. The narrow gap between the duck's small eyes seemed to leave the space for a brain as wide as a broad bean, Catriona thought.

Alice had not turned round from nuzzling her son's scalp to see what it was that Dougan wanted. The Muscovy walked to the side of the bow window, and took the chain of the cowbell that hung there, shaking it until he got the clapper chinkling inside.

'I'd better see what he wants. It'll be a sandwich,' said Alice.

'How would you know what it wants, that duck?' asked Catriona. 'How does it say what it wants? Surely it can only say that it wants attention? It'll not be sure it wants a sandwich. It might want some duck food or something. It might just like the noise of the bell. It'll just be used to your thinking it wants a sandwich. It's come to link the bell with a sandwich, or so you think, but maybe it's trying to ask for something different.'

'You think it just eats the sandwich out of good manners?' said Alice. 'Like you with that telephone call.'

'Eh?' Catriona couldn't see this link. She would have before Alice had had Fergus. Was it not that the obtuseness more usually settled on the one who had a baby, not her successful friend? So the magazines said.

'Well, you went to the bell of the phone and accepted a night out.'

'That doesn't make me the Muscovy duck.'

'No it's him that's the Muscovy duck. He's the Muscovy duck, whoever he is.'

'How d'you know it was a he? Can you sex phone calls now you're so one with nature?'

'Easier than poultry, yes I can. So can you. You were styling your hair at him down the phone, Cat.'

'So why's he a Muscovy duck?' asked Catriona, not yet understanding, but suspecting that she was in some category now in Alice's mind, as, undoubtedly, Alice was in hers.

'Rings a bell and gets a treat,' said Alice baldly, putting Fergus into his netted lobster pot and going to butter the duck's piece for him. She did one for the wee boy at the same time. Marmite for Fergus, jam for the Muscovy. The duck would do the bread more justice, but Alice could eat Fergus's bread when he'd mumbled it a bit. He was a big baby and solids weren't that far off. She wished she could talk to Catriona about this. They had dissected the minutiae of the timings of courtship – when to let him do this or that, when to start calling him, all that – but had not yet been into the delectable curricula of its consequences, weaning, possetting, bottling, burping, changing.

Catriona had kept her face angry for some time after Alice had made her devastatingly stupid comment about the man who'd rung her, Fordyce Succoth from Dysart Graphics, being like that daft Muscovy duck. It was Alice and Fraser's having moved out here to the sticks that made Alice say these things, she'd nothing to keep her on the ball. She was so dopey with the caretaking of the castle garden, the green fields of grass and sea – and the wean and the coastal views, Catriona thought angrily, that she couldn't even see when a person was insulted. 'Rings a bell and gets a treat,' indeed, she'd tell Fordyce that later when they were better acquainted. She thought of Fordyce very carefully, leaving off some of the things about him like the holes behind his layered hair on the neck, where the acne had got him, and the way he drove with the backs of his hands laid on the thick thighs of his lower half. The car though was a superb machine, and Fordyce's work at Dysart Graphics very challenging, Catriona reminded herself. Any road, she thought, I can't cancel on him now.

For she had begun to think of the skin on the back of his neck, its pitted, red, angry texture pierced here and there by thin bore holes that looked as they could take a wire right in to the body. The skin was like something she would not translate into words from the picture in her head. Dougan the Muscovy duck's shiny rough bill roofed with pustules, his two dry duck nostrils came into Catriona's mind and she got more angry. How could Alice ruin her relationship like this? Was she jealous, stuck out here with Fergus and Fraser, one of them saying nothing at all in the house all day, the other doing the same outdoors?

There Fraser was, for example, tying knots in daffodils all morning. Why was that? Was he trying to remember a whole lot of things? 'Oh deary me, I must remember Alice's birthday. Let me see now, I'll just tie back this clump of daffs. Then there's Fergus's. Can't be more than seven months off.' No, Catriona thought, it was not that, she had to acknowledge it; it was more likely something to do with the way you did things having to change if you lived in a part of the world where tying up daffodils was not just a thing you might as well do because you'd seen it done but a thing it was better never to omit doing.

Fergus was sitting on the ground now, by the coffee table, propped up by cushions. He had pink all around his lips, perhaps from some jam off Dougan the Muscovy's piece, which seemed to be broken up on the floor indoors, though the duck itself was to be seen eating up its snack on the lawn moving its neck, like a typing finger, again and again, at the sticky white bread.

Alice, big and content, independent and annoyingly incurious about the life Catriona was leading now, that is the life Alice had once led too, was busy in the kitchen chopping, rocking a knife in a pile of parsley on a board. There was a smell of new coffee and mowing. It irked Catriona that she would have to move into the kitchen to talk to Alice. In that room, so securely Alice's own, she would have to be a visitor, to take whatever conversation Alice considered suitable to her marital kitchen. Apart from Fraser, Alice no longer discussed men, as if the plurality in the noun might imply some wide-ranging sampling on her part that might offend the curtains, spill the water in a blush over the rosy tablecloth. The new, absorbing, potentially plural tribe in her life was babies, whose activities, reactions, characteristics, differences and needs were now of that relevance those of men had been.

Alice reached for two onions, tore off the skins with the noise of a cheap brown envelope being forced, and chopped them with the maddening efficacious calm that she seemed to have discovered for herself. She pushed the onion, chopped and weepy, to one side with the flat of the knife, and took out a patty of what looked like pink clay, socking it into a pyrex bowl and adding two eggs, the parsley, the onion, and a brusque grind of pepper.

'More coffee, Cat?' she said. In the old days, when they'd had a clash of mood or taste or will, Alice had been nervous that it was always she who offended her friend, and had spent hours padding up to her afterwards to check if she could make things better, in this way giving Catriona the opportunity to keep her unhappy and docile for a good while after, not relenting till she had negotiated at least one practical advantage, a lend of Alice's grey silk stockings, or a go of her perfume, maybe even a whole evening of using it right out of her own handbag, at a restaurant or in the cinema.

'That's a delicious scent' her companion might say.

'My stepmother brings it me from Paris. It's made up by a Russian,' Catriona would say, in the very words Alice used when offered the same compliments. She never felt like a liar then, just as later today, in a restaurant, she would not feel badly when she told Fordyce how she had that afternoon at her people's place in the country cooked a parsley, pork sausagemeat and onion stuffing for a duck that earlier in the day she had seen eat a jam sandwich, after ringing a bell for it.

Fergus sucked on at the heel of Catriona's candied-rose pink suede shoe, pulling the colour out of it slowly and stertorously, with his milky circling lips, till it was losing colour like a frozen raspberry lolly, all its seductive pink going down the throat of the voracious puller at the ice.

Writing on Buildings

Pushing out from the shingle in the wooden boat, Bill called to the dog, twice, 'Shona, Shona!'

Shona ran to and fro on the pebbles. Bill heard her nails tap and skid.

'Come on, girl, come on now.' Shona was a black collie with a bit of Jack Russell in her. She liked water and hated boats.

Soon she was swimming alongside, when she saw Bill would not abandon his oars.

'Too late now, girl,' said Bill. 'You get along in and go home. Home, now!' The blur of black in the water turned and Bill saw the reproach in the edges of the bitch's eyes as she made for shore. When she got back up on the shingle the water poured off her, splashing the grey stones black. She whirled the drops off herself, seeming to keep her white pointed snout still, pointed out towards Bill in his boat as he made for the small island in the middle of the loch.

In the bottom of the boat a plastic bag containing a bottle and two tins rocked between the timbers. There was a clatter under the boat as the centreboard scraped on the rocks around the island. Here it was not shingle but leaning brown rocks. It was an island you could imagine sticking up out of the floor of the loch like a stalagmite, sheer and showing only its short green summit. Built among the dull ponticum and streaming mosses, though, was a house, fourteen feet wide, fourteen feet deep, twenty-eight feet high. In only one of its seven windows was the glass unbroken. The top window was an oval, under the slate gable; in it was set a lozenge of glass, painted with a standing bird, for which Bill had named the house the Heronry.

Bill pulled his boat close in and tied the painter to a standing rock, where an iron ring had been set. He looked back to the shingle beach and saw that Shona had gone. Up the hill he saw her tail whispering like smoke above the heather. She'd be home in twenty minutes.

When he looked at the Heronry he could not believe that this small house contained all it did, an unbroken confident peace that was like a delay before certain fulfilment of trust. He could not remember in how many places he had looked for what he found here. He took his papers out and the tobacco and made a cigarette without looking, just pinching, holding, folding, licking, rolling. When he put the thin thing in his lips, he looked down the once to strike his match.

The air was so empty the smell of the match filled his stomach like meat. The black loch water promised rain. Bill listened to see if it had reached the hills. He heard the faint interference of distant weather, a premonition between the notion and actual drops on the face. He saw the settling grey cloud with its violent edge of light lie up against the hill and breathe into it. The cigarette drew blue feathers on the air.

In the first house he'd imagined had held all this one did, he'd settled and lived for two years. It had been at the gates of a ruin, just outside the city. He'd lived invisibly, as he liked. The falling big house had been a safari park in its last throes. Bill's gatehouse was in the shadow of a gigantic placard that read: 'These may be the only lions between here and Crianlarich.' It was the uncertainty that charmed the very few visitors to the place, who were diverted rather than disappointed to find the lion-headed red lemurs, often flu-ridden, in the rickety aviaries of the old house. In the hall of the house were two stuffed lions, precariously fighting, at the top of the trembling stone stairs that were covered most mornings with feathers from the pigeons that had got in overnight and battered themselves against the great bland oval skylight in the roof's height.

By the end of his time in the gatehouse, Bill had developed a touch with the lemurs, golden lion tamarins. He could tell when they sneezed if it was cat flu or worse, and he was horribly pained when their long forearms and small hands had to be folded at the end. Their hair was the glowing golden red of lily pollen. When the last one died he could not stay. The owners of the big house had yet more good ideas as to how to keep the place afloat, on the road, whatever wrong words they used, and Bill could see how each one would end. There were the usual misty fantastic ideas. In the end it was down to a dope farm or an agricultural machinery museum. Bill could see it all, the rusting thresher and the untended hemp in unsuitable pots taking over the greenhouse and then turning out to be entirely legal. He knew too well the uningenuity of the family, their suicidal love of the recessive plaster and subsiding stone.

Moreover, other people had begun to come to his gatehouse, not people he invited, but lovers and other conspirators. He heard them in the night, their voices, and, far worse, their pencils or their knives as they wrote their names, their feelings, their bodies' intentions on the walls of his house, in the plaster or, with incisions that filled Bill with grief, in the stone. He heard them enact the words they wrote. He heard Jim loves Sandra, and he heard Sandra does not quite so much love Jim. He heard Alan 4 Bruno. Leah and Daniel he heard weekly for one summer and was to a certain extent let down when it changed to Leah is Crazy Over Liam.

Daniel had used words that seemed beautiful to Bill in the summer nights. He heard about Daniel's feelings and he understood them. For once it did not make him think of the mess, the scribbling mess of it all. With Daniel, Bill could tell, it was romance, with a capital R. Leah loved it and then had had enough of it by the autumn. By the time the days were getting short, she wanted the smaller words and the quicker dates – with Liam – by the gatehouse.

There were boys buying and selling there too. He found the equipment and swept it up with his metal pan and wee wooden brush totted off a skip. The foil went all soft and black but nothing could destroy the plastic bottles and disposable syringes. He threw them out and understood as he never had before his mother's feelings towards his own unexceptionable private squalor of skins and butt ends, bottles and cans.

In a country so rich in emptiness, you would have thought there would be places to live in that'd not been written on. You'd be wrong. Bill had moved north to the Black Isle, he'd moved west to Ardnamurchan, and he'd tried out Ettrickdale. Always the place where he settled started off unwritten upon, but he began to hear the movements and the breaths and the sighs and then the scratchings and even cutting and he knew that the marks of love or commerce or loyalty to God or football were about to be made, as though people could not act or think or speak without making a record of it in writing, writing that was not especially good to look at nor that ever said much that was new, nor that would be revisited. They wrote, it seemed to Bill, in order to attach their flimsy human selves to something that would last longer than they might. They were weaving themselves into time.

'Why not write on trees?' Bill had thought of saying, one night when he heard a man who had grunted for over an hour in the porch of a folly at Achiltibuie saying, 'Ech, Moira, wait till I get my felt pen.'

Buildings had no defence against those who wrote on them. They were bound to hold the record of the visit as an ear holds a note. These were not visitors who wrote one line of verse with a diamond in an upper window, or initialled out of sight a hidden sill. They were writers who did not know more of what they wrote upon than that it was old and might last. The knowledge seemed to spur them on.

Bill's present home lay up the loch from the Heronry. He lived in the game hut of a shooting lodge. It was, naturally, draughty, but Bill appreciated it by moonlight when the silver came in through the thousand slats and he lay there under the lead bell of the roof like a bird himself, but alive. He hung boughs of fir from the game hooks and slept in the striped and scented green listening to the words of love and then the frustration of the writers when they could find so little flat upon which to inscribe their most recent version of the truth.

The nearest town, Lochgilphead, was a good hitch away. He'd a reasonable living housesitting and was getting a tremendous weekend sideline in marital counselling, the demand for which rose in the winter. From the years of residence in trysting places, Bill had an acceptance of folly that made his clients determined either to surprise him by behaving a great deal better or by trying ever harder to shock him.

Now autumn was coming. Bill had sought a new home throughout the summer but most places he found had been too comfortable, too draughtless, well-appointed, visible, to be shelters for the secret people whose lives nourished his own.

He felt the existence of these people like wiring running through a house or like strings essential to the performance of a puppet show. He loved to know that things were more than what they seemed, that you could never expose it all. It made his own unpromised life feel light and simple as a creature's. He had Shona, and he had his own ways, and that was it. It was what he wanted.

He had found the Heronry on a walk. He saw it across the water, and wondered at the blue-grey slate gable pointing out of the ponticum. It was so neat and finely finished that he was sure it must be a place that was known and full of confided transactions, written and scratched into it.

He puzzled at first about how to reach the island, but he asked one of his weekend problem-bearers sidelong one Saturday if he knew where Bill might come by a wee boat. The man had a repair yard and hated writing cheques, so the dinghy, clinker-built and trim, was Bill's, plus oars, if he'd pledge another six months of his advice and leave the boat behind when he left the area.

'Good enough,' said Bill. 'Good enough.'

When he got to the place that first time, he checked it over, every bit of its stone, and its smooth coved interior. There was birdshit and there were feathers and the light bones of mouse and bird. There was dust and fallen plaster and the odd splint of lath. There were brambles curling in at one of the lower windows and in the doorway there was bracken. Half the egg of a blackbird had been blown behind an interior door. It was as bare as that, a building apparently unwritten upon except by the hand that had depicted the heron on the oval of glass, but even it was not like the words, that had come eventually to disturb Bill at each of the homes he found.

He pinched out the roll-up, took out his army knife and hooked the lid off the bottle of beer he had brought with him in the boat over from the shingle shore. He drank it so slowly that it was never related to thirst, only to the gradual relaxation of his body and the invasion of his mind by a mild forgiving warmth. Bill did not take drink in company. He liked to receive its blessing where he couldn't be seen, when his unguarded self could come free of the outer, controlled, invisible man.

The rain on the hill had fallen out of the cloud that was now all silver. The black loch was shining blue. The floor of the island around the small house was all red mast and shooting bracken.

There was a grinding, then a clopping, and the resolved sound of a boat being pulled up.

Bill looked around. He was not thinking of where to hide himself – it was clear that he or someone must be here since there was the boat – but of where to hide the bottle.

This took on such significance that he began with his heel to dig at the soft soil with the heel of his boot. He knelt to bury the bottle, after pouring the last of the beer away.

He was arranging leaves tidily over the place the bottle lay when the new arrival came.

She was not only a woman, he knew her. She visited him at the carefully neutral drop-in centre for counselling in Lochgilphead. He could not forget the story she'd told him, though he tried to, in order to make his getaway.

'Oh,' said Ina MacIntyre, née Binnie, soon to be Paterson. 'Oh, Bill Petrie.' She'd pale hair the inside of beech-nut cases in colour and feather downiness.

'Uh huh,' said Bill. 'Did you see a dog?'

'Was that what you were scrabbling for down there, then?' said Ina.

Bill felt the beer gather in his skin and go red. Red beer filled the epidermis of his normally pale face.

'No.'

'You looked like you were burying a bone,' she said lightly. She was trying to get off the subject, but what one would they get on to then? Paw Binnie's beatings, Davey MacIntyre's drunken demands or Malc Paterson's touch of fraud with the White Fish Promotion Board?

Ina looked at Bill. She was right, she knew that. When she saw the wet dog she'd known he'd be here, and alone. He must be twenty-two, she thought. Twenty bloody two and all he's ever had to cuddle's a dog.

'Cigarette?' she said.

'No thanks, I've my own,' said Bill.

He doesn't even know what to say, she thought.

He was bothered the way she was speaking from a set of flirtatious words he had heard often enough, but never joined in with. Yet the beer on his empty stomach – he'd been saving the beans and macaroni till later – came between him and his understanding. He did not yet hear the words for what they were. The Heronry's clean face and untouched interior had taken anything like suspicion from him.

'Will we go in?' said Ina.

The small house seemed to grow. The blue bird in the top window looked curiously submissive, its neck curving down, its beak also downcast, till he saw the fish painted in the lower part of the glass, never thinking of the beak.

'You go first,' she said. 'I'll be with you right away.'

He stood in the plaster-bare high single room, its every plane revealed by daylight, and his teeth chattered, though his body was warm.

'My, it's pretty,' she said, as she stepped in from the bright door. 'It's so plain. Like only us had ever been here. Even although it's old.'

It was his own feeling, come from the mouth of another, put in words, clumsy as could be. He felt for the first time in his life that there would be moves he could make that would be a refinement over words, if he let someone help him this one time.

'Come away in over here,' he said, and in a voice he had not used except when thinking aloud. 'Put down your things first.'

In the alcove of the main room of this rich man's playhouse, built to pass a luncheon in perhaps or to shelter ladies from the rain on fishing trips, built to accommodate crinolines and painting gear and rods, Ina set down her bag, containing her drawing things, pencils of several degrees of softness, and a picnic for two, apples, cheese, bread and ham. He saw the brittle, rich, charcoal sticks in her painting roll. They seemed to urge upon him the new pleasure of writing on an expanse of clean plaster.

The boats, as they will, left alone, jostled in the small cove, unable to keep apart.

On the Shingle

Our mothers had decided that the Chocolate House in Princes Street would be our part of the afternoon, after they had finished in Jenners and Forsyths. We were to meet them at four and woe betide us if we were late back from the baths at Portobello. Anne's mother had said why did we not just away off to the baths at Glenogle but my mother was English and said there was a wave-making machine at Portobello; by this she meant that it was cleaner and did not have the yellow tinge of Glenogle, also that the higher entrance charge kept out what she surely did not describe to herself as working-class people.

On the top of our bus, Anne – with whom I was in love since she was ten and I was nine and she had a dog – and I told lies to each other.

'My dad's thinking of getting a house out of the middle of Kirkcaldy, I'll have to go to boarding school (this was our dream) and then what'll Mandy (this was Anne's dog) do? Will you not just think of that?'

'My daddy plays a dab game of ice hockey,' I replied. 'You should see him, though it's no good for his heart since he was a hero in the war.' My father was a quiet man, a doctor. I doubt he knew if ice hockey was a food or a complaint, or if it was at all. His war had been heroic, in an unmartial way; he spent two years in bed with tuberculosis, and had learnt to smock.

'Dad's thinking of getting a purple Consul.' This could be true. Anne's dad was a big man with a lino factory and her brothers were down for Glenalmond. Scottish snobbery is sweet on the tongue, its private signals words which lift the blood with pride of race – Gordonstoun, Oxenfoord, Skye, Buccleuch, and traps to keep strangers out, Auchinleck, Ruthven.

The bus went past the big power station and there were the baths, low, white, harled. They were stepped and across their square gable, in wide-spaced blue letters, thin, elegant, casting their shadow back on to the distemper in the sun, was written 'Portobello Swimming Baths'. Each letter was exaggeratedly tall and thin, half as long again as it need be. The railings of the baths also had this disproportion, and bore long iron ellipses at their tips. The tiles were raspberry red to trim, or white, edged with leaf green, on walls and floor. There was a tremendous smell of chlorine and over the entrance was a notice to tell us that the next waves would be at half-past the hour of two and that spectators would be welcome in the viewing gallery, price 2d. We each paid sixpence and went in through the turnstile which was taller than Anne, though she was older. She was so fair her hair went grey when it was wet. I was so fat that it was a great show of love to let her see me in my bathing suit. Usually, I'd only let my mother, and then in the viewing gallery, what with her bikini and her accent.

The point at Portobello was to get two goes of the waves, to get rescued and to see a grown up (not a man) with as few clothes as possible. We would get the two-thirty and the three o'clock waves which should just leave time for the other two tasks which must of course not be mentioned, certainly not to our mothers, nor, until afterwards, to each other, this to guard against disappointment.

We changed in separate cubicles into our black suits. Anne's hair was short but the baths stipulated the wearing of caps for those with long hair, even men. To be seen in cap at the baths became a paradoxical index of rebellion in Edinburgh for those years. I squeezed my two pigtails into the sore rubber helmet. We wore rubber bracelets at the wrist, to hold the key of the lockers where we had put our clothes. To reach the baths, which were open to the air, we had to walk between the rows of zinc lockers, past the attendants doing wet knitting in white overalls, and through a foot bath, tiled in white rectangles with stiff palmate shapes in dark green on the odd one. The bleach-stinking water was delicious to the feet. The big thing at this point was not to giggle at the notice which said 'NO SPITTING, NO JUMPING, NO RUNNING, NO PUSHING, NO SHOUTING, NO PETTING'. The trick was to say something dead funny just before you read the last bit, so you had to laugh anyway. Simultaneously, we said the name of a girl two forms above (who had what we called boozums) and we were off, hyperventilating with giggles. We giggled like drunks. It made us wild.

Out in the sun by the baths, we stood at the shallow end; at a foot's interval all down the baths, the height was recorded in green figures on the white tiles in feet and inches. The shallow end was 2'6", the deep end 10'. Four lifeguards stood, one at each corner, in white trousers and singlets; on their feet were white rubber shoes. The pool lay, a flat pale blue rectangle, banks of seats on three sides. At the shallow end was the viewers' gallery. It was in the tall clock tower of the baths, and beneath it was the mighty pump which made the artificial waves, yet spectators could have tea and pancakes and not feel a thing, looking out through glass at their intrepid friends or children breasting the regulated waves each half-hour. Portobello is by the sea, but we were never tempted by its untimed grey breakers.

Anne could, of course, swim. I floated very nicely, my mother said. We went up to the place 5'6" was marked, as tall as me and a lot taller than Anne, and we clung to the edge waiting for the two-thirty waves.

There they came, rolling, smooth, every seventh one bigger, so high you could see through it.

Was it every seventh one? There was a magic number, but I forget it now and surely the rhythms of those warm false waves cannot be those of the lunar paradigm awaited by surfers in the real seas? Our waves were warm with the extra heat from the power station; now it might be called recreational pollution-cycling. Between waves, we toiled up towards the shallow end, always combed out and back a little deeper by each inevitable buffet as it came, hitting us in the chin and lifting us so we stood like soldiers held in the apex of each wave, before sliding down its lee-side and readying ourselves to breast the next. By the time the five minutes of waves were done, our eyes were red and our fingers white and crinkly at the tip. We were also hoarse with screaming, and ready just to splash in the shallow end for a while, biding our time. We sat on the red Dumfries sandstone steps, rough on our bottoms, and watched the youths and girls (Anne said 'girrul') whose play was as formal and pointed as a dance. We did not *look* at the youths; this would be too rude. But we did watch the chests of the girls with the attention of doctors. The big boys would splash at the girls with their feet, or dive near them and rush up through the water to stand breast to breast in the warm blue which might rock them into touching, skin washed innocent of heat and hair by the water. The girls made much play of ignoring the boys and when the boys looked away the girls redrew their eyes with particularly ostentatious displays of indifference. One girl moved her head and clapped her hands more than the rest. Even in the rubber cap her face was pretty; on her right hip was a tiny embroidered diver. When she shrieked, she took her hand away from her mouth as though holding a cigarette. She was not chicken-wired with pink veins on her legs like Anne, nor was she freckled like me. She was pale nut colour all over, not the nuts my mother had with her drink, but the sugar brown of tablet. Her breasts moved after she stopped, and she wore tiny rings in her ears. In Edinburgh, it's the Poles and the Scots-Italians who do that.

'You're right stupid, that you are,' called one of the boys to her, in a yearning voice. 'You canna even do a duck dive. Get on, have a wee go. I'll help yas.' His voice was about seventeen.

'Och leave her, Ian, I'll give you a race,' said another boy, with an older voice and a ringleader's way to him.

The girl looked up, and lifted both hands to her rubber head, touching it lightly as though it were curls. All in the same moment, she pushed her hands flat to her head and steered her elbows simultaneously out and over her head, never moving her eyes and lifting her front, so two solid hemispheres rose between the scoops of her collarbones and the navy cotton of her bathing costume. She stared until the boys had gone, knowing they would be back, and went to clutch and giggle with her plain girlfriend by the side (4'6", just right for spying out the lads without getting bombed by the bullies). Anne and I were going to discover radium, or something of the kind, so we'd not much time for boys, but I did see a glimpse of how that girl could burn in the water, incandescent even in her rubber hat.

For some weeks Anne and I had been doing research in our laboratory; my mother naturally got it wrong and called it the nursery. There we stirred shoplifted fizzy sweets into water and sealed the solution in test tubes; we each had a Letts' chemistry set, though the copper sulphate had run out long ago. We had dissected a shrew and felt a breakthrough was not far away; the teacher who was as near as we had come to Madame Curie was Miss Lindsay. She was firm but fair and wore a blue coat for chemistry, a green one for biology, and thrilling twin sets for assembly. She had quite a front and was said to have had a fiancé who was lost in the Western Isles, so now she was dedicated to science. I did quite good imitations of Miss Lindsay saying, 'If the surface of the Earth was six inches deep in sand, the number of grains would not yet equal the number of molecules of matter constituting a milk bottle.' Atoms came in the next form up.

Was that, I wonder now, so only the girls who were ready for it would learn of the divisibility even of the atom?

'Don't look now,' said Anne, nudging me, and rolling her eyes up. Starting from the shiny tiles, I saw two pairs of feet, one hairy, one smooth. Looking further up, I saw the flat modesty apron of an older lady's bathing costume, pulled over wide hips. I was above looking at the parallel part of her companion, so up I looked. Miss Lindsay! She was arm in arm with a man, a man about as old as my father, well, old, anyhow. She was staring into his face and some red hair was coming out of her hat.

'How rude,' said Anne and I'd to agree. We stared as hard as we could and felt horribly let down. They slipped into the water at 6', separating to do so. It was three o'clock and time for the new waves, our last of this afternoon. We weren't that thrilled any more. So, Miss Lindsay was not dedicated to science. We watched her and the man. This man would never be lost in the Western Isles, he was too noisy and hairy for that. His head burst out of the top of each wave like a dog's, hers beside it, pink and laughing. We were glad that we would never be interested in men, being committed to a life of seeking something very important, separating it from its baser element, like Madame Curie with the pitch-blende. We bobbed and floated, but I, for one, was above all this now.

There was a furious yell, and all four lifeguards rushed to the deep end, white clothed and muscly on morticians' feet. 'Here, yous, that'll do, ye can git oot if there's ony mair o' that, d'ye hear me the noo?'

Miss Lindsay and the man were very red in the face. He patted her and said, 'There, there.' She ducked her face into his neck as though she were a child waiting to be carried to bed, and gave him a great smile, her face shining. She looked more naked than the girl in the earrings had done. She did not look a bit rude.

I'd lost my taste for getting rescued by now.

'When these waves are over, shall we get the bus?' said Anne.

'Uh huh,' I said, a noise my mother said was as Scots as 'Em' for 'Um'.

When we'd had the compulsory shower and I'd wrung out my pigtails, we rolled our costumes in our towels like Swiss rolls and went off to wait at the bus stop by the shingle. There was a drunk old woman crying on the sea wall; she had a Shetland collie at her side, all nerves and petticoats. Mandy was a Sheltie, so Anne stroked the dog, though our mothers frequently told us not to touch strange dogs.

'Oh look at the two of yes, a lifetime to go, two wee girruls and a' they years tae love.' She smelt. Her hair was in a red and yellow Paisley scarf in the bitter wind. The white sunshine showed her blue cheeks and the scum on her teeth. 'Pain and grief and the vale of tears and it's no go the merry-go-round and ma gude man dead in his chair with his pipe in his teeth and the teeth sae clampit they' tae cut it oot Oh Christ and whaur's the sense two wee girruls tell me that and I'll gie yes the bus ride aye and the moon and stars an' a.'

Anne was all right, because she could look very hard at the dog. She gentled its allsort nose in her hand and looked out to the grey sea with its real waves. Her hair was drying back to white. The wind smelt of salt and the bleach from the baths, the old woman of pee and dirt and drink. My mother said the crones in the Canongate drank a mixture of meths and Brasso, called Blue Billy; she herself drank Cinzano Bianco, 'And devil take the hindmost,' she'd say.

I was fair to giggle or cry and I knew the old woman (or was she old?) was going to touch me; it was a race against time, would the bus never come?

It rocked around the corner, maroon and white, 'Nemo me impune lacessit' on the side, just as the old woman's hand came for my arm. 'Grace, he'd say, Grace, we've just time, here, now, here, against the wall, quick get yer skirts up.'

Later, though we'd had only milk while our mothers had frothy pink chocolate and cinnamon toast with their feet crunching among the bags under the table in the Chocolate House, I was sick, and I saw that stinking woman tied with string waddle down to the grey sea, her dog beside her flirting its petticoats, nosing in the shingle at the edge of the cold real waves.

Wally Dugs

When she put her hand in the peke's ruff of silky blonde hair, you'd only to think of her lifting the wee dog up to her old head and pulling the thing down over it like a wig to get some notion of what Grisel Carnegie had looked like when she had been the prima ballerina *assoluta* of Esme Stewart's heart. Now you could see her skull's shifting plates through the spun-up hair, and as she chewed, there was a clicking sounded like a frog looks when it swallows down some midgey morsel. She took her lunch in by degrees, making dolly meals on the fork and then edging it up to her mouth, avoiding her nephew's eyes when she actually snapped and swallowed. Beauty was ever ill-served by the act itself of eating. Esme had loved her little appetite, saw it for an expression of that sweet passivity so light and downy and otherwise unimposing in a ladylike woman, a woman with whom you would be proud to be seen and with whom you need never converse save anent that which was pleasant. Esme had been an advocate, lovely on his feet in the court, Grisel imagined, as on the dance floor, with his long robe making much of his gestures, the little wig not undignified but proper to his office. She had naturally never witnessed him as he strode and ranted and dealt out fiery justice in the court. But he was well spoken of, she remembered that, and she could still, all these years later, induce people to mention him, frequently favourably, and that was like a sip at sugary tea. She was a sipper, never wishing immersion in sensations. Those sips did her fine, as they always had.

Glenbervie was not a Home. It was strange how unreassuring the word home could become once you were older. Anyway, Glenbervie wasn't, so that was all settled. As a matter of interest, Ailsa and Carl had looked around a considerable number of Homes before deciding that Glenbervie, a warden-supervised sheltered development, would be superior in every respect. She'd a patio, a hot plate for keeping dishes warm when she'd guests, a terrific view of the whatname hills and a button to get through to the warden all hours of the day. And night, but she could not imagine having the bare face to use it. Ailsa visited a bit less now because the baby was walking and she said she didn't trust her around the trinkets, she'd never forgive herself if Rhona smashed a piece in the famous china collection. Grisel had a lifetime's aviary of china birdies, all up on the sliding-front cabinet where she kept the glasses with the capitals of Europe written on them, with a landmark on too, that tower for Paris, a ruin for Rome, and a guardsman for London. Madrid had had a bull as she remembered but it was long broken, not in the move to Glenbervie but at some fairly riotous gathering where a hem had caught the glass and sent it flying. Skirts could do that then, sticking out and solid with net and Vylene, full of starch as an ashet of mashed potatoes. They were becoming though, to anyone with a dancer's bearing, like herself. The stiff skirt would encircle its wearer like a big flower, making her little legs just wavy stamens among the rustling petals of petticoat. You'd to crush the skirt to yourself at night in a car, both to get in and so as not to impede visibility. The rustling petty was right up there with a life of its own misting up the windscreen and rising like boiling sugar to fill the side windows before you knew it. The way to control those skirts, Grisel Carnegie knew, as the girl who had broken the glass with Madrid and maybe a bull maybe a cow on had not known, was to furl them like an umbrella, the way a bindweed flower is turned on itself before its first time of opening, the time after which it just flushes up in colour then falls limp like a thing forgotten, a hankie maybe. To furl up your skirt you stood with your hands by your side and turned your hands against your upper legs as though you were twisting the top and bottom of yourself in two at the waist. The bell of the skirt followed naturally. It was like that with garments. You either did or did not know how to make them do as you wished. Grisel could honestly say she had never known her clothes step out of line. Gloves had remained wed to each other, her appropriately treed shoes had not pinched, and no button had ever broken with its hole.

She'd not been young either when she had favoured those big skirts like flowers, but she had taken good care of her appearance with the result that she'd the waistline younger women had lost to the reproductive urge. Not that old, mind, but approaching an age about which to be discreet. Esme had understood that, of course.

What age Esme had been Miss Carnegie did not know. She could have made enquiries, there were plenty of folk must have known him at school and then at the University, but she preferred a little haziness, a little of what she liked to refer to as romance. The more veils it dons the closer romance sidles to untruth, but Grisel was for beauty over truth, fortunate, perhaps, when all was said and done, at Glenbervie.

The china birds were cast in attitudes, the attitudes of real birds, which no real bird will hold for longer than an instant. The effect of many colourful frozen creatures, shiny, without the softness and blur of feather, tapping a coy ceramic snail or arrested on a frosty twig, was lightly deathly. The birds were demanding when it came to dusting, more demanding than one living bird might have been about its seed and water. But Grisel had forsworn living pets when she left her Pekinese with Ailsa and Carl.

'Taking that dog, it's like a matrimonial visit,' Carl would tell Ailsa when he got home. God, he was pleased to get home, too. You never knew the meaning of the word 'home' till you'd been to a place like Glenbervie for the best part of a day, including the drive. 'She holds on that tight to the bloody dog' – he set it down now on the coir matting in their front hall – 'and it has nothing at all to say to her and looks guilty and embarrassed and desperate for a cigarette.'

Neither of them disliked the dog that much or they would not have relented about having it put to sleep when the warden at Glenbervie explained that dogs were not ideal for the ambience of the residential complex. The baby weeded at the dog's rich coat for hours, and kissed its squashed face. The Peke permitted liberties from the baby it would have bitten off at the knee in anyone else. Indeed, the dog's and the baby's size, gait and expression were increasingly similar: each could look outraged or appealing, each was prone to soon-forgotten rage. But the animal would keep its glamour as young humans rarely do, although baby Rhona was one of those changelings who astonish by their dissimilarity to plain parents, so dog and baby were a strange, bewitching pair, frailly matched for the time being.

Once Carl had his drink and Ailsa was sitting over from him on the other sofa with the dog and the baby in a tangle at her side making, it had to be admitted, a regrettable state of the sage velvet stripe, he began his story of the day. The way to tell it was to save the marrow in the bone till the end, to worry at the tale until it split and the nourishing part was there at last. For Ailsa, so certain of her own freedom from dependence – even upon Carl, who was after all only a man – the cream of the joke was always Esme, how he came in to the fortnightly encounter of her husband and her aunt-by-marriage as they sat in the sheltered chalet in the shadow of the whatname hills surrounded by china birds and pecking at food intended as festive and failing in that intention, an inch of fish here, a jot of jelly there, and lashings of Carnation milk for a treat. The Carnation came in a lovat-green earthenware jug marked 'Brora'. Not that she'd been any of these places, the old coot, but it did make present-giving simple enough. Just keep your eyes peeled for a place-name and snap it up. Sensible un-dependent Ailsa had no patience for bits and bobs, it was like clothes, a waste of time and money just to give yourself allergies with the dusting or, in the case of clothes, acute discomfort. Ailsa favoured the untailored, the non-iron, the elasticated.

It was appalling to see how Grisel still kept all that nonsense up, with her assisted hair and the kitten heels to her old lady's shoes. Surely she could shut down on her appearance now? She'd been playing that tune all her life. Might it not be a relief to change stations? Tune out of being feminine, tune in to feminism maybe. Ailsa loved her feminism, it was so dependable a comfort. She knew she would cope fine if Carl was inconsiderate enough to leave life before she did. She was a natural coper, so she thought. She knew what was what, she often said, only very occasionally acknowledging the disappointed voice within that asked if this was it, was there nothing more, nothing along the lines of what she sometimes glimpsed in her sleep or heard in music or flowing water, a sheen in the air.

Carl was spinning out the drive, making it all as boring as possible, partly to make Ailsa feel bad but also, she hoped, for they were not on bad terms, to whet her appetite for any fun to come. 'So eventually I get off the A9 anyhow and cruise down to the Alpine Village itself. Usual smell of rubber briefs and grey potatoes and a wee dab of cologne for the Sabbath. I'm dying for a drink, of course.'

She knew what to ask. 'Gay Paree? Romantic Rome?'

'It was London this time, and a sherry. She must have laid it in for me. Mobile shop service looking up.'

'Just the one?'

'Two out of her and one solo in the kitchen.' That'll be five in all, thought Ailsa.

'She serves out the dinner slow so it's cold on those ferocious hot plates and sizzling but chilly, the Brussels still frozen at the middle and smelling like cats on the outside. I put Carnation on the mashed-potato balls just for some variety. Christ, have me put down by the time I'm old, will you not?'

I will, Ailsa thought, don't worry. Illness had no place in her understanding of the world. But I, she continued in her strong mind, intend to live for a long time after you are gone, and always to be myself and do as I will. It did not occur to her that she might ever become an old lady in a colony of old ladies, cooking bland food for ungrateful connections, and shopping from a van full of tins. She would be splendid, and wilful, and eat garlic. No one would discuss her after visiting her save with admiration.

'Yellow jelly?'

'Red jelly.'

The baby tried to copy her parents, 'Ledlellyälellylelly.' The parents dismissed this primitive vocaläising. The dog jumped down off the sofa one end before the other, it was hard, beneath the hair, to tell which, and shimmered over to the fireplace. There was no fire in the grate but a white paper fan, made anew by Ailsa annually to fill the fire basket in the summer months. She was good with her hands, undomesticated but stylish.

The baby followed the dog to the fireplace with the vehemence of reunited love. The two, dog and baby, big-eyed, snubnosed, took up their places before the empty fire. It was not yet dark outside, the city had not settled down beneath its skyline. Carl made to get another drink. Ailsa took his glass from him. In the pocket of his jacket was the remains of a packet of dry roast nuts he'd got at the filling-station. He tipped the lot into his mouth while Ailsa fetched the new drink. She made it weak. It wasn't so much the health side of his eating and drinking that bothered her – what would be would be – but she was put off when he had overmuch to drink. He grew slobbery, asking for reassurance, even declarations. To make up for the weakness of the whisky she caressed his neck when she returned and pretended to be more interested than she was in his relating of the day at Glenbervie. She concentrated with the top of her mind on recollecting, detail by detail, the living-room of Grisel Carnegie; the rest of her mind she allowed to swim. She didn't need a drink to find an easy drifting movement to her thoughts. Unadmitted dissatisfaction had given her a talent for dreaming that she would have denied utterly. But the truth was that alongside her marriage to Carl and the tiring business of having Rhona, she ran dreams in her head like films without end. Their matter was not dramatic, but softly eventful. She was not a heroine but an object of curiosity, even longing, to unspecified, unnamed creatures, perhaps not even men. The glow of anticipation and undisturbed aftermath was the climate of her lower, denied, dreaming.

What Carl and sensible Ailsa could not take about his aunt was the way she made of her eventless life a romance, as though that life had been enough for her. It was a way of rationalising a totally pointless existence, they agreed. The titivation, the unconsummation, were all part of a sickness which only in recent years had been shaken off by women, that much was obvious. Now women not only knew what they wanted, but went after it and got it, not like Grisel with her net petticoats that had netted nothing, and her silent china companions and dreams of a man who'd lived with his mother and gone to dancing classes in his fifties. Illusions, breakable illusions, was all Carl's aunt had, he thought. Look at Ailsa, now, she'd never wander like that in her thoughts, yearning for something nobody could put a name to. He prided himself in knowing what was in Ailsa's wee mind, he really did. Like now, he knew it would be the room at Glenbervie, the flock of motionless birds.

Beneath that picture, which was indeed in Ailsa's mind, hovering at the surface of it, something stirred and fluttered, never quite roosting. The texture of her dreaming was light but dense, like a field of high flowers, like a net in slow water. Something was approaching her, something wonderful, over the meadow, through the water.

'I gave her the dog to hold and she held on to it as usual like grim death and it pulled its wally dug face.' They looked up at the china dogs, one either side of the mantelpiece, their snub noses, big eyes, painted whiskers, unbearably appealing pathos. Each dog had a clownish sorrow to its face. The baby and the living dog played below the china dogs, the pleated white fan behind them in its fire basket. The two were staring into each other's faces, seeming to grow more alike as they stared. On the mantelpiece the china dogs made a quaint guard for the drift of invitations and reminders ranged along the mantelpiece. Carl and Ailsa were a busy couple. It was unthinkable that they would be halved, one half or the other bereft. Death wouldn't get an appointment squeezed in, their schedule was that busy.

'She's ageing fast, now. The winter might just do it.' Carl was realistic. Everyone had to go sometime. They'd put the dog down then with an easy conscience. Rhona would for certain be too young to notice.

The baby gave up the staring match and grabbed the dog by both ears to pull its face to hers. The pair kissed and began to roll about and yelp and wag before the grate empty of warmth. The china dogs had a wily look to their faces if you looked harder. The painted freckles on their flat muzzles were just like those of the Peke. Fluent painted lines feathered their china feet. Ailsa knew for a fact wally dugs were not the same as china bluetits. They were vernacular Scots ornaments, not substitutes for love.

Something quite warm and tender was about to take place in Ailsa's dream. She felt its approach like the opening of a door which has been ajar.

'Esme came in to it a new way, today,' said Carl, turning the pinky finger of his left hand around in the deep hairs of his left ear. He'd been feeling furred-up, slow, lately. 'I wasn't even angling for him yet, and up he leapt into the conversation. The old thing just looked me up and down after I'd eaten and said, "Esme Stewart was a lovely-looking man, slim, with remarkably mannerly ways." How I had put her in mind of him I don't know, but I took it as a compliment.' He cleared his throat, pulled up his trousers by the belt which encircled the flesh below his belly, and rose to fetch another drink.

Catching on the silky loops of dog and baby at his feet, he tripped heavily, only saving himself by grabbing at the mantelpiece and keeping a hold on it to keep from falling on the two small creatures. Shocked, child and dog disentangled in one movement, like springs, and sat up alert, paired, huge-eyed, frozen by the hard tinkle of china all about them from the smashed wally dug whose widowed companion stared Ailsa hard in the eye as she felt the beautiful, romantic thing that had been approaching her recede.

'I'll get you another drink,' Ailsa said to Carl, angry enough to want to kill him.

Homesickness

'Doesn't look too good, does she?'

'Nor him.'

The women were not talking quietly. They were loading up for the week. They did this together, after yoga. Gert was a lot older than Sophy; Sophy admired Gert because she had had cancer and got it beat. That took mind-effort. Gert had taken up yoga after the cancer, in gratitude for God's irrational dispensation. She'd taken up Sophy then too. She found Sophy funny, she was so eager to have something to believe in. Gert believed in a number of things, none of them comforting. She was trying out fads now, things about which she as a rule felt sceptical. She was relieved by the short lives of fads. She did not believe in the future.

Now they were at the healthfood shop. Gert could not have cared less about carob chocolate substitute; she had been raised on bread and dripping, so meatily, richly, delicious, its memory gave you a wet mouth. But coming to the healthfood shop was for Gert like going on safari. You saw a number of alien and touching pieces of the creation. While Sophy was stocking up with sacks of organic puffed rice and pots of smooth cashew butter for her three boys, Gert collected her own requirements for the week. She had throughout her life eaten modestly and without much interest. Yet she had somehow managed to induce, encourage and nourish a poisonous growth within herself. She felt responsible for her cancer, as though she had become carelessly pregnant. Now she continued to eat modestly, but she took an interest. She read labels and lists of ingredients. Provenance concerned her. She felt that, at least, if she were to get another go of cancer – for her it had no nickname – the monster would be fed on good food. Meanwhile, she did wonder how well her diet of moulded glutinous rice and seaweed extracts was maintaining her self, the self outside where the cancer had been. She found the notion of such care expended upon unimportant choices intriguing. Would she have chosen thread with such care, or paper? Where did the discriminating consumption end? Was not everything in the end corrupted and poisoned? She had been taught that the pollutant was original sin, but now she was told to believe that sin had begun again, with the partition of the atomic apple. A bite taken from the rounded whole, and invisible poison, considerably less visible than sin, had seeped out, burned those close to it, and stained all air.

Who was to say where it ended? If we are all to live in fear should we not find each other equally appealing in our common humanity, victims together, illuminated by the flare of threat?

The truth was, Gert found the couple who ran the healthfood shop very unhealthy looking. She was amused when Sophy, who was of their generation after all, agreed with her that they did not look well.

'Doesn't look too good, does she?' asked Gert, conscious she was breaking a convention, and was gratified to hear Sophy reply, 'Nor him.'

The broken convention was twofold: it was not right in Sophy's opinion to make judgemental remarks; it was not good to imply that a – presumed – diet of perfectly screened foodstuffs conduced to anything but a perfect body, not perhaps in terms of beauty, but of health.

Sandy and Janet had come down from Kintyre to run the shop. There weren't many shops like this one up there, though there was something of a community of beardies round Oban, and a big demand for tofu from all the Chinese in Stornoway. But round Campbeltown there wasn't much in the way of a herbivorous movement. Pasties, bridies, mutton pies, puds and saveloys in batter were the thing up there, and bags and bags of crisps, also the kind of ice-cream which looks like turbans made of fat with a Tunnock's snowball on the side on a good day, making an ice-cream oyster to be eaten in the hand. And 'broon coos', the same ice-cream in a big paper cup of Coke, like frothy gravy to look at.

What made Sandy laugh was when folk down here said, 'You must miss all that delicious fish.' He knew they were thinking of sturdy fishing smacks and fresh cod like a steak of sea-meat. No dice there, with the French diving deeper and deeper for clams and sending the stuff down to London places. Anyhow you've to do a hell of a lot to a fish or a mollusc or whatever till you get it a convenient morsel fit for leisure eating. Only dead-rich folk want to bother with food that's hard to eat, lobster and oysters and all. Crab sticks was the shape of the future. Sandy had two aunties who gutted white fish on Barra and hadn't felt their hands in years. They couldn't fancy fish but when it was in finger form, out of the deep freeze in the post office.

As for heritage foodstuffs, sod that. The laird's well-hung haggis with venison and blaeberry on the side, and 'partan bree' and 'crowdie' to you, missus, three bags full, would madam care to pay in guineas?

But health food down here in the south, now that was big big money. Janet laughed most at the ones who came in the shop in fur coats to get their meat-free roasts. But she was fair-minded, mind. She sniggered right enough at the ones who wore raffia shoes in case of cruelty to leather. The guys of those couples always seemed to be pregnant and did they belong to a secret society that telt you not to clean out your ears? Janet was careful about her appearance, she liked stilettos in white patent and Sandy liked her curvy. No one down here did their hair like Janet. She'd the top bit puffed up and longer bits all down her neck, the Slade look it was known as in the clubs back in

Campbeltown. Slade was a great group, a bit old but great for dancing, dead rhythmic. She'd not found someone to colour it the very way she liked it; Shena'd done it for nothing in the house twice a month. But there were advantages to not living with the family as well. It didn't matter that much for example that she and Sandy were not married, though maw's letters made such a hefty deal of not mentioning the situation it was amazing the envelopes didn't bust with the effort.

Not homesick, or not very, Janet would say to the people who picked up on her accent, saying it was that attractive and how it reminded them of some holiday they'd been on, never in winter and never with a holiday job packing kippers for dirty Donal Forteith.

'Never mind four teeth, he's four hands', the kipper girls would say. In the lounge bar of the Argyll Arms hotel, dirty Donal had said something about the smell of kippers to Janet's father who had stopped the holiday job, 'Forthwith, Janet, forthwith, and that means now even if I've to employ you myself.' So it must have been bad, because there was nothing at all to do in Janet's father's shop in the winter unless you counted the odd poke of rock to some daft tourist the bus had left behind in a portaloo in the summer months.

Health food, now, that was not seasonal. People seemed to fancy trying to feel well all the time. Sandy said that they felt better because they lost weight the instant itself they left the shop. It was a weak joke. The goods were dear, it was a good living. Sandy and Janet even ate some of the foods, the ones you could ginger up till they tasted normal. Still, neither of them felt quite a hundred per cent.

Maybe this was just how people felt down south? Was it how people felt anywhere at all now the water wasn't recommended for drinking (even watered down) nor the air for breathing? Did Janet imagine it? Had she once felt better than this?

'I don't feel too good,' Janet said to Sandy.

'Nor me,' said Sandy. It was not a proper feeling of illness, just not feeling perfect. Not as bad as sickness, more a kind of ache.

'Everything's touched with poison, you can't be too careful,' Sophy was saying to Gert. The little wooden birds in her ears had been made by children in Chile. Sophy had bought them from the Quakers at their meeting house fair against war. Two bright little wooden birds against war.

'It's everywhere the sickness, in our bodies, our homes . . .' said Sophy.

Gert had heard it all before. She was glad she had had that solid bit of death inside her instead of just the vague sense of pervasive mortality these young ones had.

'Do you think it might be homesickness?' asked Gert.

The Buttercoat

This story is for Peter and Kathryn Kuhfeld

'It's perfectible so long as you keep it wet and moving,' said Lorne, and he made a beautiful subduing swoop over the wall to flatten the blushing plaster whose chalky convalescent smell filled the half-tamed room.

Intrigued by the idea that her lover, her betrothed now, or she herself might say the wrong thing in response to Lorne's words, and hoping that neither of them would at quite this moment, but might use the very words later, Nora idly offered herself the idea of being about to live with the gentleman-plasterer rather than his employer, whom she would wed and who had done so well hereabouts in animal feeds.

Gavin *had* done well. Here was the pink-faced house, two hundred years old, at the head of the sealoch to show for it, and frail tough little Nora to put in the house.

Thornshields looked out down a low belt of islets that seemed at dawn and twilight to be attached to one another. The sea between them at other times was defined in colour in apposition to the mood of the little drops of land themselves, that often was itself at odds with the temper of the mainland. You could stand in front of the house and collect eight ways of seeing blue before your eye had met the furthest island, to which Lorne had moved with his dog, his dinghy and his son long before Gavin Whelan bought Thornshields from old Lorne.

Lorne's parents were relieved but shy about the transaction. Since the sale, having driven into Campbeltown on a weekday morning to see the world, Grizel would hide from those she had most hoped to see, from the butcher where she had for forty-three years bought old Lorne's favoured cuts of meat, from the tweed ladies over whose counter she had never bought anything but thread, from the postcard-lady who had a past and smoked behind the counter of her shop, where there was a sign: 'Patrons will understand it is discourteous to Smoke inside this shop.'

Having lived at Thornshields for her entire married life, having been raised only a nibble of shoreline along, but three and three-quarter hours away by the road, Grizel could not bear to explain what might seem a sudden defection, her husband's and her own subsidence in the face of their son's apparent exhilarated uninterest in the house since his widowerhood – and Gavin Whelan's friendly, cleansing, money.

What Grizel made of Nora Cronin was not clear, and she would not have uttered it even to her confidantes, those people with whom she enjoyed the conversational luxury of uninvolvement, to whom she was not related by blood or obligation. She lived, as do many women of her class, under the sense that she was closer to those who were innocent of her life's actual drudgery, thinking it easeful and slow as pears in a bowl, than to those who knew how she swabbed and stitched and sat silent over papers that would not agree with each other as the place swelled in demand about her.

Indeed, she had unhooked most of these last people from her own and her husband's life. It was somehow draughty to be seen and erroneously pitied by their old friends.

'Like it?' asked Gavin, not asking, but instructing, his handsome face resting quite comfortably on his chin as he moved around.

Nora couldn't speak, so she enlarged her pupils. She assumed his question related to the moment.

'It is a nice house, isn't it?' said Gavin. His hair was just turning from gold to silver, thick, bimetallic, glistening. Many things about him were moving from their natural state into silver or gold. He had never felt stronger, more defined.

They were not yet living at Thornshields, but had flown back to the city, which was airless but exciting, like almost being wherever you want to be, off. Tomorrow was to be the day.

Gavin redisposed all the limbs within his reach or power. Now she might speak.

'Who are you thinking of?' asked Gavin, which was the question he was wont to ask at such times.

As Nora did, she told not the truth but gave the answer required, demanded by the sort of good manners that make a hedgehog feel good by addressing it as a porcupine.

She was thinking of many things at one time, barely of a person, but she knew whom he admired and modelled himself upon and gave the name, and later, when he was sleeping, she looked at him and felt that routine would bring her to love. In the night he cried and never woke up and she lay awake with worry for him till he cracked open the new Glasgow day with, 'What'll we get the day?'

It was an idea, she thought, to purchase a present for the day.

Actually, had she had anyone in mind, it was him alone. But that might have bored him. He wished more for magnification than reflection.

Gavin grew up strong and miserable, tied to ways had helped his father stay upright. He saw the life he wanted and he went to get it, with his hands at first, and then stopping as soon as he could, turning to a more inflated currency than labour, the capacity to sell.

When he saw young Lorne using *his* own hands to get away from that same life Gavin burned for, his centre buckled. It was pathetic. It was lucky Gavin had a feel for personality that is like a feel for ripeness or putrescence. He and Lorne were going to pass one another, slowly, maybe painfully, in their divergent ascendancies, he knew that.

On his borrowed but chosen slot of land in the narrow loch, Lorne looked over the small isles to Thornshields, up at the crook of the sealoch. It was a house he knew too well to give a different skin, even of so friable a substance as plaster.

His past life there would, he now saw, spin out into the rest of his days. He would never, though, not be imagining what went on in the house, its cellars and yard, and the cold merry corridors where light gave way to shadow and comforting nightmares and ennobling dreams lay, and offchance kisses.

He wanted not to own the house, but to know it, touch it all over. Plastering its walls was like watching a beloved skin grow old, and filling that skin once again with youth. He did not need to live at Thornshields to save its skin.

When he turned to his father, Lorne's small son looked up with bored adoring trust.

'Can you let me make a mess tonight?' asked Lorne the youngest.

They went out to the wall where the wind over the garden-sized island was least chill, where there was even a last flag of sunshine on the salt grass.

Lorne equipped his son with a fist of rosy plaster, a flat square to hold it upon and a jittery diamond-shaped knife. Together they set about the soothing of an area of dark drystone wall.

'No use,' declared the youngest Lorne.

'It's harder with a smoother wall,' said his father. 'You can see the problems here. They're plain to see.'

His son, at seven often seized up by ambiguities, did not reply, but stuffed the juicy barely gritty stuff into deep but tidy crevices, and from time to time made fanning effortful gestures, getting the plaster to lie like icing over baking that has not yet achieved its full distension. Plaster looked as though it would taste good stuffed in to your mouth, but it did not. It sucked up your spit.

The work of the youngest Lorne had a happy temporary look, as though a group of small children was waving through his plastering from within the wall, about to break out with whoops and powder and clatter of burst stones.

Once his son was in bed and asleep, Lorne blew out the last candle in the steading on the small island and got into his dinghy.

He rowed, without his dog, who would have alerted the child, over to the unlocked house, sixteen square stacked rooms looking empty through their pink shell on to samples of land and reaches of sea.

He made fast the dinghy at the jetty under the shadestruck tangled garden. Within the walls of the vegetable patch acanthus rattled. The only birds he could hear were misled by the uncommitted Highland summer darkness, that would settle for barely three hours in the night.

Lorne began to work, Thornshields having electric light, in the room where he had explained that morning to the new purchaser of his mother and father's house that in order for mobility there must be wetness, until he had made one wall as flat, as poreless, as butter. Before he did so he wrote on the wall in carpenter's pencil his letter to Nora Cronin, a letter born perhaps of loneliness and too much proximity to one child alone and the similarly incessant demands of the sea, but also of the moment when he had seen her think, after he spoke, that she could move in either direction, that she was as yet fluid enough to do so.

So he claimed his house and made clear what he might husband as his love, a secret warm for himself and helpful too against the tiring, loving interest of his parents.

Seven miles inland but forty-nine miles by road away from Thornshields, Grizel and old Lorne sat down to dine.

'The rest of the world may now eat,' said old Lorne. She had never said it for him, in all the three hundred and sixty-five multiplied by forty-three evenings, with the leaping lunar extra days, just as he had never corrected her pronunciation of the word 'orchestra', that she spoke with a hard G at heart. By such sharps and flats they made their way. When she looked at him over the table she already missed him. It had been so too when they began.

'You'll be reasonably pleased about the news,' she said, leaving it loose so's he could respond.

'Television news?' he asked, 'or real?'

'Lorne's news.'

'He rents a bit of land in unpredictable water not his own, how is it we can be sure he has not found a woman just the same type as the house he makes the boy inhabit?' he asked, pleased with the conceit, not applying the analogy. 'And I mean inhabit, not live in.'

'He said he was in love, Lorne,' said Grizel, 'And he never tells us anything.'

'It's not natural,' said her husband.

Grizel, who had watched her husband grow layer by layer, who feared for him in case of some ugly demolition or careless exposure of his careful self-restoration, thought of their son's calling.

He made walls smooth with his plaster, made them themselves again. He sharpened and restored detail unnoticed unless absent. Briefly jealous of the person, whoever she was, in whom her son had settled his affection, she speculated with interest and with a horror of knowledge, and came up with possibilities so conventional that she realised she was herself, in her own eyes as free as a cat, not merely conventional but of historic curiosity.

As an intimate formality, she offered her husband a second water biscuit. In the glass she watched his face, willing him to repeat himself.

'Do you know, I think I won't,' he said, making her happy. So they sightread through their time, virtuosos by now in their marriage.

Gavin Whelan chose his own breakfast and that of his wife to be, who was upstairs in the hotel putting together her day's appearance.

One of the things suited him about Nora was her unchanging mutability. She looked a new woman every day. It was hard to think of being stuck with a woman who just looked the one way and let time eat her up.

He dealt with the foundations by ensuring that her first meal of the day would set her up without spreading her out.

He gave himself the pleasure, extra heady in a hotel, of referring to Nora as his wife when he gave the order to the waitress: 'Full house for me with double Lorne sausage and burned tomatoes, skin off the black pudding if you would.'

Senga the waitress saw his handsome head and fine tall body and acknowledged to herself that this was the ideal. A man ate like a man but looked like he did not. She supposed some people were just lucky and burned it off. He gave her the set of his face that had made him an excellent salesman when he'd commenced in animal feeds, a smile just restrained behind the lips and eyes, a smile it was impossible not to feel dawning in answer behind her own skin.

'My wife'll take a selection of fresh fruit, a yoghourt shake and six prunes in a glass bowl. Prettier.'

His smile came through on the last word and gave the waitress the feeling here was a man loved women. She left the table writing on her wee pad and feeling she'd received a compliment.

In the kitchen, she gave the order to Callum the griddle chef and watched him cut the slices off the Lorne sausage that was of special catering size, as long and thick as a stocking stuffed with remnants.

'What meat is the Lorne, mainly?' Senga asked Callum, pretending to be retying her frilled pinafore while he took a nip out the vodka bottle he kept in the muesli drum that was the size of a cement mixer.

'Basically, it's the bloody zoo,' he said. 'That's rare. The bloody zoo.' He was already on the second stage of his morning's drinking, the confidence. He'd be tearful by the time the last reek of kippers had been and gone and they were back to salad and Parozone.

Now she looked at the brick of plopped meats, she could make herself see the bits in it, bits of tiger, parrot, cow, pieces from the cage floor, the bits from between the teeth of grinders, old used-up animals and vigorous ones that had succumbed to stress in the modern world.

'It's like felt,' said Callum. 'Ken, felt, it's formed out of all the cloth never made it into clothes, ground up and plastered together and rolled out smooth. It's meat felt, Lorne sausage. Right enough. Felt meat.'

The Smirnoff had made him hungry. He caught a sizzling slice of Lorne sausage up on his spatula and ate it off the smoking metal keeping his lips away from his teeth.

Something made Senga think of horses.

'You look gorgeous,' said Gavin, finishing his breakfast with the rich sweet knob of eggy black pud he'd saved. He changed it to a word she preferred. 'Delicious.'

She looked up at him through her fringe. Today she took her colour from the buttery caramel suit she wore, and the contrast with her rural fresh self of yesterday was like a gift of time to him from her. Today she was a woman poised to spend. He repeated his exciting if idiomatic question of the day's beginning.

'What'll we buy the day?'

'Poor man,' she said, finishing her last prune, and raising to him the look she saved up for such moments, when she knew what she wanted so much that she dared not say. He interpreted this look in a way that satisfied them both.

In the tiny plane like an egg whisk that was taking them back to spend their first full night as the owners of the refurbished Thornshields after the day in the city, Nora stretched, her wrists crossed and gold-burdened. In the boot of the aeroplane, it was really no more than a boot, were piles of cloth, silky pink and lime yellow, for their bedroom, where they planned to sleep tonight in the new-plastered room, that should by now have dried.

It was a company plane. Animal feeds were an industry bursting with health just now, Gavin reflected.

He was hungry and full of desire, made legitimate and therefore more lewd by what would be their first night in the big house he could see now out the plane window, floodlit as he'd told young Lorne it should be for their arrival, although the Highland dark was saturated with light.

As the plane came low over his candlelit steading, Lorne looked up at its modest size, pondered its concentrated value, reflected upon whom it held, by what it was kept airborne, expertise and physics and meat and money. He realised that the love letter under the buttercoat was not so much for the woman now over his head like a tinned angel, but for the house that opened itself up to him at the tip of the glistening sealoch, open, wide-faced, entirely known, secret.

A Revolution in China

In China, that day, all seemed well. The customary moves towards communication were made, none going so far as to be built upon for more than one fragile day. The usual codes of conformity and transparent speech were observed. Hierarchy and the understanding that its imperilment would have certain horrible consequences lay behind each move and every word.

A new batch had arrived, kitchen services for cheerful families fond of animal antics.

Unwrapping an oversized mug from the corrugated-card box that the china had come in, Else held it up to show Miss Montanari, who lifted her chin a very little. This meant that the line would move well, but that Miss Montanari would give a sigh as she sold any item from it, a little sigh of disappointment as she took the money or the cheque or the credit card. She was a woman all shades of rose and grey, and her sighing was part of her colouring, like the susurration of a copper beech. Miss Montanari was the china buyer; her skill was for locating designs for which she did not care and being sharp enough to know that what she did not like was what people wanted. No one knew of the revolution that had lately taken place within her.

Benedetta Montanari was looking at the new, garish china, as it emerged from the box, with eyes that could no longer look with disdain upon anything.

People had said that she was a woman with taste, that what she had was 'good taste'. There was a short gamut of things that she found acceptable, a boundless flux of things that she did not. All shades of grey and beige suited, and all the many whites, more than in the vocabulary of any Eskimo. Black came into it, but must not be allowed to engulf a room or a body. Black was a white flag of surrender, Miss Montanari had said recently, and no one laughed, any more than they understood.

One morning seven weeks before, on her way to China through the old department store, Miss Montanari had lingered in Hardware. Her hair was a nutmeg red with two wings of pinkish grey, one at either corner of her white, high, forehead. Her skin was thin, her nose proud, and she was held in awe of an old-fashioned sort, meaning that most of the shop's employees recognised her and none had seen where she lived. She dined with the store's directors at Christmas, for it was feared she might put the celebrants off their stride if she were to attend the staff party everyone came to and to which she never alluded. The directors of the store were three cousins and their spouses, none of the six that far above seventy. The cousins would offer a catered meal, usually, in deference to Miss Montanari's supposed foreignness, rather greasy. Once or twice, a visit had been paid to a restaurant where the cost had proved a matter of concern, amid brave play for the bill among the old cousins.

On hooks under a bright display of unbreakable picnic beakers in the hardware department there hung a row of hot-water bottles, some of them already equipped with hot-water-bottle covers. These covers were made of differing materials – plush, fur fabric, a napless velvet like a shaved Angora cat, or a shiny fabric that glistened like cretonne. The covers were made to resemble animals. They were a puppydog, a furry tortoise, a hippo in specs and a russet orang-utan that held a banana you could unpeel and re-enclose, thanks to the miracle of Velcro.

Miss Montanari looked at the outpushed sad lips in the felty face of the ape. She picked up one of its small hairy arms and folded it with the other arm, arranging the banana towards the lips. She gave the raised shaggy knee of the little false animal an encouraging tap and said to the morose face, 'Aren't you a case, just?'

The monkey continued to hang by its neck tab, a security docket clipped through the warnings printed on the clearly printed label about not using unnecessarily hot water when filling a hot-water bottle. Miss Montanari smoothed the stiff whiskers of an adjoining ginger cat bottle-cover, and walked on towards China. Her seniority stayed behind her momentarily as she passed, chilling conversations, interrupting them, turning them over to speculation about her.

Her fault and her interest, in the general opinion of the other buyers and assistants in the store, lay in her quietness. She uttered those sighs, she gave intelligent replies to the questions of customers, but she never told a thing. No one had asked her either, for Miss Montanari was one of those people for whom others invent a story. Her face, which was startling, poised, somewhere off beautiful, equipped her with a character that might not have been the one she possessed. She was polite, or perhaps she did not know the person whom others had made of her.

Benedetta Montanari had come to the department store in order to fold silk scarves and earn enough to feed herself as a young person of twenty in 1954. So she was still young now, four years off the millennium, she thought, hardly sixty at all. No one had dared bring up the question of retirement since no one liked to admit they knew what age she was, or that she had an age.

The day after she'd been amused by the monkey hot-water-bottle cover, Miss Montanari dawdled in Hardware again. She made a purchase; a pink copper jelly mould, brittle with lightness and casting pink shadows. It was large, fluted, domed, with a twist to the fluting that gave it a smart look of near-movement, like the contortions in a cartoon.

'What's its capacity?' asked Miss Montanari.

'It's a jelly mould; for jelly and that,' said Joan, who was a new mother. She was marking down a gross of jam-label sets and already fit to weep, she was that tired.

'It holds three pints,' said Mr Gilbert, who ran Hardware as a tight ship, but had a soft spot for babies and had known Joan since she had been one.

'Very nice,' said Miss Montanari, ticking her nails inside the glowing copper mould. 'I'll take it. And has it any little ones?'

Joan was sent off by this into thoughts of the needy baby at night. She just looked, calm as a cow, at the older woman, and said, 'Four ninety with your discount.'

Miss Montanari paid.

'Three pints jelly is a rare amount for a woman lives alone,' said Carol Beveridge, who got by alone on sardines and gin and Lactulose.

Mr Gilbert did not react to this, but said to Joan, 'It's good, isn't it, when there's still blossom about and you get a bit of sun? Not that we see much of it down here, but it'll be great out in the old pram, I expect.'

Joan returned to the jam-labelling sets.

'Take a seat,' said Mr Gilbert, and he fetched the kitchen stool they used for reaching the top shelves where were kept the things no one but the aged and country dwellers wanted – peg-mending kits and trivets and onion-bracers and sink tidies.

The next day, Miss Montanari appeared again in Hardware. Joan had stuck up a picture of her baby, Carl, just below the counter, so she could look at it while she counted out change. Carol Beveridge was thinking what she might bring a picture of, tomorrow. She had no photograph, but perhaps you might buy them. She didn't want a poster-type thing. She wanted a photograph that had the messy look as if a moment had been cut with nifty scissors out of a full and busy day. In the photograph of Carl you could see all sorts of things, a shawl, a toy rabbit, a small wool boot, the side of what must be a three-seater sofa. There was a lot of pattern, and the signs of other lives than Carl's, too, a mug with playful animals on it, a scarf, some keys, an elderly hand with a wedding ring. There was even a plant in a pot, with flowers growing out of the plant.

'May I have the family?' asked Miss Montanari.

Mr Gilbert knew what she meant, before either Joan or Carol Beveridge had to fill the silence with the particular response each might have made to how she had heard the words.

'All the other moulds of that particular pattern? Yes indeed, if we hold them. I may need to fill any gaps by a rummage down in stock. The copper dessert dome, Carol, in the Sandringham pattern; all sizes down from the three-pinter, please.'

The clattering, shiny moulds came one by one out of their tissue to make a procession of pink metal turtles across the counter.

'The lot, please,' said Miss Montanari.

She made the Hardware department nervous, with her air of transforming things into other things, her unliteral deportment – as though she were someone in disguise – and amused look of being disappointed. It wasn't easy to think of her making sequences of milk puddings with her new family of empty moulds.

It was not long after her purchase of all the degrees of jelly dome in the Sandringham style that Miss Montanari began her daily morning visits to other departments of the shop.

She had never before been a person to venture very far out of China, unless it had been to visit her acquaintance the pharmacist, who had a short lunch hour because of the responsibility that went with her calling. The two ladies would meet for an infrequent but pleasant meal. They shook hands at Christmas and exchanged gifts of good soap. Their hands were cool.

In Linens, Miss Montanari's browsing went on for several mornings. Jessie, whose gypsy hair and leaning bust frothed and toppled over the linens counter with its inlaid brass rule for measuring sheets, thought Miss Montanari wanted something, over and above just bedlinens, and said so to Karen, who said through prim cold lips, 'Don't I know what?' and felt the pulse of the love bites under her rollneck blouse.

'It wasn't that I meant,' Jessie said, shaking her dripping pendant golden earrings. Her hair was so thick it caught their chimes and held them so they stayed silent. 'I mean she's hanging about. Like she wanted to talk. Like the ditherers.'

The ditherers were old ladies who came in, like drinkers visiting far-flung off-licences, infrequently but regularly, and discussed for hours very fine points of pillowcase size or duvet pattern or handkerchief-adornment for some much younger relative, usually rarely met or even, Jessie feared, invented. Infant bedlinen attracted the most.

'She's never a ditherer,' said Karen, eyeing Miss Montanari's careful waist and ankles. 'She's got a secret, more like.'

Miss Montanari, though, had wanted to talk, and went, with Jessie, into some detail about the items she eventually did buy, two dense, light, creamy blankets bound with slipper-satin around all four edges and several pillowcases embroidered with strong wild flowers as if off someone's national costume. As an afterthought, Miss Montanari also bought six bags of cedarwood chippings – 'to keep linens wholesome in the old country way' were the words screen-printed on to the sisal bag – and a bright green sleeping bag sewn into segments, screen-printed with the cheerful, if optimistic, features of a holidaying caterpillar at the head end, and all down the segments with a double run of merry caterpillar feet. Jessie tied up these bulky items and asked if they should be delivered.

Miss Montanari said, 'What a blissful idea.' It was what she had heard said.

'Not natural, that woman,' said Karen. 'She behaves like a customer.'

Miss Montanari arrived later at work than usual the following Thursday, delivery day for the department store. She took delivery of the parcel from the place where she worked.

'Come in and have some coffee, Arthur,' she said to the delivery man for the firm. Although she had known his name for over twenty years, she had never used it before. 'I am grateful to you for bringing my parcel. It was rather heavy for me.'

Miss Montanari made some coffee and stood while Arthur drank his, since he seemed not to want to sit down. He saw the line of twisty pink metal helmets all sizes, just cluttered about in the sitting-room. His wife would never do that. The whole flat was dead bare, modern you'd call it, apart from that procession of the things that looked like nothing better than pudding moulds though he'd swear she paid an artistic price for them – and now the parcel. She could hardly wait until he had gone to open her big parcel, invitingly taped and bound with twine.

She thanked Arthur fulsomely. He had left most of his coffee and the almond biscuit she had put on a plate beside it. Miss Montanari realised that she had given him what she would have prepared for herself. She had not adjusted. She felt this slippage of good manners in herself as acutely as a symptom.

Miss Montanari began to open her parcel of purchases from the shop where she had worked since 1954. She enjoyed punching a knife through the brown tape over the joins in the box and drawing it fast along the crevice, feeling the blade tickling tissue within. She flapped open the cardboard lugs of the box, unpeeled the stickers that held the tissue paper furled around their secret innards, and lifted out each weighty, cool folio of pillowcase with its vehement floral edge. She smelt the cedarwood although it was still wrapped, and could almost feel the warmth of the blankets buried within the box. She would leave the giant caterpillar until later. Maybe she would still get to take it on a great trek through the north, or maybe it would just rest until one day it would solidify, harden and crack and a great fabric butterfly emerge.

She sat among her shopping for a time, enjoying the feeling she supposed was no longer noticeable to those who regularly received deliveries, or, indeed, post.

She dressed carefully, rinsed the delivery man's cup, ate his almond biscuit and poured a few of the cedarwood chippings into a handkerchief, which she knotted and slipped into her handbag.

Miss Montanari was losing her touch. She was beginning to cease to know how to define what things it was right or wrong to like. She would have known before to give the delivery man from the store the coffee he would have liked, the biscuit he might have liked. She would have known unerringly, by gauging her own depth of distaste, by asking herself what she would not have liked, to what degree and how, and offering whatever, according to this negative and unerring canon, proved apposite.

But her distaste had fled. She was prey to an uncritical enthusiasm and curiosity. The possible cause struck her, and she dismissed it from her mind. She had not the time.

On the day when the parcel arrived, Miss Montanari was not able until her tea-break – she forwent lunch since she had arrived late that morning – to make her trip to a department of the store. She found herself in Toiletries. She conducted a long and quite friendly conversation with an assistant who did not seem to know who she was and treated her with the indulgence bestowed on customers, even when she asked the girl what soap she recommended for dry knees and elbows, even when she decided not perhaps to go for the soap but instead to buy a petalled bathing hat and some nail extensions for a daughter Miss Montanari was moved to pull out of the air by the sudden materialising at her eye's far corner of her acquaintance and occasional luncheon companion, the pharmacist.

'She's quite like you,' Miss Montanari said to the assistant, who had dark hair on her arms, white skin and strongly apricot black-rooted hair on her head. 'The same colouring.'

'Clever girl then,' said the assistant, whose young green eyes had received four compliments, that's two compliments each, in the club last night, and who was hoping to knock off when this old bird was through.

'Have you tried these temporary tattoos for your daughter?' Clea tugged at her orange hair and sized up Miss Montanari. Not all that weird, wanting to dress young in private. Not when you'd seen what Clea had seen. There was blokes come in here in frocks looking for depilatory bold as brass, a pair of twins at it one week, splendid ladies in tweeds with a dog they'd handed over to the commissionaire and hands like bloody octopussies, all fur and fingers. This old bird was just suffering from being too correct. It was understandable she might want to rush off home and dress a bit nylon. Maybe it was her good man wanted her with the nail extensions. Perhaps Clea should recommend the Eyelure diamanté-tip lash extensions fashioned without cruelty to man or beast.

Miss Montanari fumbled with her change and moved swiftly away, having thanked the assistant with the orange hair, more unsettled than she had thought she could be by the presence of the pharmacist.

These forays into territory beyond China persisted for several more weeks, each day bringing with it at least one conversation during which Miss Montanari managed to shed the coolness that had accompanied her throughout her life in the department store. She achieved certain small triumphs, from time to time being almost certain that her interlocutor did not know who she was, that she was causing no ripple by her break with her own habits. She was speaking, whenever she could, only to recent employees, the youngest boys and girls, who had not had time to form an idea of her, perhaps even, mercifully, did not know who she was.

'She's missing having had children,' said Mr Gilbert of Hardware to Mr Stuart of Photographic, who had never once taken a film from the hand of Miss Montanari and who therefore had no idea of her home life, leisure time, or loved ones, which was not the case with the other employees of the department store.

'She's missing, *not* having had children, do you mean?' asked Mr Stuart. 'Oh no, I see what you mean, right enough. She's a mystery woman. But good at her job. And handsome.'

'Somewhere near beautiful,' said Mr Gilbert, who kept Mr Stuart right on these things since Mr Stuart was not, as he put it, in the business of appreciating women in the very flesh. Mr Stuart lived with a friend whose widowerhood had come like balm in reward for forbearance. Mr Stuart and his friend kept quails in their greenhouse and went on water-colour courses around the coast of Great Britain. It was a beautiful life, when the only thing you ever need complain about was rain or cats, Mr Stuart said to his friend. He described Miss Montanari often to his friend, for her air of foreignness, her dislocated elegance, 'Like Garbo's,' he said, meaning something about her private life that he could not say aloud. And that could explain her talking to the young girls quite so much lately. There was only so much hiding a body might take.

'It'll be she's Italian,' Mr Stuart's friend said.

'She's born in Inverness even if the blood has garlic in it,' replied Mr Stuart, wanting his own romance of Miss Montanari to be kept intact, as Mr Gilbert wished her to be pining for the bonny babes she never was mother to.

'It's not unusual for a woman of the older sort to take on. Especially if she's sailed through the earlier part,' said Else to Lindsay Kerr in China, one day when they saw Miss Montanari smiling at some night-lights in the shape of mushrooms and moons, as they were all about to leave.

'See that,' Lindsay shrieked, muffling it at once. But Miss Montanari, putting on her new overcoat of mauve and russet mohair with a swing back, purchased in the Outerwear department two weeks before, did not turn around.

Else and Lindsay Kerr looked with astonishment at the neatly filled-in order form that was inadequately hidden in a pile on the China cashdesk. Miss Montanari had put in an order for mugs with a message on them, a number of such mugs, the very mugs that she had made an infernal fuss about permitting to be sold at all through her precious China outlet.

'I've a good mind . . .'

'Oh, leave it, Lind,' said Else. 'Leave it, leave it. Any road, you've not. Leave it with me. Come away out of it now and we'll go and get blootered at the Deacon.'

'Ech, posh,' said Lindsay Kerr.

In this way Else kept events in China on an even keel until the day when Miss Montanari, having unpacked the last of the oversized kitchen crocks, decorated so gloriously, radiantly, appealingly, with animal antics, slipped upstairs to the staff ladies to check the neatness of the wings of grey in her nutmeg hair and her thin formidable face and to wash her cool hands, before slipping downstairs back to China, which she wanted to leave without fuss, simply handing over to her colleagues in token of farewell the personalised mugs with the name of the recipient and, crammed in rather, the words 'From Benedetta (Montanari)'.

Later, when Miss Montanari had been scattered, the most elderly of all the three cousins spoke at the service of remembrance. He spoke as though the store were a ship or a great school or a regiment. He spoke of all it had given to Miss Montanari, how it had been for her more than a home.

At the stand-up drinks after the service, she was quick in the memory of the youngest people there, who kept saying to each other and to the older employees of the shop, 'She *was* someone, we thought she *was* someone.'

'What,' said Else, loyal now she was in charge of China, and tipsy too on the wine Miss Montanari had surprisingly left to be drunk on this occasion, 'and not just a shop assistant?'

'Girls,' intervened Mr Stuart. 'Girls, indeed now, stop a minute, would you? Lend me your expertise. Are these flowers not a surprise in themselves? Bearing in mind like what she was . . . Benedetta?' In death Miss Montanari fitted her long-hidden Christian name.

Tottering-flowered blue delphiniums, bunched siläverleafed stocks and heaps of rowdy roses stuffed in containers all anyhow filled the borders of the church hall, ruffled bright coarse flowers embroidered roughly around the edges of the plain white hall in which those who had known Miss Montanari for the longest still slumbered in the illusion that it was they, not the people who had seen her in the last weeks of her life, who knew her best.

'We should perhaps have known it was the end,' said Mr Stuart, who had brought his friend, the widower.

'My word,' said the widower, 'a real party, this is. Wine, and *several* jellies.'

Sweetie Rationing

'In the main a discriminating man, Davey, would you not say? Not the sort to get in with . . . leave alone engaged to . . .' Mrs McLellan's voice fell and joined those of her companions, good women in woolly tams.

With its freight of sugar ('freight' pronounced 'fright' to rhyme with bite and night in those days when the Clyde was still an ocean-going river), the cake-stand flowered high among the women. At each of the six tables in the tearoom there was such an efflorescence, encircled by blunt knives for spreading the margarine, and white votive cups. The celebrants sat in small groups. They had all been born in another century.

'Old ladies, that's the business. There's always more of them. The men don't hold on the same way. Then there was that war, too.' Erna's mother had told her right when she nagged her to take over the tearoom, even though it meant a move into the city. Erna's mother was known as a widow. Erna had not met her father. He was gone long before he was dead.

'What are you, Mother, if you're no' an old lady?' asked Erna.

'An old woman.'

Erna wondered about the difference. Her mother wore a scarf munitions-factory style and had brass polish round her finger-nails from cleaning the number on the front door. Out by the lochan they'd had no number, but good neighbours. Now, in Argyle Street, the old woman went to kirk to get her dose of grudge at whatever new daft thing God had let happen. She had a top half which she kept low down in her apron-bib till the Sabbath, when it went flat under a sateen frock with white bits under the arms in summer and a serviceable coat over that in winter. Erna had always had shoes.

Well, now they had the tearoom, and Erna's mother had silver polish round her fingernails, from all the paraphernalia ladies use to take their tea in style. Cleaning the cake-stands was a long job because of the ornamental bits, curly at the top and four feet like the devil's at the bottom. Without the silver plates for the cakes, three of them getting smaller towards the top, the things were just tall skeletons. The plates were all right to clean. Wire wool made them shine up softly, like metal that has been at sea. Erna's father was said to have been in the Merchant Navy. Erna did not know whether she herself was destined to become an old woman or an old lady. Marriage would tell. It would be soon, she guessed, from the way he was on at her.

At Mrs McLellan's table, the cakes on the bottom level of the cake-stand were almost finished. Not that it would be right to progress upwards until every crumb had gone.

'Discriminating?' Mrs Dalgleish, as though her hand were just a not totally reliable pet she had given shelter among her tweeds, took the penultimate iced fancy. 'You might say that, Mrs McLellan, but I might not.' The last cake, pink like nothing on earth, was reflected in the silver dish which bore it. Its yellow fellow was in the throat of Mrs Dalgleish, and then even more intimately part of her. When she had truly swallowed and licked all possible sugar from her lips and extracted all sweetness from the shimmery silence she had brewed among her friends, she went on.

Miss Dreever, who was excitable, never having been married, could not stop herself; she took the pink cake. She forgot in her access of pleasure to use the silver slice, but impaled it on her cake fork with its one snaggle tooth.

A doubly delicious moment: the ladies were free to progress up the shaft of sugar and to slip deeper into the story. Mrs Macaulay eased off one of her shoes at the heel. The ladies wore lace-ups perforated all over as though for the leather's own good.

They were good shoes and kept up to the mark by shoe trees and Cherry Blossom; the good things in life do not grow on trees. Mrs Dalgleish had at home a shoe-horn, which she sometimes showed the lodgers; the late Mr Dalgleish had given it her, she explained, before he died. Only one lodger had ever dared to respond, 'Not after, Mrs Dalgleish, then?' The shoehorn was to save her bending. 'Though a widow has to do worse things than bend,' Mrs Dalgleish would say. She was not having a joke.

Nor was she today. 'Davey is no more discriminating than any of them when it comes to . . . women. And he's been cooped up in engine rooms for half his natural life. All that oil and steam. Not to mention foreign parts.' Mr Dalgleish too had been to foreign parts, but without the fatal admixture of oil and steam. Davey was an engineer, the sort with prospects. After the war, he'd done university.

'But the girl's not foreign, is she? Is her mother not from Kilmahog? Didn't you say that? And the wean brought up on Loch Lomondside?' Miss Dreever had a grouse-claw brooch which she touched with her own thin hand as she spoke. Since the war, she'd not got about so much, with her mother and the breakdown, but she did pride herself on her penetration beyond the Highland Line. So many people lived in a country and didn't know the half of it.

'Yes, but a father from where, that's what I'm asking myself.' Mrs Dalgleish looked down at her wedding ring. 'Maybe I'll just try one of those coconut kisses.'

She gave a hostess's inclusive smile. 'Will you none of yous join me?'

In stern order of precedence, Miss Dreever last, the lowest in order below the sugar, the ladies took the cakes. The coconut was friable and soapy as Lux flakes, which the ladies hoarded to care for their good woollens. Today, Mrs Macaulay was in a lovat pullover, Mrs Dalgleish in ancient red, and Mrs McLellan (who had always been a redhead) had a heather twinset which had lasted well. Miss Dreever did not dress to please. She had the proper pride not to be eyecatching.

'Would the girl's father be an islander, then, Janice?' Only Mrs McLellan was allowed to call Mrs Dalgleish Janice. Sometimes they took tea in each other's houses. Mrs McLellan had a tiger skin on brown felt backing, which had seen better days not long ago.

Although the second rung of cakes had been reached, Mrs Dalgleish was not sure that the perfect moment for familiarity had arrived.

'Not an islander *or* a Highlander, Ishbel. And now we've all had quite enough of nephew Davey. What of your family, Miss Dreever?'

It was a bony, unappetising topic, though it had to be tackled at some point during these teas. Miss Dreever was an only child. Her fiancé (had he existed? the other ladies wondered) had been killed. No meat there, of the sort at any rate which you could really chew. Certainly no fat.

Miss Dreever's mother could not be discussed in safety because she intermittently went mad which upset Miss Dreever who had been raised in a tenement and bettered herself through reading. What a true relief for her to get out and about like this then, the once a week.

'You know me,' said Miss Dreever, 'always busy. There's Mother and the teaching and there is a chance I'll be the one to take the form outing this year. We're hoping the petrol will stretch to a beauty spot.'

Magnanimous, placated – how dull could be the lives of others – Mrs Dalgleish turned to Miss Dreever and looked at her. She was a poor skinny thing and probably had nothing in the evening but her books. Mrs Dalgleish had any number of activities. She never wasted a thing, not a tin, not a thread; there was all that putting away, all that folding, saving, sorting, to be done. She often had to stay in to do it, specially.

'Miss Dreever, dear, take that cream horn.' Mrs Dalgleish referred to a sweetmeat on the topmost rung of the cake-stand. The horn was of cardboard pastry and the cream was the kind whipped up from marge and hope and dairy memory, but it was a lavish token. The horn stood for plenty. The sugar on it was hardly dusty. In reverse order of precedence, the ladies took their cakes. Mrs Dalgleish was grace itself as she hung back.

Erna took away the teapot and freshened it in the kitchen at the back. She had torn the sole of her shoe jumping on old cans to flatten them for the dustbin man. She was glad she could get away with just drawing a brown line down the back of her leg to look like the seam of a nylon. All those old ladies had gams like white puds, and then there'd be the darning. With her shade skin anyhow she'd no need for stockings. He said so. She'd let him draw the line once, with her eyebrow pencil, but it got dangerous. Then it was her had to draw the line.

'Seemingly,' Mrs Dalgleish said as she distributed the tea, 'seemingly – though it could be talk, to do with which I will as you know have nothing – Davey's girl's father wasn't all he might have been. In the colour department.'

Miss Dreever wondered, in the instant before she understood, whether this future relative by marriage of Mrs Dalgleish could have worked in a paint shop. Then, clear as in a child's primer, came the bright image of a pot of tar, and the soft, dark, touching tarbrush. She bit the sweet horn.

A Jeely Piece

'Never in my wildest would I have, would you now? Would you indeed? Or would you not?' It was restful to converse with Rhona; the energies that went into the necessary emotions, outrage, offence, dignity, were all hers, but there was an aspect of her talk that was demanding, on this warm day, to Mollie. Something to do with having to keep an eye on the subject, that was apt to change, tuck itself in and rethread with the imperceptible flicker of an invisible mender's needle.

They had known one another all their lives and soon they would be dead, thought Mollie, undisturbed as a teenager in love by the thought of death, whom she thought of as a friend of the family. Dying, though, was more hard to get on with, she could not fancy that. Her ideal would be to be taken after a morning's gentle exercise, gardening perhaps, or a turn round the park, something that would tire her out and reward her curiosity with something to puzzle over so that she would be happily distracted when she was taken. Rhona would die talking, of course, ambling around the subject, approaching it, changing it, holding possibilities up to the light like negatives to check them for light and colour and shade.

Sixty years ago they had spent the night together in a plum orchard. If that was the word? Maybe prunery, or *pruníre*? Anyhow, it had been in Rhona's father's plot which he had down to plums, and in which he had built a playhouse for Rhona, with a ladder leading up to a wee platform where you could just fit two camp beds. Downstairs there were three chairs about right for porridge-eating bears, a small dresser and a toy cooker that cooked when primed with paraffin. Matches, though, were to be used only under supervision, so Rhona and her friends tended to take things out to the cooker already cooked, insert them and remove them after a while with expressions of relish such as, 'My word, what a crust,' and, 'You must let me have the receipt for that one day soon.'

An indiscriminate archaism was part of the game of the playhouse. Its limitations of scale and equipment demanded further refinements. Especially when the girls began to grow up and to become aware that they were doing so, they worked at setting the playhouse and the games connected with it in times safely past, if they had ever been. The small house in this way became a hallway to expansive ideas and tall dreams.

Rhona was one among brothers, handsome boys with big teeth and eyelashes, who wanted to be lowland farmers like their father. Of course the farm could not be divided, so two of the boys would eventually have to find their own places. They would never go to England, that was a certainty, a place they had been raised to consider the source of all that was not right in their lives, a coward country that, like all cowards, was a bully too. India had been mentioned, and tea planting, if it was not to be Scotland. The number of Scotsmen out there planting the tea was something amazing, it was said, so a man need never be lonely seeking his fortune with the tea.

The timbers of the playhouse were proofed against rot by a protracted soaking in a bitumen tank that was in the woods behind the barn and the byres in a dark grove of ponticum. Over the tarpaulin roof Rhona's father had laid over-and-under pantiles, curved like letter S's lying down, tucked one into the next with a snugness whose pattern satisfied like that of the feathers on an ordinary bird. The windows of the house went out on casement latches that curled at the end like creeper trails.

Rhona's father had an unnecessary streak that made him do things more ornamentally than other men. Her brusque mother was not like this. It could hurt Mollie to see Mrs Gordon overlook on purpose some fillip the farmer had added to the breakfast table, nasturtium flowers in a bowl perhaps, or treacle initials written on the children's oats. Mollie had seen the farmer's wife stir these initials to a blur one day before the children came down, her face disproportionately full of something close to vengeance. She made bread on a Saturday and the farmer liked to make a single plaited loaf that he would decorate with seeds halfway through the baking. When it was done he would lift and tap it as though it were a warm instrument of percussion. He sang out of doors; Rhona said that he was an atheist who kept his eyes open during grace, said by her mother. Mollie had several times spent Christmas with the family, when the farmer said grace himself, looking holy as holy and bringing a kind of conviction to Mollie that did not usually assail her, a desire to be seen to be extremely good, more especially in the eyes of Mr Gordon than the terrible eyes of God.

In the First World War, he had been wounded and one time, not meaning to, at the seaside at Gullane on a tart summer day, Mollie had seen the wound. Or rather she had seen through the upper arm of the father of her friend. It was his right arm, white, and when she saw the hole, which he was drying carefully by patting it with a beachtowel as one pats a sore baby, it reminded her of the separate flesh packets, muscles, that composed the drumstick of a chicken. Mr Gordon had spectacles and a temper, he was tall and thin and grey, but the fear Mollie felt for him did not make her want to avoid him. This feeling grew in her when she saw him drying thin air on the brisk beach at Gullane while they sat on rugs among seaholly and thrift and sharp grass watching the sternly inert sea.

The sandwiches had been meat. Mr Gordon had whittled some driftwood into a dragon shape and shown the children how to extract the bitterness from a cucumber by cutting off the tip and turning it round and round on the cut end till all the white gall had been milked out. He then scooped out the seeds, halved it along its length and handed around sweet chunks of the cold cucumber, improved beyond its vegetable self, transformed into fruit.

When the boys were building follies with their composition bricks or sitting up in the copper beech tree's maroon chambers, Mr Gordon would sometimes join them. The longer he stayed with his sons the more like them he seemed, although to Mollie the boys did not have the charm of their father, being easy to understand. An indirection in him held him in her thoughts more than she knew, although he looked her in the eyes when he spoke to her, encouraging her to flourish in his difficult gaze.

Rhona Gordon nagged her father, who could not do enough for her. When he made little loaf pans for her and crimped dishes for tartlets out of metal he had pressed and cut himself, she told him, as her mother might have, 'These are sharp for a child, do you not see that?'

The night in the small house was a warm one in late summer. Rhona and Mollie had been awaiting the occasion with a pleasure that had sufficient alarm to it to be interesting. Darkness came at night and who knew what it might contain? Not Germans, after all this time (it was the middle thirties and the two girls were brought up ostrich fashion), but Englishmen perhaps, over the border for a rieving night? Aged fourteen, the girls were children enough to confuse fear and interest.

No one had told them anything more helpful about these sensations than that the male pigeon is moved, when the mood comes upon him, to 'tread' his mate. A picture of this obscure conjunction did not help. The she pigeon looked compliant, the he pigeon smug. A pointless attention had been paid to the particularities of their plumage, their iridescence, and so on. It was like being shown how to roll an umbrella when what you wanted, if only you knew it, was a voyage in a hot air balloon.

Rhona and Mollie had done their teeth in the farmhouse. They brought out with them a candle and a drum of matches that were not to be used save in an emergency. Through the garden under the waxy trailing leaves of the copper beech, over the rabbit-netting into the fruit cage and out into the orchard's long grass they walked as though they had not been there before ever. Each girl wore a camel dressing gown and carried a stone hot-water bottle wrapped in a piece of blanket. They had provisioned the playhouse earlier with apples, bread, butter and splintery-pink rhubarb jam.

Small and burdened the plum trees seemed to gnarl as Mollie walked in the dark between them; they were seemingly changing in shape as though being cooked from beneath, or twisted at the roots. So damp was the grass it was like paddling through wet ribbons as the two approached the playhouse. Mr Gordon had hung a Tilley lamp and shown them earlier in the day how to turn off its light by rolling away the flame.

It was like a cabin inside, warm and close and appointed with no superfluities. The two beds were made up, white as open envelopes.

In bed, the lamp extinguished, the windows opened at a distance nicely judged to take into account both health and marauders, Rhona and Mollie said their prayers and then began to go through the girls in their class, judging who had been kissed. There were seven Fionas in the class so attention had to be paid.

Rhona had not been kissed, in her own opinion, she said. You did not count the Lorimer boy because he did it to everybody. Mollie had not been kissed, although she moaned at her mother's handmirror sometimes and offered her cheek to it, sometimes even her lips. The girls fell asleep after a satisfactory bout of giggling that came to them as a mercy just as they began to talk about ghosts.

In the aware early sleep that leads to dreams, Mollie instructed herself not to talk in her sleep. She did not know what secret she contained, only that one was there. Although Rhona was the talker when they were awake, Mollie spoke out at night and woke herself often at the height of these dreams of puerile adventure and high colour that did not sit naturally with her quiet waking style.

When she awoke later, it was neatly, as if she were about to arrive at a station. She moved out of the cosy bed in two cool movements, casting a glance she realised was duplicitous at her sleeping friend; walked backwards like a sailor down the steps that led to the childish dining set, unlatched the door with the discretion of luck, and went out among the plum trees in her nightdress. Her feet were bare. The trees no longer appeared distorted but ordered in an abundant pattern full of blue, starry all the way down to the shining grass. She took a plum. In the day they were yellow fleshed inside the glowing red skin. By night under combining stars this plum was blue skinned, white fleshed. Although it was not quite ripe and still clung to its stone, she bit it and chewed. A shiny knot of resin had seeped and settled where a wasp had been before her. She wiped the stiff globule off with her thumb and looked up into the face that was higher up than most of the burdensome fruit.

'I woke you with my lamp, did I? Are you cold?' asked Rhona's father, and her absence of fear completed itself.

Sixty years on, after church, Mollie listened to Rhona and watched her as she nagged at the world and set it to rights.

'Would you have done that, though would you, Mollie, I'm asking you, would you ever have been so foolish? Would you not have had the presence of mind to run? Or even to try to do the man some reasonable harm? The good men have gone, the men of honour, the men you could trust, the men like, did you know him, Mollie, my poor father who was wounded in that First War and never the same, so Mother and I, it was hard for us, hard, we had to protect him from his own peculiarities. Of course, I recall now you did meet him. And one night when we slept the night through in my garden house, it was blossom time and the trees were white with the blossom, it made its own light like surf, I'm remembering it now, you said his name in your sleep. You said, "Mr Gordon." It was blossom time, I'll never forget, and we made jeely pieces before it was light. With plum jam. It was a rare night.'

Mollie contrived to maintain the air of uninterest that was the response most familiar to her old, betrayed, dear friend; there was no need at this late stage to look into the roots of the friendship's heartwood, a tired man on a night of nights kissing a young girl next to a deep tank of tar, some days before it came to the time of gathering plums.

For After the Trains Have Stopped, a Woman Owes it to the Outside World to Take a Proper Pride in Herself

'I owed it to myself,' said the first client of the morning, 'and to the outside world.'

'Do you see much of that, the outside world, then?' asked Diane, who was adjusting the bands and pads and clips that led to the machine.

'Not in so many words. But there's my husband. And the family.'

'Oh nice,' said Diane and Josephine Cochrane knew that the beauty operative (for so said the words embroidered across the breast of the overall Diane wore) had stopped listening. She braced herself for the torture that would begin when Diane began to activate the machine. The convulsing twinges of electricity that were intended to brace and tone Jo Cochrane's body till it would bounce if thrown any distance, the unpleasant tingling-hot, trickling-cold feeling of the soggy pads against her skin, the crabtip clips leading from them, bringing the increasingly strong electrical impulse, the live wires trailing over her deadish winter flesh, all these were bearable. Diane's talk, though, was harder to endure.

Jo put her book very close to her face and tried to look as though she was reading, to *convey* that she was reading. Reading carried out in the usual way wouldn't look like enough of an activity to transmit itself to Diane. Jo tried to look as though she was thinking, too. She was doing neither. Perhaps because she was actually willing Diane to keep silent, the other woman sensed this and began to talk; Jo had brought about the event by thinking about it, like a person eaten out by a secret until that secret is legible on the skin of its bearer.

'With me it's the little things. Nothing's too much trouble. If I give my heart, it's given, and there it is. The first one is the only one. If he asked me back, I'd be there over broken glass before you said knife. My mother's the same. Been like it all her life. You can ice a cake in only so many ways, but the trim's different each time. And the message on the top. And that's what keeps me at it. When I seen him dancing on the floor with Andrina I says do I let him walk all over me in public or do *I* walk? The kids was all behind me and they're attached like pins, all in a burr, close as 'edgehogs. Nothing's too much trouble for them. I won't let them lift a finger. That's how I am. Can't have other people do things for me if I could do them myself. Every little last thing.' She paused. Her speech did not break naturally, being excitingly unplotted, but whenever she intended to do something, she stopped, as though she were not geared for simultaneity.

Diane twiddled the knobs on the machine that delivered the convulsions that were meant to make Jo's body fit to be seen by lengthening and shortening her muscles like so many slugs with salt dropped on them. The central panel of her trunk lifted, tightened, sank. Her sides sucked at her rib cage. The currents that were to deal with her knees attacked with cramps that pulsed at her with the impartial venomousness of jellyfish. Diane spoke unblemished English save for its content and the irregular, almost genteelly specific, loss of an H at the start of a word. The drift of her speech, its lowness of muscle tone, soothed Jo but worried her too, since she was left never knowing when, or how, to respond. She became as jumpy as a deaf actor waiting for a cue. All her senses compensated for her confusion, rallying to try to divine the sense of what Diane wanted to hear.

The cubicle was built of Scandinavian-type wood, with big knots and the odd hole, that Diane had filled with plugs of cotton wool. She'd had the idea of fragrancing these one week in winter when things were slow. The walls were not secure, nor was the bench on which the seeker of beauty must lie to get her shocks. Each seeker got a fresh length of recycled-quality kitchen towel (turkey width) to go under her. This gave a good impression, Diane said. She saved the lain-upon paper towel for her kitchen, where it was meant to go in the first place if you thought about it. Diane's life was full of such logical considerations. She let her kids stay off school some days because if she had not they would be anyway. That way, she could be sure they went *when* they went, so she said.

Diane had a vision that was not Josephine's. The fragrant cotton-wool balls kept off stray glances, from the numerous men who passed through, Diane said also. Jo had never seen a man at The Beauty Spot, except for the postie who flung and fled, and it was not easy to see how a stray glance might angle and fix itself so as to penetrate the knot holes in the light wood. Poor man who did achieve this. What he would see might scare him into joining the Church. The Beauty Spot was a walk up the road from the other focus of the village, the disused station, where crafts were sold in the season and home baking all year.

Lochanbeg was an abrupt wee border village pressing close to the sides of an old road that it refused to allow to grow wider. Women came to the village in great numbers, having done so from the first day Diane arrived with her electric exerciser. There was reputed to be a larger machine over near Dumbarton, it was said, but it was situated in a great open place with mirrors and other individuals in need of improvement, according to one customer of Diane's, who came right the way over from her guest house by Peebles and swore by Diane's machine. Other ladies, too, agreed, that the charm of The Beauty Spot was its smallness.

'It's homey,' they would say, a word always used when a place is not a home, or not a home of choice. The chief charm of The Beauty Spot was its near invisibility. The social word might have been discretion; the fairer word was incongruity. Yet women drove in their cars rather solider than those locally reared from all over the lowlands to be subjected to the electricity that was directed by Diane through their unloved fat and into their disused muscles. Diane herself was a curiosity. She had arrived from England with her machine, with a clutch of English children by her first husband. She was to be the second wife of Gibson Renfrew, who owned the big local garage where they did a steady trade in 4-wheel-drive vehicles about five months of the year, and made up the shortfall in sandwiches and souvenirs come the season. It had been a thinning living till Diane appeared with her slimming machine, after which many profitable contacts had been made.

When you stepped on to the forecourt of Gibson Renfrew's showroom, the asphalt gave. Beneath it, the heather was waiting, as it always did unless you gave it no hope at the root, to come back. Gibson was a big man with a small mother; he was easily led astray by women, but his mother saw to the sorting-out. Diane had come from the south to the house of her mother-in-law and the children of her husband's first wife, and she had them all subdued and happy right away. A baffled happiness had furred up the usually sharp relations of the Renfrews. No one could say why, but the effect was noted. Mrs Renfrew senior had said, and to be heard, that 'Diane was a woman of her word'. It was thus become a known fact.

Jo Cochrane said, 'I'm reading.'

'Why did you ever not say? I can't be expected to read your thoughts, can I now?' Diane spoke kindly. She never took offence. She was chewing lo-cal gum and eating a nice Rice Krispie and syrup flapjack to her elevenses. Rice Krispies fell with stunned sweetness to stick to the wide rubber bands that bound Josephine round her least taut parts.

Josephine Cochrane thought of the confusion undergone by the modern body. She considered the state of Diane's gum as it must be when she had reached the end of the day and its snacks. Diane turned up the power of the currents leading to Jo's legs.

'You're not reading now, are you?' Jo waited. It came when she had hoped it had passed. 'Aren't you having yourself too good a time?' The current at the top of her legs was as high as it could be. At least the girl-talk was over. No worse to come but this rather bracing self-inflicted – and costly – pain. But Diane continued, 'Too good a time to waste it reading?'

'She only says it because it's what she thinks I want to hear,' Jo said to herself. She was reading ferociously now by dint of counting the number of 'fors' on the page. It being a book by a Scotswoman, there were twice the usual number for the word has more than just the single use.

'Flapjack?' said Diane.

'No, thankyou just the same.' Jo thought she might try a joke. 'I'm here because of too many flapjacks. In principle.' There she went. Why could she not rest without being strict for the truth? Who cared if she didn't precisely eat flapjacks?

'They're high in fibre. I'm surprised you got that way,' Diane indicated the many surfaces of Jo, 'by just eating flapjacks. After forty isn't it, you've the face or the figure, not both. They say. That's what they do say.'

Jo wanted to ask her why, if this was so, she continued to sell the notion that you could have both with the collaboration of an electric current and some almost Victorian-seeming paraphernalia to harness and apply to the vexed face and/or figure.

With a laxness shocking and pleasant, the current sank and was gone. Already Josephine heard the voice of the next seeker.

She was speaking to Karen, who did electrolysis and waxing and was off on a course to Wick, to learn thalassotherapy and the physiology of the nose.

'I do it for myself alone, and not the outside world,' said the voice of an older woman. Emerging from the insecure wooden booth without her tights, Josephine stopped for a moment, dazzled by the freedom her limbs had forgotten in their fifty minutes of constriction. She looked for the speaker in the low front room of The Beauty Spot. Mrs Renfrew senior was speaking. 'My daughter-in-law,' she was saying, 'gives people what they want. She's a girl in a thousand.'

If she had lived in a city, Mrs Renfrew senior would have said, 'She's a girl in a million.' As it was, a thousand was a million to her. Lochanbeg was never busy, and since the railway line had gone it was less so. Tourists came like bright ghosts of day in cars and buses but vehicles that had brought them took them away. There was not the old pleasure of holding people strange in the village till they had buried at least a generation. Mrs Gibson Renfrew senior set down the box of frosted butterscotch furls she'd made for the home bakery up the road. Her life was fuller now she'd Diane in her family; there was more in the way of things to do.

'Of course, I'd to test the icing for it was sweet enough,' she said to Diane, 'and fresh sponge out the oven on a cold morning fills the inner man like a cladding. Anyroad, it was good right enough I knew I was coming in to you, dear, so's I knew it would do no harm if I'd a wee taste.'

Diane was ushering her mother-in-law into the booth where old copies of *The People's Friend* lay stacked on top of one another, the pages stuck together – as the pages of recipe books sometimes are with grease and sugar – with massage cream, patent slimming gel (drawn, so it declared, from the wasps of the Yucatán), baby powder and the crumbs of home baking.

Josephine muttered to Karen that she wasn't going just yet, went into the leanto outside lavatory, put her tights over her tingling and insulted hind quarters and wrote out a cheque. She preferred to do this where Diane wouldn't see her and feel a touch insulted, somehow less artistic, for being paid.

For that was Diane's secret. She was an artist of what people wanted to believe. She kept life on the move. Well might one ask what was the point of coming many miles to be attached to a machine of unproven efficacy in the diminution of the expanded flesh and then passing down the grassy street to purchase fresh home baking, but Josephine understood it now, in the shining tussocked meadow behind The Beauty Spot, looking along the steely row of stone village houses with the telly aerials too big for their chimneys.

Diane speeded up the cycles, making guilt fresh for all her ladies, helping them to notice their ordinary pleasures by making of them sparkling vices. Or that was what she did for Josephine. For her mother-in-law she apparently was a magician who could make something not have happened, who could magic away, even absolve, the sweet peccadilloes either past or anticipated. It was a curiously Roman idea in this stern bosom of the nation. To each her own sweet self-deceit.

Time had stood still in Lochanbeg, and now it was being moved along. Where once the comings and goings of the trains had marked the days of the men, the domestic round the rhythms of the womenfolk, it was now the electrical nocturne of the screen that occupied the men, the fight with natural appetite that gave bite to the lives of the women. Diane was the reminder to live to consume, the modern equivalent of the bad conscience, the siren of redoubled gratification. She was democratic in her temptations. Pensioners, the unemployed, sick, or full-time education sufferers all received the chastening attentions of her machine – at very much reduced rates. Diane was a corroboration of human weakness, an indistinct tempter, a blur of deleterious sugar to take or leave like fairground cotton candy. Her swarm of speech, its cloudiness, was like her attendant spirit. Clichés and half-ideas, good but inconclusive impulses struggling perpetually with overmastering appetite, were her familiars, a cloud of sprites, confused, modern, unavailable for marshalling, afraid of the stern light of scrutiny and discipline, the old hard virtues of every village like this one; until recently.

Up in the sky the clouds spanked along behind the hairy soft green hills. The wet blue road to larger towns, to wider roads, to other lives, to the outside world, led over the hills.

Josephine Cochrane, electric with appetite, set off through the dazzling smirr for the railway station bakery where cakes lay in the place of journeys and intention, things to be consumed in the place that had been the focus of work and hungry curiosity.

SEVEN MAGPIES

The train was passing between still, high fields of standing corn. The light over the fields had a talcy glow that lightened and ceased to shimmer a yard or so into the sky. From time to time a small area of field flicked under a switch of wind, the specific unanimated flick of a creature's pelt. Rangy wild oats over the wide crop and flimsy poppies at its edges were the only intimations of natural disorder. Nothing much was moving but the train through this thinly chivalric part of England.

'Girls are like people, I realised it late on,' said the younger man to the older, who resembled him too much not to be linked to him by blood.

'It will have been my fault you did not see that before. Though I can't see the good it will do you to know it now.'

'Why do you say *now*?'

'You've already done your harm and it is late to begin any undoing.'

'You know more than most that there is no undoing. At least I need do no more harm now.' The young man spoke as though harm were something simple, like hammering.

The older man stood to open a window, with such urgency that he seemed in want of new air. The air that entered the train brought nothing new with it but dust more rural than the dust within.

'You dramatise yourself, Findlay, a pointless thing to do in your profession and very tiring in hot weather.' Sitting down, the older man pinched his trousers and flung his right leg over his left as though this gave depth to his paternal but unfatherly dictum.

'Gum?' rejoined his son, loosening a white tooth of chewing gum from its packet with his thumb and offering it gingerly to his father. It might have been the elegant old man in his cream linen who had been uncouth. But the reprimand was lost on Robert Meldrum who sat now looking at his son over his own, just touching, fingertips.

Knowing that his father was waiting for him to offend, Findlay shot five bits of gum into his own mouth and began to champ until his throat was flooded with minty saliva and his jaw was aching. Would it be the professional or the private life that was coming into the old man's sights, he wondered, with the same dishonourable curiosity that led him to encourage people to repeat themselves indefinitely and to tell him stories he already knew.

'I followed a trade all my life and I fear you are too good for that.' The word 'good' carried none of its customary decent replete weight. Nor did it imply its opposite, merely something lightweight, skittering, inconsiderable.

'Father, your life is not over,' said Findlay, hoping to divert attention from his own life, still, he felt, hardly begun. He almost forgot himself and began to flatter the hard old man, as he might have someone he loved less and trusted more, enticing him into discussion of the past with some welcome slipway down into memory, 'And what a life it has been, eh . . .'

'No, you can't catch me like that. Are you hungry at the stomach or is it the chewing you favour? If so, how odd. How unnatural indeed. You are like that.' Findlay knew his father meant 'you' the young. He himself was seventy-two; Findlay forty years younger. 'You are all appetite and no hunger. All temper and no rage.'

Only a man as stagy-looking as his father, black-browed, blue-eyed, white-haired, elongated but without idle languor, could speak in this public manner in a private place without self-consciousness. The natural dignity of his appearance had throughout his life lent authority to the actions and sayings of Robert Meldrum. Replacing the words in the mouth of a notional short man with clumps of hair, a man whom Findlay had begun to keep about him as a companion in subversion as a boy, was the way to subtract the awe inspired by his father's stern Scots glamour. Although he would have denied the word, the older man exploited the quality, as a preacher might have, in mixed vanity and good faith.

Findlay was slighter than his father, but like him tall and blue-eyed, the eyes seemingly set in the sockets by sooty fingers. His hair was black as his father's had been, but with needles of white at the back and sides. He was less dapper than his father, and as evidently clean to the pitch that actually repels dirt, rather than the holiday smartness that draws it and is ruined. Neither man wore a colour much beyond the neutral, although there was in Findlay's inner jacket pocket, when it flapped open, a row of pencils, crocus yellow, each with a small pink eraser bound to its top with a band of gold metal. Once or twice his right hand went up to these pencils and rolled them like a toy or an instrument. Their small geared hexagons made a noise only Findlay heard.

None the less he failed to notice when his father, in a train, in summer, in England, leant his fine head against the rough blue nap of his seat, drowsed, slept, and, sometime before arrival at their undesired destination, died.

'It's unfortunate you married a man so far superior to yourself,' said her husband.

There was a choice of replies to be made, but since it was breakfast time and their two children were watching Morag to see how she took Daddy's joke, she said, 'That is so, I'm afraid.'

Edward's comment had been made in front of the children before, but never before, as now, stripped of the pretence of levity. It was clear that today would continue the bleak barracking of the night before, until he was out of the house. On his return it would, as clearly, resume. She began to attend to his wants with an assiduity that was part of the ugly bargain she had some months ago made with fate: she would tend to him scrupulously if one day she might be delivered from him. She squeezed oranges down on to the juice extractor as though they were the breasts of the martyred St Agatha.

The table had no place, indeed no room, for her, and it was her pleasure to wait on her family. The thought of eating with them confused her; who would fetch things if she sat down? If she did sit down, she would surely have to rise, so it was easier not to. She thought these small acts of abnegation would attune her children at an early age to the deceits of family life and, even more importantly, the real place of women: these inoculations she, being ironic, took as salutary, and they, being innocent, took for example.

When told she was inferior, it came naturally to scrutinise the superior object. Morag was inferior to a large man nearing forty who sat like a stranger among his possessions and children and whose umbrella, had this been a normal day, he would later forget, causing him to return and feel obliged to kiss her.

In the garden below their first-floor kitchen window a cat moved with rumpy stealth towards a fit-looking magpie that had settled under the denuded roses, among petals lying profuse over the sodden grass. The cat kept its belly from touching the ground, as it would not have on a dry day. Its dark tail and ears cast their shadow in the fresh wet sunlight, its creamy body appearing too blurred and soft to be stockinged and tipped in so sharp a mode. All through the grass were spiders' webs still, though where the cat had been there was a bright trail though the webs' slick silver.

When the Siamese laid low the maggot-pie the squawks and cawings came from both. The cat batted the smart but loutish bird, deriding it to death, then crunching at it with a besotted look as if to say, 'Doesn't it suit me?' The big bird, now without its life, looked frivolous as a hat, but for the dainty giblets and bladders the cat was discarding from its feast. All the while wet petals fell with no sound and up in the kitchen the children, silenced by this pleasant domestic diversion as they had not been by their parent's contained wretchedness, watched, staying their eating only to exchange old saws:

> 'One for sorrow, two for joy,
> Three for a girl, four for a boy,
> Five for silver, six for gold,
> Seven for a secret that's never been told.'

Morag caught the boiling milk as it reached its height and poured it for her husband on to the freshly brewed decaffeinated coffee. On noticing that there was a drop of coffee on the saucer, she fetched a clean cloth and wiped it, making sure that she took the cloth from the pile that was composed of cloths that touched clean surfaces only; not floors, the sink, the table or anything that had not already been washed at least once – a system instituted by Edward.

So as to prepare Edward's breakfast without distressing him, for he had washed his hair this morning as usual, she lit a candle, and set it in the sink to consume the frying smells from the children's breakfast. No one could say she had not colluded in her own demotion from love object to servant. The extravagant acts of obedience and enslavement had, she thought, been a conduit of intimacy between them. Now these actions had set into resented habits and their certainly fetishistic significance had fallen away. Sometimes, when Edward was far from home and she was able to think about him with the balance bestowed by distance, she suspected that she had invented some of his more demanding stipulations in order at first to have more ways of pleasing him, and at length to have more things to blame him for.

She extracted the unsalted butter that only he was permitted, and cut off a small nut or knob, as the books told one a small piece of butter was dubbed. It was not to her especially lubricious stuff.

The butter went into its own brick-shaped, lidded pot, to avoid taking on the smells of other substances. The openness of butter to corruption is extreme, Edward had taught her; only let it see garlic, or melon.

In the early days of their marriage the serene freedom from confusion that her husband had represented, with his distaste for muddle or inappropriateness and his almost mystical sense of what was proper, had been a relief to her: like entering clean sheets for good. A man who knew where things should be put was a man to honour in untidy times.

Now, though, Morag had come to think of mess as having an energy if not sublime at any rate fully human. She had begun to cultivate people who lived in a manner abhorrent to Edward, so that she might sit at their sticky kitchen tables to hear them unpick their troubles as they cleaned their children's faces with their own spit and a paper handkerchief and shook out cat litter, birdseed, flour and currants with impartial, unwashed hands. She fancied she saw a nobility and vigour she did not find in her own house in whose kitchen she never entertained.

'What are these?' Edward asked one evening after his bicycle ride home, his first bath and their wary kiss, during which he smelt her carefully and could guess almost her entire day from what he smelled.

Morag had once made an ebullient – the word occurred to her as she pitied herself for living with a man who did not love fun – an ebullient flower arrangement that included beautiful, fat, complicated globe artichokes. She had thrust their thick architectural stems deep into a vase and starred them about with blue cornflowers and asters the colour of plain chocolate.

Edward flinched when he saw it, at the whimsy as much as at the waste.

She set today's egg before him, and ten toast soldiers. He had never stipulated that he liked ten, but in complaining to a friend one day of her husband's ways, she had invented this one, and found herself complying.

'A man so attentive to detail must be attentive in other ways,' her friend had said, not wrongly, but displeasing Morag who was attached to her hobby of resentment. Her friend was anyway not to be trusted in the matter of men, changing her walk and lifting her tail and walking round the room only to stop, and softly pick things up to hold them against her cheek in the manner of a girl in an advertisement.

'You two go and clean your teeth,' Morag said to her children. She had retained enough tact not yet to enjoy displaying the faults in her marriage to its children, a stage that comes as a rule when the children can least begin to bear it.

Hearing her voice change, she said to Edward, while she took the crusts off his second piece of toast, placed it on a clean plate, and took away the used things before setting down a fresh knife, 'Would you like a second egg?'

He had never said 'Yes' in answer to this question and did not do so now. He did not take more than three eggs in the week, making sure to include in this tally units of egg that might have been incorporated into other things he ingested, for example cakes. Morag's question about the second egg therefore had to his ears something of the murderous in it.

'If you want to kill me,' he said, 'continue to behave precisely as you have done for the past three months. You will find no one as good as me . . .'

She left before she heard this sentence end with the words, 'for you.'

She left the house with her raincoat, her handbag and a pair of painful silver shoes she had worn to annoy Edward that morning, but which by the end of a day that included the plane south, a journey on the tube that had been almost alarmingly smooth, as though she would never have human feelings again, a hot train journey through a part of England that made her homesick already for Scotland, and a promising period of eavesdropping that ended with one of its participants' disappointingly quiet death, annoyed her much more and burned her too, by virtue of their metallic finish.

Hard along the house's dusty yellow length the scaffolding was set, carrying all the blows taken to fix it tight together up to Jean's open window in the form of longitudinal shudderings and breathy irregular chimes. She was resting in a position that she had taught herself during the years of living in other people's houses. Braced everywhere but the neck, her body was arranged in the least comfortable chair in the room. This choice might not have been understood by people unashamed of their own ease. Her wrists and hands curled, ready at any moment to push her up, over the chair's splint-like arms. The plumbing of the house clanked and hissed without cease. In the sash window-frame of Jean's thin high room lay flakes of paint like peeled bark. A tentative persistent lichen grew in on the sill. The scaffolding seemed bold, an expression of someone's intention to hold things up against time.

Fresh yet heavy with the summer that sleeps low around an English river, the air brought into Jean's light sleep noises that came always at this time of day. She did not know she heard them but her closed eyes told her pictures as each noise came. The pictures were clear as illustrations in a first alphabet. She saw a cow, yeast-coloured, on a green field. Pigeons arrived in pairs behind her eyes as their cooing took her back to other houses of which she had become a part, and then fallen away at the given time when another job at the heart of a family withered.

Behind her warm lids, a train came, complete with funnel, condenser, signalman, smuts. She awoke with a start and a taste in her mouth like sucked coin. Morag was coming to stay here. She was arriving this afternoon, in the train.

Jean woke, remembering that Morag had left behind Edward, and, more deplorably, Ishbel and Geordie. She wiped the sleep from her face with a rough flannel as you clean the bloom from a plum, and prepared herself to see her daughter and look her straight in the eye. Morag would no doubt make free of a taxi from the station. Edward would already be beginning to pay for whatever his sin had been. Jean was made unsteady by the reasons Morag gave for leaving, as if there could be reasons for an unreasonable thing. The confusion of love with marriage was no help. Jean held love, in Morag's sense, to be what you felt before you knew a person well enough to know when they were lying. What came after that knowledge might have less fire but it was warmer also, she on principle imagined.

She filled her kettle from the wash-basin and made a half-cup of instant custard, watching the glowing pink flour melt to a suffused yellow, breathing in the smell of vanilla, sugar and starch. Quickly the custard set, with the spoon upright, as though in a cup of plaster of Paris. She powdered her face in a sketchy way, looking at the mirror's flecks and motes and not at her own, which did not interest her. Before leaving the room, she spooned and smoothed a layer of cooling thick custard into the half coconut that hung at her window for the birds. She could not bear to give the birds nothing, and had not the facilities or way of life that produced bacon rinds. It was a vegetarian household, had been so for eighty years.

'Mother, come down, I'm arrived. Or we are.'

The voice came from under the window. Jean looked down through the scaffolding.

'Do you want me to climb down to you?' asked Jean, in an admonitory whisper that subtracted the intended irony. In the heat the creeping plants that embraced the house were reaching tendrils towards the scaffolding, pitting their minute continual subversion against the clumsy man-made optimism of its structure. Should it remain too long, the plants would wind it about and bring it down.

'Shall I actually come in this way?' said a male Scots voice, perhaps drunk. Jean looked along the house. Just to the side of her own bathroom window, over the workroom of Ludovina her employer, was a man over thirty standing rather crouched in the hot box of air between the first-floor scaffolding bars. His colour was bad. It was hard to believe that here was a romantic motive for Morag's morning dash from Edinburgh, but it was Jean's duty to ask.

'Had you intended sharing a room? Ludo would not mind but I am not for haste in these things,' she said to the starling-coloured head of her daughter below. Morag was standing thigh-deep among blue agapanthus and the long belts of their leaves.

'Mother, I left my husband under twelve hours ago, and not because I don't love him. I may.' Morag began to look for a cigarette. She had taken up smoking in the last two hours. It had seemed impolite not to smoke in all the dejected rooms she and Findlay Meldrum had been put into after the finding of his father's body. There had been so little all these strangers could offer, it would have been unkind not to take their cigarettes.

'Have one of mine. You light the end that you don't put in your mouth,' said the man in the scaffolding, dropping a cigarette that fell some feet wide of Morag, and seeing the ineptitude of his throw, he burst into tears for the first time that afternoon, and fell limp out of the rungs down on to the deep lawn of moss where he lay on his back weeping at the English sky in gasps for his father as Jean and Morag looked down at him from their two heights, and, from her workroom in this house where she had been born, Ludovina heard what she had not for more than twenty years, the intractable grief of a man.

The obvious thing, to gather him up in comfort, was evidently up to Morag; but she only knew more about him, she did not *know* him any more than did her mother or Ludovina. Shy of any first touch, she wanted him and his misery, and the way it might bind them for even these hours, to be gone.

She had chosen this as her own day for drama, and events had eclipsed her. Things do not know when to happen, she thought, they are ruthless like children. Cheated of a weeping declamatory scene with her mother, she did not at that point choose to consider why she had not minded becoming involved with Findlay Meldrum's long distressing afternoon with the railway authorities, the police, the hospital.

Curiosity had made her listen to Findlay's conversation with his father. But the sight of him had passed into her with a speed and heat she had forgotten through the years of discipline and some kind of peace with Edward. This made harder the thought of gathering him to her as he beat his head back on the ground – to put it out of its misery, it seemed – and poured tears for his loss of a man she did not know. If she had thought of holding him it was not to give ease, or not at once.

In the end it was Ludovina who dealt with Findlay. Her presumption of competence always endowed her with it. She was good at the extreme states of others since they offended her sense of the stable, measured, discreet and sober way a rational life should be led. She was a satisfied atheist, a type that will take swift decisions without later compunction; her greatest impatience was against timewasters and ditherers. The rock of her unbelief had never once let her down.

Letting herself out by the apple-house door, she moved over the lawn in her sandals and djellabah, her stout decisive form at once becoming the focus of the group; the other two women were distraught at the sight of a man unmanned. Ludovina took over. She was at her best in a crisis, her certainty and bossiness becoming buoyant and purposeful, not chilling.

She thought aloud in the drawling unembarrassed tones that had served her perfectly well through eighty years of privileged activism and rash adventurous travels: 'Jean, you make a bed and a drink for him, if you would. Somewhere he can shout and howl without disturbing us. What's your name? Ah interesting, you are a Scot too then, at any rate at the start of your history. I live here because this is the house of the parents of my mother, and the house where I was born, but I owe myself to Scotland.' Here she spoke of what she found best in herself, her toughness, her independence, her sentimental effective brusqueness.

Ludovina remembered the urgency and stopped, delighted to be at the heart of things that were happening, not to have to kill time with talk. 'Morag, this is sudden, but I am pleased to see you. Since he is not your lover, don't be so foolish and hold his head to stop him doing that.' Ludovina knew well that a mistress would hold a lover who wept. She had herself conducted passionate rational adulteries throughout her long successful marriage.

Findlay had rolled on to his stomach and was beating his head down on the edge of the grass where it met the path of gravel and cinders. His shiny hair was dimmed by black dust. He began to like the distracting pain of smashing down his head among the sharp small stones. Morag squatted, sank and caught him under the arms so that his head was held in her lap where he lay tense and resisting until the reminder of life that came with being held for no reason but humanity entered him, and restored to him the superficial social emotions of a man watched by a short, composed octogenarian woman as he breathes in a stranger through her skirt wet with his own tears. Ludovina nodded as Findlay calmed down. She took her time. Her hard but inky hands were on her thick waist.

She had the thread of a new story almost in her grip. She could not wait to return to her pen, with which she had a further three hours to spend that day, before she went out to dig the evening's potatoes.

'I'm sorry,' Findlay said, apologising also to his father who, he thought, would have deplored every one of the actions taken by his son since his death. 'I had not known it would be like this. You are kind.' It was not easy to say these things lying down and into the lap of a woman he did not know, who smelt of lemon soap, ironing, cheese and pickle, blood and, on the fingers of her right hand that was now stroking, not holding rigid, his left shoulder, the beautiful autumnal domestic dirty smell of extinguished candle.

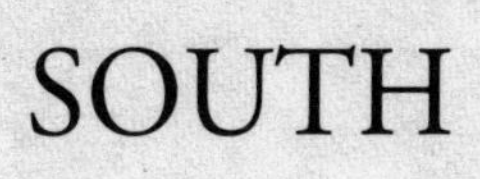
SOUTH

Strawberries

'Church or chapel?' would ask my nurse, and my parents would set their mouths. My nurse was asking if my high-church father or atheist mother would care for an arched piece of bread from the top of the loaf or a squared-off piece from the bottom. Whichever either chose, it would be buttered to the edge and smeared with fish paste. We were having tea in the white day-nursery, which always smelt slightly of singeing. My parents did not care for each other, and they detested Nurse, but could not agree as to her disposal. I loved her.

As though massively exhausted, my father began, 'Nan,' (this was to convince himself that he had come from generations of people who had employed servants) 'Nan, no more can you impute the Romanesque line of that particular crust solely to churches than you can suggest that our friends the Welsh worship in boxes; or, if, by "chapel", you mean something more Romeish, while the Gesú in Rome could conceivably be considered squat, I cannot myself be sure that it might be seen as a square.' Did he talk like this? If not in fact, certainly in flavour. He never stopped, never definitely asserted, incessantly and infinitesimally qualified. He was an architect but however did he draw his straight lines? How, once he had begun it, did he stop drawing a line? He might continue, 'The fish paste, Nan dear, is, I must acknowledge, an apt touch for the believer when one brings to mind that ichthyic ideogram for the name of Our Lord scrawled on the lintels of Byzantium or in the sands of Palestine; this reduction, indeed, of fish, this distillate of the deep, this patum of piety.'

Did he speak in his intolerable manner out of hatred for our unadventurous nursery world, the humiliating occasional necessity of spending time with the son he had somehow got on the stony woman sitting low in the nursing chair? I am certain he did not speak from love of words, for all his polylalia; he issued his words as though they strained the sphincter of his mouth, and sank, drained, whenever he at last completed a sentence. To ensure freedom from interruptions, he moaned at not quite regular intervals, as though his speaking mechanism were running down. He also breathed energetically and gobbled at his cheeks.

My mother in contrast was so quiet as to suggest illness. When she spoke, the remark would be of the sort that made me pleased I had no brothers or sisters. The thought of anyone having to hear the things my mother said made me embarrassed. Today she said, 'Did you know, my pigeon, the firescreen is worked in silk from worms which have eaten nothing but the white mulberry's leaf?' It was her overworked absence of banality which made me uncomfortable. I do not now think she was affected, rather, I think she may have escaped into willed eccentricity, which combined with an already eccentric nature. I have inherited her warmth towards esoterica; she had none for people, but she loved her dreadful facts.

Unlike my mother, I have always felt inhibited by the idea of displaying curious information in daily converse. I find it hard to imagine dropping into a free, swiftly moving conversation, odd bits of factual knowledge; they seem to choke the progress and clarity of the thing. I loathe those men who just happen to know about monorchitism in dictators or the curative properties of the toxic members of the potato family. I like best knowledge which comes from comprehension. I do not care for ornamental knowledge, as worn by my mother. Expository or even revelatory knowledge are what I like. Since I became an adult, the mathematics of space and time have been my particular weakness.

But then, on the rug of knotted grey and green cotton rag, concentrating on the knotting's soft randomness to drive time off, I was years from my final resting place, the study of finite dimensional vector space. I have mentioned that I was an only child. I had no friends. If you have bundled and divided the genetic fibres I have offered you, you will not be surprised. But I did have, on my father's side, some cousins, and I liked them.

We were to see them the next day, for the funeral of a great-aunt of mine and of theirs. She had died alone in her flat by the river. On my last visit before her death, accompanied by my mother and by Nurse, my great-aunt had been alert in her freezing flat. She was as sane as a horse and my mother behaved normally for at least an hour. Nurse was scandalised by the cold, and told my mother so. My mother replied, 'Cold is so very good for keeping the more highly-strung tropical blooms fresh.' There was a very small posy of flowers at my great-aunt's flat, and it was made out of wire and buttons. It lived in a vase with a blurry view of a castle painted on one side, strangely out of register, as though the transfer had been done by someone trembling badly. Beside this vase lived a photograph of my four cousins and me. This photograph pleased me in two ways, once warmly, for love, and once in a hot mean way. We were richer – in money – than they, and my coat, even in a photograph, was clearly better fitting, better cut, and of better cloth. I would be wearing this coat to the funeral.

Tea over, Nurse bathed me and read a story to me, a story too young for my age in order to foil nightmares. We also conspired to keep me a baby, so my parents needed her and she could hold my own helplessness against her dismissal, when it came.

My parents overcame their fraught lassitude for long enough to give me a good-night talk on the warping of furniture ferrules in comparative latitudes (my father) and the lost-wax art of a man (am I tidying the past unmercifully?) called Gloss

O'Chrysostom (my mother). If he had listened, and she had momentarily emerged from her hypochondriacal trance, they might have found one another quite interesting. As it was, he worked at home, there was not yet a war to take and glorify him, and she simply had too little to do. I, as a child, was not sickened by all that rich leisure, since that is a child's state, to judge its own circumstances the norm. And children have not learnt to measure time. Nevertheless, through observing my parents observe time and its passage (clocks, watches, timers, tolling, chiming, sounding, and the terrible mealtime gong), I was fast losing that innocence.

I said prayers to Nurse, having rescinded to my mother the elaborate pieties she knew I had enunciated to my father. My private prayers were simple, 'God bless me and God bless Nurse and God bless the Morton cousins.' Their Christian names were easier than mine, John, Bobby, Mary and Josephine. Noel Coverley was my name. I have two middle names which I will tell no one. They attest the intimate spitefulness of my father, who has ensured that I recollect his coldness and his pretensions every time I fill in an official form. Thus he has slung my adult self about with the unhappy overdainty child I was. My grandfather had been the brother of their grandmother. It was the sister of these two who had died in the cold flat by the river. Another thing I love about mathematics of the sort I live among is the way that they blunt the points of time's callipers, by stretching them so far apart, into other sorts of time. Families do the opposite, all the relationships marking time so clearly on that short wooden ruler.

She lay in her coffin and the flowers held out in the steady cool for the whole service, which was long, and presided over by Anglican nuns. My parents and Nurse and I (in the coat) were driven in our grey Morris. The cemetery was beyond Chiswick. The cousins and their parents had come in a car they had hired for the day. Our driver sat in our car. Theirs went for a walk and bought a paper and a bag of pears. Nurse, who was a thorough Presbyterian and averse to what she called 'smells and lace', shared the pears with him. She was partial to a little fruit.

It was my first funeral. Several things about it were unbearable yet intensely pleasurable. The only completely awful thing was the thought of a person in a box. The words of the service went to my head, so my tears were delicious. The 23rd psalm seemed to paint a nursery Arcady where a nurse and not a parent was in charge. We would all be good and fear would be cast out. For the duration of the funeral, I ceased fretting. I did not once look at my mother's defiant white cerements, her alarmingly druidical hat.

The mother of the cousins wore a woolly mulberry thing and she gave me a nice smile when the sermon was threatening to break the richly religious mood. Each of my cousins wore a navy blue felt hat. I had almost chewed through the elastic on my own hat. I could feel its petersham ribbons on the back of my neck. I was a skinny boy with blue knees and pale red nostrils. I had the strength of ten. I was always hungry, though I did not eat in front of my parents if I could help it.

We crossed the road that divided the church from the graveyard where my great-aunt was to be buried. I was prepared for this burying to be the most shocking thing I had seen, worse than my father battering on my mother's door, worse even than seeing a dog shot. So I was better off than Mary and Josephine whose faces crumpled as they saw the spadeful of earth land on that box containing a person. Perhaps they had suddenly realised that they might not live for ever. There was a wind, and while there were fewer motor cars in those days, the dirt from the Great West Road was worse. Our eyes filled with grit and our noses with the smell of cinders. John and Bobby did like men; they screwed up their faces so that no tear could possibly find its way out. I, being 'delicate', was expected to cry, and did so with unmixed pleasure.

The only thing which shook me was the presence of another, unknown, child at the funeral. She was standing with two adult people. She made them look ridiculously large. She might have been my sister, she was so thin. She had a smirk behind her becoming tears. Her mother and father looked sleek and almost impolitely well-groomed. The small girl was dressed in a blue velvet cape with white fur like a frosty Eskimo doll. From the blue velvet bag she carried she extracted, still crying with her face, a peppermint disc the size of a florin. I smelt it amid the wool and naphtha. I looked reverent and stared hard at her from under my lowered lids.

It was not only the mint of which I was jealous. Would this child come back to the cousins' house? Would she offer them more highly flavoured snippets than I let them have from our different way of life? Was she related to me? Or to them, and not to me? I sent up a prayer which mentioned my great-aunt only incidentally. Its main petition was that my cousins did not, or would not, excessively care for this child.

My mother took my hand in her gloved one. The kid felt like the lids of mushrooms. I knew what she was going to say and had a pretty good idea what she was going to do. Piously, for health reasons, against burial, she was about to break a glass capsule of eucalyptus beneath her nose, and blow it loudly. It was only since I had become seven that she had ceased doing the same for me in any exposed place. She then said, 'While we have a moment of peace' (what a moment, our family at prayer in a windswept graveyard) 'my dove, just take heed of your mother when she reminds you simply to rise above the dirt and devastation at the house of your cousins, who are by no means as fortunate as you. Naturally, for reasons of politeness, we cannot fail to attend the proceedings, but I know I can trust you not to have any needs or to give in to any temptations you may encounter.' She meant don't go to the lavatory and don't eat.

One of the two lessons of that day was that death makes me hungry. It is as though food, the staff of life, were a spell against falling into dust.

The burial done, my parents and I joined Nurse. She had the sweetly acid smell of pears on her. Her grouse-claw brooch had already that day achieved much in the way of irking my mother. We all got into the grey car. It slunk through the small streets near the Morton house. The driver could not park in their street; he would have blocked it. We had passed on the way a vehicle as long as a lifeboat and red as a fire engine. Its chauffeur was upholstered in cherry red, with cavalryman's boots. A whip would have been unsurprising. My parents, who until now had exchanged no sentence, only my father's accustomed latent speech and my mother's dammed silence, looked at each other. That in itself was unusual. They spoke together, 'Victor and Stella.' My father continued, my mother no doubt wrung out by the effort of speech. 'And the odious child, a vision in coneyfur. I wonder they did not drown it. Of what possible use is it to them?' My father was in this way approaching one of his favourite topics, the childrearing customs of the Spartans. He did that turn especially for Nurse, who could not control her outrage, even when she knew she was being riled on purpose. My mother remained silent, thinking no doubt of the struggle awaiting her in the Mortons' house.

Their father I called Uncle Galway. He taught history, cricket and Latin at a nearby school. Aunt Fan taught part time at the school, when she was not busy with her children. Her subjects were botany and maths. She occasionally taught dressmaking, though even the pancloths she knitted were out of shape.

Their house was attached to its neighbour. It gave the impression of being a big cupboard, perhaps because nothing inside it was put away. In the sitting room, the temperament and pastimes of the Mortons were apparent. The room was stuffed with books, rags, wools, jigsaws, a tricycle, a tank of tarnishing but sprightly goldfish, a cat on a heap of mending, jars of poster paint, a shrimping net and some wooden laundry tongs lying on top of a crystal garden in its square battery-jar of waterglass.

Upstairs, I knew, there would be clothes everywhere, in optimistic ironing baskets, over bedheads, stuffed into ottomans. Everywhere were clothbound books, yellow, maroon, tired blue. In the bedrooms there was a good chance of hearing mice; the Mortons were allowed food wherever and whenever they wanted it. They kept apples and sweets in their chests of drawers, where socks might have been in another house. They were a family which shared its secrets.

The sitting room went straight into the kitchen. Today both rooms were occupied by those who had come on after the funeral. Why were my family, with so much larger a house, not entertaining the party? Their sallow social tone might have been suitable to the decorous gloom conventionally required by a funeral. But they had not offered. It seemed better, at the end of a long life, that there should be not my parents' mean, ordered luxury, but what I saw spread out almost indecently in the kitchen, soft cheeses, deep pies, steaming fruit tarts, jugs of custard and of cream. Aunt Fan was dispensing the food with a battery of unsuitable implements, pie with an eggslice, trifle with a silver masonry tool, cheese with a palette knife, cream from an Argyll. It was a bright mess of colour and juice, squashiness and superfluity. Nurse and my mother stiffened, the one as she saw good food in quantity, the other as she perceived the prowling spectre of uncontrol with its attendant bacteria, spillage and decay.

My cousins fell on me, wagging like pups. Each of them held a thick slice of well-buttered black cake, so by the time they had greeted me I was an object of horror to my mother. She took a long look at me, winced, drew herself up, ruffled and settled her shoulders, and bent, in movement like a river-bird, to unbutton and remove my now Mortonfied coat.

Nurse fetched a plate for herself. My unspoken arrangement with the cousins was, as usual, to get myself upstairs unobserved. I think now that their parents colluded in this against my mother. The house's muddle was a considerable help. I now, too, surmise that my mother's desire to be free of me was even stronger than her dedication to germ warfare. And on this occasion it was clear that she could hardly remove her glare from the pair of grown-ups who must be Victor and Stella. They were tall and, separated from their curiously superior child, clothed in blatancy and confidence. My itch for vulgarity responded to those glittering froggings and facings.

But what concerned me was their daughter, now free of her velvet cape and revealed in a white cotton dress smocked in unfunereal red. The collar was embroidered with very small red strawberries, natty *fraises du bois*. The buttonholes down her back were sutured in the same bright red. Her hair was long, thin and white. She had no front teeth, just two gum spaces. This gave her a lisp. Bobby introduced us. She was Coverley too, her grandfather my grandfather's brother. How had my father overlooked, in his passion for overinformation, especially where it touched upon himself, a whole knot of family? My cousins obviously liked this girl. So I hated her.

'Hello,' she said. 'Is that woman your nurse?' I saw Nurse, for an instant, without love. She was piling a large plate high with food, all mixed up. Her skirt was wide as a fender.

'Yes, she is. And where's yours?'

'Left, they always have; can't bear it.' So she was one of those bad children who rushed through nurses and showed off about it.

'What do you do to them?' I asked, not in admiration as she might have hoped, but prissily.

'It's not me, it's my father, and I can't possibly say. I don't know exactly but shall soon enough, my mother says. The last one broke his ivory hair brushes and tore up some of his clothes. My mama says it is something I shall learn all too soon. Men have a rolling eye, she says.' All this with the toothless lisp. In spite of her chilling self-command, something gave me a hint of fellow feeling.

'Is your mother mad?' I asked. From observing Aunt Fan, I knew that my own mother was not typical.

'Is yours?' asked the child. 'She looks it.'

'Come on, you two.' It was Mary. She stood between me and the other cousin, whose name was apparently Lucy, taking her left hand and my right. Mary was shorter and sturdier than we were. Nurse came over and blocked our way to the stairs. She did not mean to; she was just that fat. I looked up and saw she had two plates, spilling with good things, leaking over the edge. I read the names of the china in her shiny hands, 'Spod' and 'Crown Derb'. Her fingers covered any remaining letters. Each of the plates had been broken, at least once. Now they were riveted, and should not have been used for food. Where the cracks were, a deep purple was beginning to appear, the juice of black fruits.

Nurse was a small eater, but she heaped her plate at the Mortons' house.

'Just go and fetch a cup of black tea, dear,' she told me. She was not smiling.

'And would you,' she spoke to Lucy, 'get a slice of lightly buttered bread?'

Equipped with this thin meal, we returned to Nurse. She wore her bowler-style hat indoors. She peered out from under it. The coast was clear.

She filled the narrow stairway as she led us up its druggeted steepness to the bedroom where our cousins had made a table of Josephine's bed.

'Pass me the tea, dear,' she said. 'And before either of you' – she spoke to me and to Lucy – 'starts on your meal, it's bread and butter. Sit down.'

We sat at opposite sides of the child's bed and she placed in front of each of us a gleaming incoherent feast on broken china. She looked at Lucy, who appeared less menacing up here. She smiled at her and the little girl smiled back, showing side teeth like buds.

Taking a white cloth from the holdall whose cane hoops lived at her elbow, Nurse said to Lucy, 'Lift up your hair, love, and Nurse will tie this round your neck. You don't want fruit juice on those smart strawberries. Eat the bread and butter, the both of you, then you can say you had bread and butter when you're asked. Church, Lucy. Chapel, Noel.'

I explained to Lucy what it was that Nurse meant. All those nurses, and she didn't know a single thing. Eating opposite me and bibbed up in the white cloth, Lucy became at once an ordinary little girl, hungry, skinny, released for an afternoon from the obligation to be odd. By the time we had finished our tea on the bed her untoothed gums were purple and I loved her.

Already equipped with the deviousness and instinct to flirt of a grown woman, she had been dissembling ignorance, she told me years later, when she pretended not to know what Nurse meant by 'Church and Chapel'. 'I was putting you at your ease,' she said. By then we were smokers, and, as I held up a light for her, we looked through the pale flame to the bright red burning tip of the cigarette, bright in the dark like a wild strawberry on dark moss.

You Can't Be Too Clean

I'm the woman lives on the step of the bank and eats soap. That's my name and how they speak of me when they fold away their eyes and move a wee bitaways off their track even though it's the bank they've come to see and they'll have to pass me. Often I see them holding their noses without even lifting their hands, which is odd, because I think you can't be too clean.

I've other names but they're put away and I can't see when they'll come out again for they're locked up in the other bodies I was. For the moment I live on the step of the bank, unless it's winter when I get a bit closer and move in between the portals. Dog's'll not pee there, it's too skeetery. It's mosaic on the floor between the portals, very smooth till you lie on it and then it's all small corners and you lose the picture in close-up like that. If you stand away from it you can see that there's a picture of a woman all made of squares pocketing her wages with the help of a lion and an owl also made from these small hard tiles, each with the four corners when you lie on it. I settle down after the bank's stopped getting visits. Then God's in his small corner and I in mine. I can take the mosaic if I put my blanket down on it. This blanket is the main thing. The blanket and the soap.

This blanket I brought with me out of the first life and right through the other ones up till now. It has covered the many forms of nakedness I have lived inside as the time and the place changed. The blanket had its moment of glory in the shop, where it was part of the list of things I thought came with being married and the one I was about to marry agreed and marked the box next to 'Pure wool Witney blanket, 72" x 84", cream, satin bound' with a 6. We'd a house with three double beds that soon. Maybe it was then I should have heard a red light. All the beds got used, so the wastage didn't seem like it might to me now I've been poured through the many lives. We'd people in to lie under those blankets several times a year, and we kept the beds ready to be made up, covered with white counterpanes over the mattress protectors, the folded blankets and the sleeping naked pillows.

The quantities of unused linen, clean and folded, that lay ready for my use then makes me feel weak like remembering kisses used to. It all comes up into my chest and heart and I raise up my head and smile right deep into the eyes of what's in my mind – and it's clean sheets in there, clean sheets radiating whiteness and the smell of soap you'd so much of you kept it folded in its paper between the heavy cold sheets, the scented soap just lying there ready among the sheets that were ready too, waiting to be extracted, flung and soothed over beds that were aired three times a week and mattresses that were turned each month.

I think of the stuff I've used up without thinking as I've gone through and I wonder how the world can take it, the weight of materials needed for a person to live a modern life.

The other moments of glory belonging to the blanket are various and include some happiness. Its label is soft now and it's only got threads going across the way. The sheeny blue and yellow words about Made in England have all unwound from the sturdy threads. It's a blanket from the time of market towns and church attendance.

For sleeping in the threshold of a bank, though, a city like this is by some way superior to a market town, where there's not enough to do so then they turn to those of us who repose outdoors in most weather conditions.

The blanket came in a lorry from a shop to the first house, boxed up with five others and paid for by a guest at the wedding who had hopes of some business arrangement with my intended loosely to do with an implement for crushing used cans. Later he went away for a while and while he was away doing that his wife took the first quite big overdose but he got out with a discreet companion from the right side of the law for a couple of days of compassion during which she achieved a more efficient job of counting and succeeded in her ambition so then he received a little more leave during which arrangements were made for the children who became swiftly used to the habits of their grandparents and learned how to turn off lights and keep their voices down.

So in the end they got a good education though I was worried lately when I saw in one of those catalogues that people don't notice falling out of their magazines as they walk along looking at the shiny pages for what to buy next that someone else has brought out a contraption for crushing used cans, not the man who introduced the blankets into my life, or I should say, the blanket. *Empty* used cans, these machines can compress, though few householders understand empty in its full form, meaning containing nothing, not a scrape, not a lick, not a wipe or a dribble of food.

I cut out food practically when I achieved my present way of life, though I keep up my fat intake with the soap and have managed to rectify my dreams at one and the same time, the soap giving a safe taste to dreaming. It's probably not an indigestible food and of course you sleep all clean inside. I'll take you through that when I've set it all straight about the blanket. Soap leaves nothing lying around inside you, that much I'll say. Inside me it's calm and empty as a basin.

At the time of receiving my blanket I did not pay it sufficient attention. I slept under it, certainly, or under what may have been only one of its fellow blankets, that were so like it, but at that time I slept under my blanket, or even, in winter, blankets, with the intervention of a sheet. On top of it all, like cream over a sweet and rich pudding, lay a sack of feathers sewn into furrows and trapped in there with flowers printed on to cloth.

The depicted flowers that were so plentiful in that first married house didn't do more than give it pattern and colour at first. There was no scent of course. A shocking absence of decay soon gave a hint of the truth about these blooms. They turned their heads at me, the roses, the lilies, the auriculas and gillyflowers, and watched and turned again to each other to pass remarks on the state of my appearance and see how I compared with them in being pressed into flatness and colour and odourlessness.

They talked at first only when I was out of the room. The harebells on the cushions confided in the curtain hydrangeas, the ivy on the trellis silk-screened on the paper throughout the hall began to close over the areas of white, so I grew short of light and air while the leaves approached one another to exchange the words the flowers and leaves all spoke from the walls and windows and beds of the house where I had been taken to live. The flowers despised my changeability, my moods, my unreliable way of being alive. They were unchanging, open always even in the absence of sun, firmly forward-looking.

I had worked out the way out of the bower by then. I lit it up to shut it up. The fire was stubby and noisy and I was right – it did talk louder than the flowers. Soon after it had started to win, though, he arrived home from where he went in the day and duffed it up with a blanket. But it left a good gasp of smoke choking each flower in the room where I was meant to sleep, so at least that kept them quiet overnight while I pruned all the chintz curtains downstairs and took the throats out of the floral cushions, which got me peace of a kind when he drove me in the car at night against all these lights coming at you with the promise of colour over your face coming in stripes till you felt it must lie over you in ribbons and I parted the ribbons of light I'd collected in the back of the car and walked out into the place where they sorted the first body I'd had and ushered in the next one which began after the doctor laid me down and helped me to sleep without talking or behaving at all like a flower and even replaced the blanket after. My own blanket.

The place had a room for sitting and a chair for sitting too in that room for sitting, also a television and a notebook for writing what you wanted to watch in. There were people staying there wanted to watch things I can't stop seeing now right inside my head even if it's so cold in the portals of the bank you'd cut your side open just to get your hands on the warmth inside. Not all of the people at the place wanted to watch things you'd get on actual television I didn't think but he said, the doctor said, that we keep these ideas inside us at our peril. So that is how I got some of the ideas someone had put outside of themself inside me and it is why I wail from time to time in the doorway of the bank, not able to sleep the idea out of my head or wash it out no matter how much soap I use in and out.

They were logical things and all very practical and written in the slow helpful way a recipe is made out: Take a woman and bend her double till you see right up through her so you're looking out of her mouth at the stars and then you take the one and then the other and fold her up small and put her in the pan and boil her up three times bearing in mind that the cheeks and forearms yield up the best and finest fats. To keep the next one young-skinned use this rich substance made from the previous one's smoother parts.

Leaving the place was sad enough though because of the doctor and the way he listened to the flowers too when I had explained, coming close on the pillow to hear when the embroidered buds chattered among themselves on the hem of the linen sent from home to this place where they provided me with a bare room that was the least talkative as to the walls I've slept in ever. I have more faculties than those who do not hear the flowers speak and the leaves spread their rumours, but others can't take the news I have for them – that we should ward off decay by sitting motionless and keeping clean and remaining in the proximity of money.

The last luxury, my blanket. And the other that is an essential, the soap. I eat it without water, in the slice, but for washing I do use some water from the Ladies round the way. I never wash with the eating brand, or vice versa.

From the bank in the morning come noises like the sounds in a deserted zoo. The sleeping money is unbarred, its movements and territory marked for the day. It breathes and its breath is not warm, though that of its suitors may be.

After that time at the place with the doctor the old body got lost and the new body grew big at home and unloosed its little prisoner. I felt the blanket cover him and me and the new one and wished the world away. The walls and windows no longer commented. In my absence they had been frozen white and iced cream. Only in the room of the new one were there flowers, metal, in a bunch, and they blared pleasure out of all their bulbs of light over the bed where new small blankets covered the third one of us.

Not knowing where we began and ended was what I called love but they went off into their own bodies more than I could allow so I bound us together while they slept and he sat up and that was how their selves got caught and fell and the rope pulled tight although it was not thick, indeed thin being made of the strings that feed electricity to light bulbs and help them keep up their shouting till you turn them off by rocking their tonsils or flicking their tongues.

So the smaller one was pulled up by him as he sat up. The smaller one hung there from the vein that fed the light and twisted round and round at the neck till the light was very uncomfortable, it was pulled so tight by the heavy baby hanging there.

All the strength from the poor lights failed. The little one rocked there for a moment between us and we were all held close in the dark and I knew love bound us in this house where the flowers had stopped their talking.

The little one made a noise himself and then swung and the man started making a loud noise which I did not like since it interrupted the love. Even more so when he was pushing the little one hard all around the heart and eating its face. And I tried to take the little one away and make sure it stayed clean, with no dribble on it. But there was an ugly thing at the neck of the little one, so I said, 'I must go and get some soap to wash away the mark around its neck.'

Then he said much that another person might have regretted. He took the little one and folded it in the blanket that was off the bed where the three of us had been. He laid the little one down and begged it to move.

After I saw it stir, I told him, and he was jealous I had seen it first, I suppose, because he screamed at me and pushed me over and held me down and made me a nice necklace with his hands and I knew what he wanted and set about helping him and he screamed again and threw me like a bale of bitter weeds across the room. All along I was reading what was happening but could not translate it. It was certain that the little one had done something very wrong, or it would not have been so sad and still.

When it moved, and he saw it too, he fell on his knees and called out to God. How I loved him then. He was forgiving our naughty little one, as a father should. The blanket began to fold and wrinkle as the small legs moved inside it. I saw that the blanket held everything we had.

Later in the next room that they found me for sitting in on my own with visits and gossiping trees outside all the windows, he brought me a blanket. I do not know if it is the same one that held the baby, but it is certainly similar. I fold it at night around the soaps and over my head and I lie in the portals of the bank. The soap hardly stirs or breathes but how it glows.

I am only a little disturbed by the tedious statements of the traffic lights as they mark the passing cars. The blanket and the soap never trouble me by talking. I see flowers carried sometimes by those who come to visit their money, but the flowers don't speak to me now that I have faded to a state where I am no longer their rival.

White Goods

I like to think we're happy enough. Certainly we're not too happy, so that must make us happy enough, I guess. It's at the times when I stop and think to myself that I want for nothing that I feel that small gap. It's like something I've forgotten, but which didn't much matter anyhow, the words of a bedtime prayer or the shade of a lipstick worn by my mother. Small things which could lead on to bigger things if I'd the energy to think. I mentioned this feeling to Geoffrey.

'Something in the tea,' he said.

'More likely something on the TV,' I said. I'd heard some lively debates on the telly about television and what it does to your mind. The overstimulation, apparently, is what makes me feel switched off much of the time. My horizontal hold, too, has all but gone. I wouldn't say that to Geoffrey, though, because he'd be sure to take it personally.

Reading, seemingly, that's the great anecdote to telly. All fine for those with a free hand and free time on their hands. I mean you have to hold the book up and give it your full attention. I've got out of the way of the train of thought. It doesn't stop here. We girls do miss that train, if you ask me. You're forever going in six directions at once, doing the meals, cleaning the pots, finding Geoffrey's glasses which he can't find without his glasses, thinking about dead-heading while you're brushing your hair, looking pleased to see people when they come by, even though what it means is foot-marks, disruption, and a wrangle with Geoffrey about the carpet which is, I freely admit, not a practical colour. Our recollections of who selected it differ, so consequently it's a minefield. The thinking behind the carpet was that, since we live up here on the clay cap, we'd have a nice shade of russet. So that if we did have company and if that company had walked or had cause to get out of the car at all (Geoffrey has a logical mind), the mud or, if it had not been raining, dust, on their feet wouldn't show up on any carpet we might purchase. But there was a shade which was on offer and it was a sort of ginger, called Rottweiler, I think, or something romantic, and the shop showed a photo display which did win me over. It was one of those full colour pictures of the past, showing the carpet in various locations, being crafted by craftsmen, walked on by sheep, and so on. The carpet being walked on by the sheep was green, naturally. Well, dyed. It's OK though, I mean they were grazing the green carpet, but nevertheless it wasn't cannibalism, was it, because the carpet was wool-type, not the pure new thing.

It's easy to care for, granted, and I still get a thrill when I tell new acquaintances I call it teal or terracotta or curry or whatever it was. But it shows up clay and the crumbs of Bourbons like Albert Ross at the wedding in the poem.

Makes you want to bite the carpet sometimes, vacuuming in your head already while the visitors heedlessly walk on the carpet and gorge on biscuits prepared by your own fair hands. It was the past which sold me that carpet, I'll admit it. I love the past, the way things were. Things were nicer in those times, more quaint, picturesque is the word I like to use. Things used to be traditional. There was time, for everybody. The rich man at his castle, the poor man at his cottage. There were values then, and standards. You knew where you stood. I don't remember the past. It was before I was born.

Geoffrey has no time for the past, all the little touches which recall it. Take cooking, for example. For the modern wife it should be a leisure activity. I purchased myself a device which is said to be especially useful in the preparation of crowdie, bannock and other receipts of yesteryear, and with it came a kit for making batik. Batik is a craft as practised by our forebears, who wore robes richly devised with its motifs. I have made several useful gifts and an unusual kneeler for gardening.

Geoffrey, though, doesn't care for my new device, or for the batik I have made with such care. He calls the one modern and the other fusty and he says life is for living. Well, that has to be the case, but I've never quite managed it, not recently at any rate. I mean, I know I'm alive because I hurt if I drop the hot wax from the batik kit on my hand, for instance. In fact it's at times like that I do know I'm alive.

Let's think of other times I've lived life to the full, like when I get a little bug of hot wax on my hand, and it makes a blister the same size and with the same softness just a bit later. But you can't flick the blister off, so it's extra lucky really, a little ladybird of skin to remind you you have lived. Other times? I feel quite alive when I've got every last thing done and I know there's a clear half-hour before Geoffrey gets in. I've dusted and vacuumed our starter flat – Geoffrey says Hoovered is not a real word, would you say I've Haytered the garden? Well, I would, of course, because I have hated it all my married life, but I wouldn't say because that would be off the point, even I can see that. What Geoffrey is minding is, he tells me, often as not unprompted, the misapprehension of proper nouns, or somesuch.

Geoffrey teaches. I made the bag he takes to school. He hides it in the car and really uses a different container for his documents, a leather briefcase with spinning lock-barrels and a combination. I like to think of him doing all that transferring of papers in the car. When this small pleasure goes a bit dim, I make him tuna sandwiches. Geoffrey dislikes odours and tuna lingers longer. I give him mayonnaise on the tuna because Geoffrey dislikes all forms of mayonnaise. Or he says he does, and has been saying so since we married. He says it's messy and unnecessary and makes things all the same. He rants on when he hits this topic. The pasteurised culture, or something like that.

Though I could do with more fields, myself. Sometimes, if the bag-swapping ritual has been omitted, the sandwiches settle and develop a culture of their own in my home-made bag. The bag isn't batik, it's Amerindian folk art sort of thing. I emblazoned a simple beadwork and chamois pouch with Geoffrey's initials. For this purpose, I made a small branding iron with copper wiring, held in my mum's old laundry-tongs to avoid getting my fingers burnt. I heated it up over the naked flame of my hob.

The flames are like blue flowers when they're up high. Geoffrey says no flower is blue. The meconopsis poppy, found in the high Himalayas and in the environs of Inverness, is in fact blue, Geoffrey, I refrain from saying. I found this in a supplement on exotic honeymoon locations. We walked Hadrian's Wall on our honeymoon. That's Geoffrey all along. I wasn't snippy like this till we were wed, and then I saw clear as day how it's all effort and perfection and homebaking and fresh undies.

When else do I live life? Thinking about it, what the occasions have in common is a kind of brightness and heat. Sixpences, which were coins in the bit of past I was present during, though it did not feel like the past at the time, well, sixpences were thin coins the size and lightness of the circle of card at the top of the pack in those tubes of Horlicks tablets. Think how exciting your life must be I don't think if you pop Horlicks tablets. Sixpences were not worth six pence, nothing being what it seems. But I loved sixpence, cunning little sixpence, because with it you could buy gas for the fire. The fire was made of a kind of honeycomb of chalk, bevelled off like little white knucklebones. You'd put in the sixpence and turn a smooth brass key which smelt of Brasso. There'd be a bang as you struck your match and applied it to the suddenly thick air, and a big pale purple and orange sheet would billow out, then suck itself in behind the chalky honeycomb. The little white bones would begin to glow red.

People like watching open fires, for the things they see in the flames, peacocks, chariots, lovers, the future. I watch gas fires. I like to sit in the dark and watch the way shadows exaggerate just a bit and things shiver before your eyes in the rising heat.

I love those drinks waiters light. They seem to promise a night of heat and dark. Italian, they are. You can have that one in the glass like a small schooner and the coffee bean goes berserk on the top. A glass of flames, blazing like a thistle. I like the smell of burning, come to think of it.

I like to know things. To this end I attend occasional classes at our local clinic. I like first aid. We pass around the doll and give it mouth to mouth and by the end there's a taste of curry on its plastic lips. But fire drill's my favourite. I have swift reactions and have never known the fear of flames. I like to know what not to do. Sodium, now, you must never attempt to quench its flames with water because water makes it burn. And they tell you to roll your children up, like kid kebabs, in a largeish piece of carpet you have handy. Not our carpet, though. It'd adhere, being synthetic.

I have felt alive on other occasions which I should enumerate. I would never wish to flout myself but I was on one occasion the queen of our local steam fair. This was before Geoffrey and I moved up here, when I was still at home with my mother and the other girls. I had some shoes that summer which I dyed all colours, starting with a pale yellow at the beginning of May and ending with midnight blue and silver at the close of September. There was a primer for the shoe dye you could breathe and get all sleepy and excited. It was also highly combustible, it said on the bottle, though you could tell from the whiff which skinned your throat much in the way of that Italian drink which I was saying. The coloured shoes took me through the summer. In the morning I'd do my little sisters' hair. They had brown hair and it brushed like water, dead straight. The little one still had creases like a pup at the back of her head, and if I brushed for a long time, she'd nod off, with her head on her fat elbows, forgetting her breakfast jam sandwich. The middle one would pick off the strawbs from the jam like a thrush with snails. It was nice those mornings.

Then I'd dress myself, paying every attention to detail, and spend the day with my girlfriends till the little one finished school. Spend was the word. We spent time. It seemed there was always more.

My only regular obligation was church. I sang in the choir. One Passiontide the vicar told me that he was heartened in these heathen times to see my response to the Passion of Our Lord. Passion means suffering, Geoffrey will tell you that. Factory-farmed lamb is lamb that has known passion, don't let them tell you anything else. My eyes were full of tears as I sang. I had a poorly eye at the time and had tipped in chemistry-set tears from a dropper to help it along. The funny bit was that the false tears brought out real ones.

I got made queen of the steam fair because I hung about by the steam engines. I like the smell of oiled machines and the glow of fire. I was pretty too but that wasn't the main thing. I mean, anyone who spent that time on herself would be pretty. I was like a wax dolly, painted up. If you'd've lit my face, it would've melted. I had creosote lashes and lips red like that wax which comes on those big yellow grins of that cheese from Edam's. If you'd've toasted me, I'd've been burnt quick as a witch.

The beauty of that night when I was the queen of the steam fair was all the kinds of fire. There were children running round with nightlights in pumpkins, a single melting tooth inside a big open grin. The smells were delicious, the toffee smell of baking pumpkin and the oily smell of engines. Three barrel organs played three different tunes. There was a smell of hot sugar and the smoke of used-up sparklers added to the main reek of hot iron. Did I mention about Geoffrey and odours? He can tell if I've eaten anything untoward in the day by my kiss, which I should say is not always one of the most intense friendliness, when he gets in. We've not yet decided about children, whether they're worth the hazard to Geoffrey's nasal membranes, I mean.

So, at the steam fair. The air was hissing with deep fat and burnt sugar. There were the scents of burnt stubble and gunpowder from the squibs the boys had been letting off. Steam engines don't scare like horses. It was night-time, see, did I say, so the fireworks were fiery in the night's blackness. They went up, the one, then the other, then countless, a house of rushing and light in an exploding roof over my head. The walls streamed stars. There was no room for the cold.

I've, no, we've, bought a new fridge. Geoffrey refers to it by the full name, refrigerator. He speaks the word in a careful way as though tipping someone the wink as to how to spell it. Either that, or as if Refrigerator was a super hero, some hunk dressed in icicles and an ice-tray come to save us from the evil forces of milk past sell-by and eggs which have slept in. We had a perfectly nice fridge before, knee-high and enamelled a sort of cream colour. We bought it off one of those postcards in a tobacconist's window, 'Everything must go, no item over £8.' Geoffrey laughs at the wording and goes quiet on the way home from plundering these families who are selling their worldly goods for less than the price of a pair of shoes the lot. Most of them have a story. Quite often it is not true, for example that they have come into some money so are going to lash out on a new fridge, baby bouncer, stripped-pine orange box and set of slightly worn copies of *Woman and Home*. Often they have offered us tea and I signal with my face to Geoffrey that they are just being nice. 'How very good of you,' says Geoffrey, pleating his trousers at the knee, tossing the keys of our Fiat and our flat on to the table and looking about like a dog for biscuits. One family had a tea cosy with panels in it in case their teapot put on weight. There was a man who told us he was in a state of temporary embarrassment. The ceiling was lath. The plaster was all fallen, and remained wherever it had landed over the years. The whole bedsit was under a snow of plaster, sardine tins under snow, the tap with its ledge of snow, the Zed-bed with a tartan rug under snow. There was snow in the old man's hair, and, as we drank tea, a snow of dust fell from the ceiling. It never stopped and you could not see where it was coming from. Perhaps it was sifting down from some upper room, passing through different people's lives as it came. Always run your home, it says in my bridal book, as though the side could be taken off it like an enormous doll's house, or in our case doll's flat. God gets that view without removing the wall.

Whatever the state of the rooms and houses we visit, Geoffrey comments only on their inhabitants. At home, he can smell if the iron was on two hours ago. But he's not bothered like that with other people. I have learnt not to pass comment either, myself. In this way, I suppose you could say Geoffrey is a good man.

I have liked Geoffrey a bit since we've had the new fridge. Yes, I'm mercenary, but not for fridges. Now we've got the thing, which is white and makes no sound, while the other revved and changed down and sluiced its gums all day and night, now we've got this silent cave of ice, Geoffrey seems to have calmed down a bit. In the week before we took delivery (this is how Geoffrey describes it on the telephone to anyone from his school, called colleagues), the flat was full of brochures. Geoffrey makes it his business to know an appliance inside out before committing himself, or he has done since we were married. And you *could* get into our fridge. I knew a girl knew a man who was frozen to death in the refrigerated hold of a cod trawler. He was holding this great big cold fish, for the comfort. I suppose you would. Cod have those whiskers though, don't they?

We purchased the fridge from a white goods warehouse. White goods is the word for big things you don't buy often in a lifetime and which don't move about easily. The whole place was full of those cardboard boxes people can live in, though not from choice, a cliff face of heavy-duty cardboard. I thought of all those machines stripped of their cardboard housing, and left cold and white, some of them with the one big eye at the front for loading. I thought of all the mess and spillage, the dirty clothes and half-eaten meals and used dishes that those shiny white blocks would deal with, and for once I felt quite glad to be human. I felt quite patriotic for the human race, dirty and incomplete, but still somehow at the cliff face, holding on. There were little ledges in places up the cliff of cardboard and you could think of gulls hanging there, no nest to speak of, just like at by the sea near us. Except on these ledges it said 'VORSICHT ATTENTION ATTENZIONE MADE IN BRITAIN'. The white machines clad in their heavy-duty board seemed like something military, a machine army, the forces of cleanliness ranked all together. Yet if you could choose just one or a couple of the machines you could use them for your own ends, human purposes. There were small fork-lift trucks moving between the alleys of white goods as I thought about this. The personnel were all kitted out in yellow. We were in like a huge hangar full of peacetime machines. I looked at Geoffrey. I suppose what we have is all we have. We have spent time together. I suppose that this spent time makes up a past, even if it is a very new past.

Fire and Ice, that was the name of the lipstick. I can't remember the prayer yet, but it's coming. I told Geoffrey these thoughts in the gulch between the white goods and he spoke to me as though I was just someone we were visiting to pick up an old table, and not his disappointing wife. 'Thank God,' he said. 'Does this mean you've let up on being the perfect bride?'

I didn't understand the words of what he was saying, but I got the sense. Not that he's been the groom of your dreams. I was happy in myself on the drive home from the white goods warehouse. I told Geoffrey to stop outside The Deep Sea.

The Deep Sea is a chip shop. We had curly bits of fish as big as chestnut leaves in autumn and two little paper sacks each of thick chips. I had salt and vinegar, but Geoffrey had tartare sauce. Tartare sauce is composed of mayonnaise with good bits in. It is especially palatable with sea-food dishes. He ate his fish first. Everything smelt of deep fat. The inside of our car was all steamed up. Usually Geoffrey won't eat fried food and anything smelly has to be eaten in a gale. He has been using a breath-freshening spray for work. We sat in the car with the heater on and the wipers going to and fro making smears on the windscreen.

There wasn't much rain but we kept the wipers on high speed, for the fun of it.

Advent Windows

In the blue dark, the building's twenty-four east-facing windows were closed, with the inside shutters fast, trapping slabs of cold air which would leave melting ferns of frost in the morning.

By the orange light of a street lamp and the white glare of the Chinese chip shop, it was possible to see that it had once been more of a small street than a building. One side of it was scarred where walls and floors and chimneys had been: there were traces of flowered wallpaper, and one fierce square of purple where, perhaps, someone had expressed rebellion from the beige trellised life in the next room. For these were once family houses, extending down what was now a triangle of waste ground, ending with the shop on the corner, which had been round as the elbow of a fat woman. A sign had swung from the shop, green and gold, on a bracket like a pub sign. It had read 'Don't say Brown say Hovis'. By the time of demolition, the last word had been changed to an uglier one so often that none of the insults was legible.

Mr Lal, who had run the shop, and no longer lived nearby, was driving past the building this Christmas Eve.

He imagined the scenes behind the twenty-four windows, shuttered not against the hot sun but the cold wind. The two terraced houses had become five flats. That meant five tall green trees covered with red and gold tinsel, sheltering bright drifts of presents. And for lights, not soft points of flame in oil, but strings of hard electric buds. Mr Lal braked to allow a young couple to cross the road; their heads were down against the cold wind as though they were acknowledging a bitter truth. Both were dressed entirely in black, funny clothes which must mean something since they appeared neither warm nor attractive. The young woman held a lumpy white infant casually against her hip; at least it was properly wrapped up. He wished the couple would speed up: he did not want his wife to see the baby. If she had a baby, she would not carry it like that, carelessly.

The young couple let themselves into the building. They closed the door securely behind them. Mr Lal thought of them going in to their flat, sitting around their big green tree, probably singing some carols, maybe mulling some wine, almost certainly wassailing, whatever that was.

He drove on. Business as usual tomorrow, indeed rather brisk sales, especially to the lonely who could not always rely, he learnt, on much conversation in church.

Lara and Ben took their white burden into their flat. They went straight to the kitchen, which gleamed with brushed metal. A magnetic band holding knives and a cleaver was fixed to the wall. 'Get me down the kitchen devil and I'll deal with it while I'm in the mood,' said Lara. She unwrapped layers of white to expose naked pink flesh. She was intent, almost artificially so. They did not look each other in the eye.

'It's you who wanted it,' he said.

'I know, but you'll be glad too . . .'

'When it's over.'

'Not long now,' she said and brought the beautiful quick knife across the gizzard of the turkey. Then she cut and snapped off each scaly yellow foot; they flexed, and there was sand in the nails.

'I thought we were giving Christmas a miss this year,' said Ben. 'No tree because of the ecosystem. No presents because of the cost of this' – he felt for a derisive word – 'dwelling. And no turkey because they suffer in life and are full of hormones. Don't please tell me it's free range. If I know its biography I shall feel worse.'

'I know all that,' Lara said, 'but I suddenly thought of everyone else, all jolly, trees, presents, turkey . . .'

'Rosy cheeks and figgy pudding,' Ben yelled. But it never did to be satirical in a loud voice. The other person thought you were being emphatic.

'And those too,' said Lara, and met his eyes. Wrestling with the dead flesh had brought some colour to her.

Sometimes Ben thought he might like a child, but where would it go, among all the metal and glass? He knew of no storage system for small humans. 'I bet Tabby's had hers stuffed all week, and the tree probably has self-sweeping needles,' he ventured. Easy malice about their efficient neighbour bound them for a moment. They kissed and their kiss was reflected back to them in every shining cupboard door, silver and white and black, decorating the high cold room.

Tabby had done everything perfectly, well in advance, and now she was blind drunk. When she and Donald, her good kind husband whom she disliked, had moved to this new flat, he had said to her, 'Now, Tabitha, I'm taking a decision here; you can have the benefit of the doubt no more. The type of person who lives here will be able to identify preprandial slurring and over-lavish use of perfume.' And here she was, doing it again. The problem was perfection. She aimed at it, achieved it, resented it and ruined it. The tree was lovely; grey and green only this year, and all the wrappings too. She had peeled the chestnuts herself, with their inner skins like mouse-fur. Donald did not like labour-saving foods; he said he felt that they could not taste as good. 'If labour is so essential why not give it a positive vote and get me pregnant?' Tabby would shout, the shouting she did so quietly that no one in any of their homes had realised she was anything but over-adequate, let alone a drunk. She knew the answer to that. Until she could show herself worthy, Donald was sorry but he had to draw the line somewhere and where he drew it was the impregnation of inebriate hysterics.

Tabby remembered her own childhood each Christämas. She had grown up in Uganda and still thought of England as a country where someone had turned down all the control knobs: no bright colours, no real noise but the hiss of good behaviour pressing down damp dirty feelings to give things a temporary smoothness. She was homesick for a place which had ceased to be when she left Africa for her English boarding school.

'Though heaven only knows what they taught her,' Donald would say at dinner parties, 'since, when she met me, I've reluctantly to report, she thought shirts ironed themselves.' She'd married him to unload some of her sex-appeal, which bored her and tired her out. This evening she cut kisses in a hundred pearl-sized Brussels sprouts. She stuck a glowing white onion with the scented nails of cloves. She prayed for Donald to die, nothing painful, on his return from his mother's flat north of the river. Then she heard the small flat feet of the children upstairs and called down the wrath of God upon herself.

Upstairs things were neither very good nor very bad. Tyrone, the baby, who did not know how immanent were babies in how many grown-up minds, who did not know that it was a baby who came to earth to save us all, was nonetheless certain that one baby alone ruled the part of the earth which was familiar to him.

'See the lights, Tyrone.'

'Come to Mumma, Tyrone.'

'Tyrone, see what Daddy has for you.'

'Let me lift you, and you see the star, Tyrone.'

'It's over so quick, isn't it,' observed the grandmother, who was sugaring a big yellow pie. 'I mean they are old so soon.' From her tone you might have inferred she was indicating a crone, some venerable pipe-smoking great granniema in a rocker. But she was looking with tart tenderness at Ella, aged seven, whose legs were long and whose questions awkward. Ella sang the verse about not abhorring the Virgin's womb again and again, knowing somehow that it ruffled an idyll which her adults needed.

The MacPatrick family had invited the old lady down for punch and a dish of puss preyers, hot and fishy and sweet. She wanted to hold Tyrone, who wished to withhold favours for a time. He was flirting with her; in his blue sleeping suit he looked like the best parcel in the world. He advertised the shelly pinkness of his toes. He patted his circular black curls. He sucked his index finger, palm outwards, showing the small world map of lines on his hand.

'He's saying something, surely,' said the old lady upstairs.

'Da, Da,' said Tyrone.

'Star,' said his mother and the old lady, both of whom were devout, but who had not attended each other's churches in spite of protestations of intent to do so.

'It's Dad he's saying,' said the men.

Ella, who had uttered the same gnomic syllables and at an earlier age, was fiddling with the catch of a shutter.

The doorbell rang. It was the residents of the fifth flat, Adam and Bill, come to say happy Christmas before they went off to their separate families. They had had to be apart in this way at Christmas for twelve years.

'It's a family time,' they were saying to Mrs MacPatrick, as they handed over presents and the keys to their flat.

'A family time,' echoed the old lady from upstairs. She was a widow and her daughter had married a man who made parts for rigs and could not take a joke.

Ella was humming under her pink tongue, 'Lo. he abhors not the Vi-ir-gin's womb.'

With a gesture of revelation, she threw open the shutters.

Scared, Tyrone lifted high his arms and cried, 'Ad. Ad.'

Adam lifted and held the child in the bright room, standing before the revealed window, behind him the trees, the smiling faces, the buds of coloured light.

Eyes burnt by the white light of the Chinese chip shop, a passer-by stopped in front of the building with twenty-four windows. Raising his eyes, he saw what he wished to see, a man with a child in a room full of light.

On the Seventh Day of Christmas

Further into the wood, the ground was so slippery with fallen needles that your feet were pulled ahead of you, but the rest of you was held back by the starry arms of the pines. In each direction where a path was visible it was possible also to see a spray of new paths off that path, a replication on the ground of the branches above with their many jagged green elbows and conjunctions, ending with hair's breadth options of angle between the bristling needles at each eventual tip. If you looked up, you saw a deep furred green darkness pierced at its heights with sharp dazzles of winter sun. It was like looking up at the stars, though the darkness was made of green needles and the stars of naked white sky.

This was not somewhere to be with a person you had met as an adult only recently, and then in rooms and cars and lifts, places where account is taken of our human need to remain untouched. In the wood, there was no room for the pod of distance that thickens around us as we carry out our lives.

'This wood's vindictive!' said Nella, pulling some bare sharp twigs out of the back of her hair. 'It's taken my hair down.'

'It's only the spiky trees,' replied Christy. 'It's how they are. Further in, they get taller and there's more space. The branches all swarm up to the top of the trunk to get a look in at the sky, so the trunks are quite bare till some way up.'

'Are branches competitive now, then?' Nella asked, and Christy wondered whether this walk had been a good idea. It had been essential to do something after the news had come to them.

Christy had suggested the walk in the woods, confident that the air among pines must clear the head. Or why would people lie dreaming in green-tinted baths, inhaling the chemically agreed smell of crushed needles? Also, it was hard to see what else they might have done.

Earlier in the day, Nella could have foreseen none of this.

Now, she could not imagine how she would ever be able to extract herself from the new, unwanted, situation, newer even than what she had suspected was going to present itself as the year's first conundrum.

Her preparations for this already bruising holiday had been carefully drawn up so as to make sure that nothing surprised her.

She had made lists and timetables, rotas, stockpiles and contingency plans; she had anticipated all the mischief that might be caused by unfamiliar food, by children and dogs, including dogs and children not her own. She had tallied and balanced her wish for solitude with her fear of loneliness.

They had got through Christmas quite creditably. She did not like to catch herself thinking like that, it was as though she was turning joyless through competence, like an adequate, but no more, actress.

Now it was the first day of the new year, the beginning of the slide towards the next Christmas. She had heard the children often, wishing time away. They were as bad as mountain snobs, living for the high peaks, despising hills, oblivious of plateaux. That morning she and Christy had agreed, with the rather boastful shame that comes of exhaustion, that when it came to life, the dull bits were the best.

'All currants, you wouldn't want. You need dough, or whatever the stuff in between is called. You'd know, of course, Nell.'

'I'd know because I clearly have an affinity with dullness, or because you think I can cook? There's not much stuff between the rich bits in the Christmas pud, if that's what you mean: probably that's what's wrong with it. If we kept to dry toast, and cold water, we'd never get the aftermath. Anyhow,' Nella had said,

'I'm for the bits between the thrills, aren't you now, Christy? Less chance of biting on a bit of broken glass hid in the fruit; more chance of being ready for it if you do.'

Christy had put down the oval serving dish he was drying.

Its shine steamed. He must have hands without feeling, or he must actually often do the drying up. He took a sip of the brandy he was keeping among the plates and desiccating greenery on the dresser. The house belonged to Christy's mother.

'I think I'm with you,' he had said, 'I love the days to be predictable in runs of about one or two.'

His hair still hung over his forehead like that of a short pony. He was wearing a thick snowflake-pattern jumper. His chin was square and blue, so that it was hard to take seriously anything he said that was not totally direct and virile. Since the bent of his temperament was subversive, his face worked against him with strangers, but the combination never failed to amuse his close family, who would watch them modify their expectations.

Meals for seven days, four times a day, for at least 10, more often 12 people, almost without a hitch, and *this* had to happen, Nella thought, irritated as though the bites at her face came not from crystals of snow but from mosquitoes, as she followed the noise made by Christy passing into the wood that was, as he had promised, growing leggier as it deepened.

She was refusing herself the pleasure of the walk, she was so annoyed. Within her annoyance lay shame that she was selfish enough to feel it. So large a change in her life should do more than annoy. Was she capable now only of insulated unpassionate responses, even to news as shocking as this? Had her habit of self-protection grown over her like bark?

Christy's back, with the dark blue knitted snowflakes falling from their dense flurry across his shoulders to small diamonds neatly set at regular points in the white wool, was always a little too far ahead to make talking comfortable.

She wondered whether keeping this distance was a matter of habit for him, or if it was aimed at her; was he habitually morose or just a bit knocked back by the news? In the air, snow winked and went, never quite attaining the size or languor of a flake. The light, already sieved by the scented trees, settled on each brief point of snow and passed to the next as though it marked instants in time. Although the air was full of these particles of light and ice, nothing reached the ground or settled on the trees.

Christy had foreseen everything. He'd even sorted in his mind the big thing, which was the children. With great care, he had not sucked up to them, nor let them know that he was in their power, in a way they could not understand. He had not even let on that he was familiar with their preferences as to meat – white or brown, skin or no skin, sloppy or dry – when it came to carving the turkey which he had taken care not to carve like a man with domestic rights over the woman who had stuffed and smoothed, dried, basted, lifted and adorned it. He had restrained his impulse to fold and retain any paper that would do for another year, for in another year, who knew if he would be there? He had foreseen everything, made his plans accordingly; and now this.

He snapped off dead branches when he saw them and broke them into lengths for kindling. There was no need for this, but Christy was a man who did several things at the one time with pleasure. Because it was his habit, established over the years of living well alone, he was not distracted. He could think about one thing and do another to a more developed extent than men who had been married. In this he was self-sufficient like a soldier.

When he and Nella were children, their names had been different. In those formal years, they had been Christian and Eleanor. He had liked her and of course they had agreed to marry. At eight and ten they were parted. She had been the more wretched, or made more fuss, he remembered, perhaps because, as the elder, she was nearer the confusion to come.

Their parents had made the usual careless and public allusions to the parting. Eleanor's mother used it as a topic to entertain her friends in the street; Christy's mother to inform her new neighbours halfway up a hill in Ayrshire that there had been close friendships down in England, that there was no sinister reason for returning North beyond the coming back home. As fast as she knitted this frail web, Christy's father undid it with false promisings and borrowings and gluey stories of expectations, until he one night tore up the whole caper and did a flit. It took Christy the years between growing up and turning thirty-two to make that lot good, and see to it that his mother was sorted. Her success in novelty wools and rare yarns quite took him by surprise. He thought it must be the profitable outcome of her years of talking with other quiet women in rooms, more used to changing things with their hands than with their voices. All at once she was the woman to talk to about angora or welter-weight synthetics, the tensile strength of two-ply or the incompatibility of certain silks. She sold east and west, not only the two Scots coasts, but over the world, travelling light and owing not a penny.

There had been no plan to Christy's life but pleasing himself and his mother. On hearing of Eleanor's marriage, long after it had taken place, he felt simultaneously the disappointment of an eight-year-old and the pique of a grown man. When, five years later, he heard of the departure of her husband, he sympathised for a moment with the man, remembering how maddening Eleanor was at board games, competitive one moment and uninterested the next.

He sympathised too with any man who had to deal with a woman with so furious a passion for digging. Then he remembered that it was more than twenty years since they had spent the afternoons trying to get to the centre of the earth, 'where it is hot', said Eleanor, 'and only apparently unmoving'. They had found the phrase in a book about science. It was the pomposity to the words and their suggestiveness that got the two of them.

After meeting Eleanor again at an event thrown for his mother by a yarn king or somesuch, he had concentrated his suit upon her for those last London days before normal life put itself away for Christmas. She'd not noticed a blind thing. He was delighted when Eleanor's father, who'd lived with her since her mother's death, suggested that both families get together, for the new year. For that most dangerous sake, of old time.

Keeping in store, as he was, his great news.

The sky was harder now to find between the branches.

What had been white was a blue that was as soft as fur. In the dusk the needles underfoot were more treacherous.

Christy stopped and listened, the bundle of kindling held stiffly in front of him, his dues to improving the shining hour, like his mother's knitting. He was tired.

He turned to look down the many paths for Nella. He tried to sense, almost to smell, down which path she would come. He made her out of the dusk, element by element, gold hair, white coat, cold hands. She materialised not like smoke as he, conjuring her out of the approaching night, had imagined, but short and warm, lost, furious and there. She hit at him with relief as he held on to her, the kindling snapping between them. She asked him the question he had not dared ask: 'What will it do to us when our parents marry each other?'

Christy pulled the burry kindling off her white coat. 'There's enough of what we have to go round,' he said. They stood there till the darkness was decided, and the kindling which Christy slowly let drop made the ground under them the only rough ground in all the slipping wood.

Being a People Person

As will be clear, this story was written
before the reunification of Germany.

'And, above all, you've got to be a people person,' finished the person, addressing a number of people in the personnel room. As though, thought Patrick, one could ever get away from being so. Since the last tangle with a person, I don't care if I become a louse-person, or a concrete-person, anything at all in fact but a people person.

A person laughed in a most unseemly way and Patrick followed the sound in case it was he himself who had made the noise. Since Frances had gone, leaving the teapot warm and the paper folded at the 'How to Spend It' page of the *Financial Times*, he had suffered from bouts of disembodiment. One time he had seen a very drunk man fall down in the distant purple mirror behind a cocktail bar. Red cherries and tall cocktail spoons made a Miró of the mirror. Only in the morning did he realise that it had been himself, Patrick, who could wash in rye and stay dry behind the ears. Corny jokes come easily to admen, he thought. I think in phrases which would fit on a bus-side. Was his id riddled with quick quips and reflex associations too? He admired the notion that he might be a perfectly functioning phenomenon, a faultless free-market capitalist. A credit to any mother, though in fact considered a debit by his own, since taking up this job. She'd sooner he were a teacher or a preacher. Or anything but what he was.

Patrick was twenty-nine and he was going to live for ever. Or he had been until Frances went. In actual fact, maybe he'd live for ever anyway. That would spite her.

Now, where was that laugh coming from? Patrick minded people looking instantly towards the source of some irregularity, a lunatic on the tube, or a raving prophet on the bus, so he dropped something behind himself in order to pick it up in the most natural way in the world and lift his head, at the same moment darting his eyes to the source of the laugh.

His glance struck and stuck. If that was a person, he certainly was a people person. 'Certainly am,' the other guys in the office would say if you asked them if they were going out that night. Was Patrick a people person? Certainly was.

Catch a load of *her*. She resembled everyone's sweetest fantasy. Sisterly sexiness shone from her, asking to be licked off like butterscotch sauce. She had that kind of French colouring which looks good with lace and an old bike in some campaign shot in an attic for five hundred grand. Dipped in water, she'd just get shiny, and deepen fractionally in colour, like damp sand. Twenty-four-ish, he supposed, just turning the corner from legwear to food products. None the worse for that, though. Older is bolder, thought Patrick. It was not his own phrase, though he prided himself on learning fast.

But she didn't look bold, he thought, in relief. Demure was the word, which was how you wanted them when it came down to it, to look at at any rate. That folksy old saying about the perfect chick being a maid in the kitchen and a whore in the bedroom was the one Patrick intended sticking to from here on in; he preferred the old ways, the good ways, tried and trusted, passed down from father to son, or was it from hand to mouth?

Her name was Louella and she was a doll. No one didn't like her. Right then in the personnel room of Drive, Torque, MacIsmo, the cream of the firm's team was busy liking her a lot. Patrick couldn't think for the moment why she was there, but they often got visitors at Drive, Torque. It was the coming agency.

Several of the men in the room were plotting. They were people people, after all. How to get rid of the evening's domestic arrangements and insinuate this toasty, sugary young woman into those valued leisure hours? Work hard, play hard, that was the form. And they believed women were people, these men; certainly did. One or two of them had even learnt the lingo necessary to trap the new people women; there were certain key lines to put forth which would almost guarantee a lady'd put out. A bit of jaw about freedom, space, quality time, and the figgy treat was on the table, all but.

The biggest account held by Drive, Torque was a confectionery bar aimed at the homebound housewife; like her, Jeremy Drive was fond of saying, it was soft with little hard bits, sweet but with only natural sweetness, and could be eaten at any time when nothing more leisurely was possible. The bar's shape was that of many of the bottles to be found in any household cupboard, straight-sided with a neatly rounded swelling at the top. The product developers have long known this shape is specially congenial to the female grip. In the case of the bar the swelling was coated with chocolate over a bullet of vanilla cream, which tipped a core of honeycomb. As the marketing director said, 'Show me the bird who didn't learn French kissing on a Crunchie bar and I'll show you a nun in the Rasputin.' The Rasputin was a club where advertising men met up with each other in a leisure situation. It stayed in the swim with a total makeover every couple of years. Last time it was done over had been when the promotion for a kind of dogfood had got out of hand. It was like the dogs hadn't known how to behave at a big do.

The ice-cream at the Rasputin was said to be made by a deaf mute from the Bombay Taj. ('What other Taj is there?', the club's manager asked.) None of the members had seen the subcontinental icecream man and his legend grew. Jeremy Drive said it stood to reason, 'The deprived are the best at luxury goods, take it from me.'

The confectionery bar was called Goldenrod; its tag was 'the molten gold bar'. The teaser slots on TV, between long stories for washing powder and baby alarms, ran 'The at-home bar – guilt-free gold, in YOUR mouth NOW'. The direct reference to the act of eating had been thought a bit near the edge by one of the girl juniors in media, but the client had explained matters to her. After all, the bar contained not less than 20 per cent full farm yoghurt, the only food known to peel off pounds whether you slap it on or slurp it down. She was a big girl, and that stopped her mouth.

Late at night in the Rasputin (some tyros called it the Raz of course, but this did them no good at all among the real helium warriors who called it the Monk), the Goldenrod bar was referred to as the choc cock and the men felt they had isolated a great truth not merely about the advertising business but about women.

Drive, Torque, MacIsmo had a considerable number of accounts, but the big one at the moment was definitely Goldenrod. There was a Goldenrod guy, a man whose career was not in modelling, so he had the right homey feel. His parents had come from a small part of what was now East Germany; his name was Axel and he needed the money badly. It was good money. He wore specs and didn't look like a woman when wardrobe put him in a cardigan for C2 credibility at personal appearances.

Patrick's brief at the moment was to find a Goldenrod girl. Axel's own girlfriend, who was in fact his wife, would not do. She had to be, excuse the double meaning, kept pretty dark. Patrick liked her fine and she was beautiful, but she was black as your hat and incredibly serious. Like a lot of Senegalese, she was a catwalk model, which left her quite a lot of time for Axel. Most of the girls who lasted, she'd explained to Patrick, just looked extraordinary. Most of them simply lived their lives; it was the minority who changed racing drivers every season. Anyhow, catch Roxanne eating a Goldenrod, all those refined sugars.

Those executives of Drive, Torque who had seen Roxanne talked about her as though she were a bit alarming, like a big cat with good manners. After a few bevvies, they'd discuss her, in depth; last thing she needed was a choc cock. Axel was completing his doctorate in insects' nervous systems; mayflies were his special interest. Did the shortness of their lives make for speeded-up messages between neurones? Axel worried that his own time would run out before he found an answer.

The meeting in the personnel room had been on Goldenrod. For the first time since Frances's departure, Patrick felt sentimental as well as physiological lust, something less itchy than simple appetite. He was determined to win the nut-brown girl. It was the end of a long day and he felt he owed himself a reward, something soft and creamy and delicious.

'Meeting adjourned,' said the person at the head of the long white table, 'I'll be interested to see what you can come up with.' Patrick could not remember how the last hour or so had been spent. The words had been the same as ever, maybe in a different order, that's all. There was a shuffling and dealing of bits of paper; the secretaries left the personnel room, followed by the girl. Who would be the first to reach her without seeming uncool? Patrick hung back, and, once the room had emptied, took the chairman's private lift down, intending to catch her at the door of the mirrored building – it was worth the risk. He looked at his own face in the walls of the lift. He was satisfactorily reflected back to himself on all sides. He wouldn't take her to the Monk, he decided, careful even in his private thoughts to use the most exclusive slang. Strive to belong, behave as though you belong, and you will belong, he told himself regularly throughout each day. Act as though you are one of them and you will become one of them. It was not that hard, mostly just a matter of not speaking first, laughing in the right place, and copying their gestures and phrases. If you wanted something enough, you generally got it, and Patrick wanted to be one of them. They were sleek. They knew what to do. They weren't losers.

Not the Monk, then, but somewhere he could receive her undivided attention. He allowed his thoughts to soften. He might even have begun to feel a stirring in his imagination had he not gained the revolving glass door just as she did. There she miraculously was, in deep brown fur and pale leather boots. No one else seemed to be about.

'How do you do? I noticed you in that meeting. Where do you fit into the campaign? I'm Patrick Hunter, by the way.' He was keeping things light, important with really pretty ones. The better looking they were, the more offhand you'd to be or they thought you were a woman. Peter Torque slipped him that tip one night they'd been working late on a flowchart.

'Hello, I'm Louella Drummond, and I'm in market research.' She had quite a deep voice and white teeth without ridges. Rich girl's teeth. No sugar abuse there. There was a candied scent from her hair and skin. Her gaze had an interesting blankness. Patrick gained confidence.

'I was wondering if you were free for a bite of supper?' he heard himself asking in an almost perfect imitation of the tones he knew got results, because he'd heard them time and again in the Monk. He sounded offhand but full of potential.

'Oh, that would be really nice, Patrick,' said this delicious girl, with her fresh hair and small brown gloves.

'Shall we go then? How do you like to eat? Korean? Thai? Japanese?' First time he'd been asked how he liked to eat, Patrick had said, 'Sitting down.' That had torn them up laughing. 'God, you kill me, Paddy,' Jeremy said, hitting him repeatedly in the chest.

Patrick had not been brought up in the knowledge of foreign food and he found its demands confusing. If pushed, he could do that hairstyling thing with a fork and spaghetti.

'Actually,' she replied, 'I'm not good at fancy food. I'd really like something simple.'

They ate at a restaurant he'd picked up on from his colleagues. The cost legitimised the simplicity of the food.

All about sat refugees from complicated foodstuffs. Patrick ordered tomato soup, mixed grill, and crumble with cream for both of them. She was quite happy to eat what he ate; she drank water. Patrick had a beer. He didn't, frankly, like wines. He'd said as much once at a business lunch and there was a bit of a hush.

'Prefer a milky drink, do you?' Jeremy asked, which was quite nice of him really, to make a joke of something people like him clearly held to be serious.

Patrick was soon absorbed. She was an amazing listener. Not seeming to say, let alone tell, much, she soon had it all out of him about his mum and the house in Weston. Then she had it out of him like a tooth he was happy to lose about Frances and her stuck-up parents with their indoor pool and gins you could do backstroke in. Then it came out about Frances's ideas on women. He did not go so far as to tell this soft creature about Frances's active role in the Anti-Infibulation Association. Frances had been quite unfeminine in that way. Even to talk about those sort of matters would surely offend and confuse Louella, never mind the problem of defining infibulation for her over the mixed grill's selected inner parts and their modest parsley leaf.

He began to feel that his sensation on Frances's departure had been relief, with a dash of self-pity. She had known how to iron and Patrick, with all his shirts, had appreciated that. He missed it still.

'Not that I don't want a girl to be independent,' he was saying. This was a line which had led him more than once through feint and skirmish to surrender. He spoke to girls in this mode as though he were handing them a bag of sweeties.

'Oh, I just don't want independence,' she responded, making wide eyes and drawing her spoon out of her mouth upwards, so that he could see part of her tongue and the silver bowl tipped to reflect, upside down, his own face, made paler by the patina of the silver.

'I really just want to make someone happy.' An emotion more often felt than heard, Patrick thought. It was the sort of thing his mother believed in.

'But how does that fit in with your work commitments, Louella?' He enunciated her name as though it were a new way of twisting her for her own pleasure.

'I don't find it hard,' she confessed, and he had a great rush of simplification such as can accompany the birth of love. Worry and fret were shelved, and he saw with the flat clarity of comprehensive benevolence. He felt the complications of which Frances had forced him to be aware melt and fuse and he was home, safe, a whole man again, feeling one direct emotion towards each thing which presented itself to him. He was freed from the multiple apprehensions he had endured since Frances's first eruption into his life, and even more acutely since her disappearance from it.

At once nothing vibrated with unpleasant implications beyond itself. Everything felt fat, replete with simple happy meaning. Life seemed plotless but pointful. Everything was extra real. Patrick's senses were a child's. It was this girl.

They didn't take coffee. She admitted that she'd never got used to the taste, and he was happy to agree. He helped her into her fur coat. Its biscuit-coloured silk lining shone and the fur itself seemed to promise something about Louella. Frances's mother's fur had been a solid bank reference, Frances's own had been 'hocked' – her word, horsy cow – long ago. Patrick imagined Louella saving for her fur; what could be more natural, more feminine, than to want a soft, warm, outer wrapping? How sweet that she had earned it.

Drunk at heart, sober at head, he drove her home. Though she must at least have guessed something of what might be to come, there was a coating of innocence to her. She kept her eyes down. They chatted lightly of routes through central London. Frances had judged this topic as dull as swapping inflation stories. But things *had* been dull before, Patrick now saw, until he'd found the one, the only, the golden girl.

To his own surprise, he did not worry about his flat and the messages the girl might read in its bottles, its posters, coffee table and rowing machine. He kicked the bullworker under his new leather-jacketed sofa, tooled, the salesman crooned at him, by the very suppliers who fitted out the classic motors, your Jag, your Rolls, your Aston.

He went to the kitchen to make tea and turned to look through the hatch into his walkthrough diner/rec room. One asset the agent hadn't drawn to his attention on the guided tour. You could see your date even when you were coming on domestic.

There she sat, nice as sugar pie, knees together, hands on them, head on one side, hair touching each shoulder, just. She was pale brown all over, dipped in pale brown. He did not allow her nakedness to hurry his teamaking. You had to be cool.

He laid a pretty tray, two white cups, white sugar lumps in a bowl with beige roses and a brown jug of milk. He also laid a small white dish of chocolates, dusty truffles and a few dragées. He had some white chocs too, from when his mother visited. Jeremy had told him white chocolate was women's chocolate – feminine and not too strong. The brown teapot was from his mother. Heat came out of the tiny hole in its lid, an aromatic breath of home.

He took his tray in to the brown waiting girl. They passed chocolates from mouth to mouth for a while. He laid her down and put one dragée beneath each ear. Her ears were not pierced. He journeyed in her hair and neck. He fed her. He lifted her up and gave her tea, very milky and sweet, from a spoon. When the chocolates were done, he licked each of her fingers and dried them. He put his own fingers, one by one, into her sweet mouth. There was no bit of her which was not brown. Her irises were the darkest brown, and shining, shining.

They gorged on each other. When they woke up he wanted more. She was pepperminty, still with that slight warm-sugar smell he now knew to be her most intimate flavour.

'When can I see you again?' he asked.

'Whenever you want,' said Louella, 'but for now I really must be off.'

'Well, pulled her, did you?' asked Doug MacIsmo in the executive car-park. Another of the guys was there too.

'We had dinner,' Patrick replied.

'Stand her a spot of savoury, did you?' roared Doug.

Patrick did not really mind that he was blushing. So, they knew. They'd have to know sometime, and he didn't want any of them going after his baby. Doug and the other bloke exchanged gestures of lewd envy and looks of something else which Patrick couldn't place.

All day enquiries about his night irked and elated him, reminding him of the hoard of beauty now his.

'Pat, a word,' said the person who had been giving – was it yesterday? – the talk on people people, and beckoned him with an arch finger into the personnel room.

'Do sit down, there's a good man, have a *cappuccino*, the choc dust sprayer's been replaced. It really is something of a winning little gadget . . .'

The person stretched out his legs before him; he appeared to be burdened with a codpiece, which he adjusted. Could *that* be cavalry twill, too? The legs were about the length of the front bit of a Porsche, which was just as well. These legs terminated in strangely orange suede brogues, all the nap smoothed one way.

'About the Goldenrod girl, Pat, we've decided to pull the chain on that, but the creative boys came up with a big one a couple of weeks ago and we've been giving it a good kick around. I really wanted to ask you a few to-the-point thrusters, your views and so on.'

'A couple of weeks,' thought Patrick, 'that's how knocked back I was about Frances. I never took a new campaign on board.' He said nothing. He'd thought yesterday afternoon's meeting had been about the Goldenrod girl. He knew keeping quiet was the best thing.

'Now, Pat, I'm not sure what your thinking is here, but if we're talking a hard yet soft, get my meaning, product for the ladies, I hazard' (the diffidence was so utter as to be implausible) 'I hazard the guys want something soft all through, but easy to handle. Am I right here would you say or am I right?' The codpiece was shifted.

'Um . . .'

'I mean, while the ladies want something that's never going to get confectioner's droop, if you take me, we want something here that's never going to say no, a really soft, yielding unit, but not one that's going to embarrass us in a public place, something you can eat out of doors without feeling you're out of tune with Mother Nature, yet something you can browse from your brief-case without the other chaps thinking you're a lady. The pack's got to be virile without being so butch it's fetishy, and I think we're looking to a non-design on this, a kind of street-naturalness, you have me?'

'What's its name to be?' Patrick asked. It was awesome that a chocolate bar could have all this meaning. What had people been doing without it all these years?

'I'm wanting something with overtones of Adam's rib if you know your Good Book at all, Pat, but eventually we decided we'd open the name question pretty well up to you.'

'Me?' The creative side of the biz were pretty aloof as a rule, being creative.

'Yup. Well, Pat, you see, you are pretty much the only guy who's had the ultimate experience of all we feel our target group wants from a choc bar.'

'Me?' asked Patrick again. He was silly with new love. The person before him had very likely gone mad; perhaps he'd fallen in love overnight, too. Stranger things happen, truth stranger than fiction, all that . . .

'Pat, old thing, am I right in thinking you gave one to that little pot of honey who by chance cropped up at our yesterday meeting?' The words 'by chance' had a cheesy tone.

Of course he was disgusted, but he couldn't deny it. Nor could he see the harm in admitting to love. He loved her, would marry her, keep her always, cherish her.

'Wake up, Patrick, did you or did you not? Ah, I see you did; one better you'll agree than the boss's daughter type you were porking, all opinions and poncho?'

Patrick made as if to look outraged. He knew that a man's private life was fair game, being as it was closely related to his image. But still . . .

'Never mind, Pat, old thing, I see from your face you did get some joy from Louella.'

How did this person know her name?

'Surprised, Pat? You are an old love, really. Didn't you even whiff a wolverine when none of the other guys went for the little box of tricks?'

'I beat them to it.' He was startled into openness.

'That gag with the chairman's lift is as old as the proverbials, and you must know it. Wilful suspension of disbelief in the grip of hunger, like a man forgetting he'll get fat on cocoa butter and nougat and caramel and Uncle Tom Chocco and all.'

Patrick was just about following.

The person resumed. The codpiece seemed to be giving him a disposition problem. He moved it decisively in one cupped palm, to the left, and settled it as though for a sleep. In vain. It flexed, with assertion.

'Truth is, Louella's by way of being quite a pal of mine, been modelling since she was doing teething rusks. I thought we could put this bit of business her way.'

'Business?' Patrick's stomach moved as though he had seen into the secrets of pouch and knot and gloss inside the horrible twill codpiece. He was going to be sick, unless it wasn't true.

'Nothing nasty, dear old thing, just that I, that is the whole team, thought that she'd be the perfect peg for this new bar. You've got to agree.'

'Me?'

'Well, you know the market for Goldenrod; even though Axel's so very dandy, it's the female C2s, the gross confectionery purchasers, the checkout punters and afternoon timekillers and old bags with Hoover hangovers. And we feel the new bar has got to be for . . .'

'The male equivalent.' Patrick tasted bile as he spoke. This was their punishment of him for trying to be one of them.

'In a nutshell, that's broadly it, old son. The thing of it was, when we were all around the table, we realised (it was the day after you'd tied one on when that girl dumped you) that we were going to have to do a touch of product testing. We wanted the name for the bar to come from the experience we wanted the bar to reflect, soft, sweet, you know the sort of thing. And if possible firing a bloke up to want another about every eight hours. Not just one a day helping work rest and play, but three a day, Pat, assisting slog, sleep and shag. The long and the short of it was that we needed you, you, Patrick, because you may earn like an alpha but you're the only man in the office with the distinction of having known life as a C2. Now, do tell, what would you dub the bar, never forgetting this could carry a hefty slice of the sweet folding stuff when the product hits the shelves? How would you describe last night?'

He leered, but his real expression was one of attentive pecuniary acumen.

'Melted Dreams,' answered Patrick, knowing bitterness for the true opposite of sweetness.

With Every Tick of the Heart

The afternoon would not be moved. He smoked, she did her knitting, the cat sat waving his tail on top of the television, but nothing made the time pass. It was as though the air had braked, a great breath of afternoon had been taken and held. No person passed, either, outside the window of Denise and Norman's retirement apartment, on the corner of the busy shopping street and a quiet road full of dental surgeries. Denise and Norman rested in the still of the afternoon.

Their room was warmer than he liked it, but she suffered with cold hands and Petal liked the heat, too. Petal was a cat that would not go outside. His litter tray sat on the plastic drugget in the tiny hall and reeked. Norman emptied it once a week. Denise said she did it on the other days. He knew not to believe her, but it was easier to leave it. He indulged her like that, enjoying this late carelessness in their lives. From time to time he did not tidy the ashtray and his pipe of the night before, or they got silly together over gin and a box of Good News and as much Schubert as they could cram in, and failed to pick up the telephone if it rang, and slept in the next day. The days were brimming with a new timid freedom for the couple that made them unlike the other residents of these apartments. When time stood still they did not fret about it but admired the pose it struck. They were luxuriously idle, idle as teenagers with a meal of hours before them.

Norman was born to young parents, who raised him with the casualness of confidence. His mother would eat off his plate and expected him to do the same to her. Neither parent was jealous of the kindness Norman showed to the other. Not counting up the favours bestowed by the baby, they took them for granted. Later Norman climbed up and down the kitchen dresser by the shelves, made jam tarts with his mother in sharp metal patty pans, and potty trained himself throughout the summer of 1923, in the back garden of their cottage in Lancaster.

After the War, his father came home with a plate in his head and a limp. He couldn't settle but roamed around like a man hearing a fly and never coming upon it. He had a job in the bottle factory and Norman's mother worked in the haberdasher's further up the town, next door to the refreshment and tea shop. After her work was over, Norman sometimes went to collect her at the end of his day with the piano tuner and they might go in to the tea shop.

'These aren't Stan's bottles,' she often said, screwing the stony stopper into the dimpled glass of the lemonade bottle. 'Stan's are for something stronger than the pop.' They might have cold pie or they might have railway pudding, a big cube of dry yellow sponge in a bowl of custard whose level sank as the pudding fattened up.

'Just drinking up the custard,' Peggy would say. 'Listen to that pudding sup.'

'She's a wise woman. Wise and good-looking.'

An old man was talking to them. He sat down. He had on a tie and braces, buttoned to the trousers with leather ears. How did he get those trousers off? How could he pull them down without pulling his shoulders down too? Norman did not care to think about these things, but they just came to him, like the passing need he had had as a boy to say something rude about Jesus in Sunday School.

Not like Jesus, this man, as far as you could tell, though he seemed to have been there when the five thousand had been fed. Or he seemed to have stopped the poor five thousand getting a look in.

Now there was a lot of trifle on the table. In a bowl, on the table it glowed, covered with cream and sugar strands.

'No carrageen in that cream at all. All comes out of my girls,' said the old man.

Norman's mother asked first. Luckily Norman had not got the picture in his mind fully in focus before his mother said, 'Girls?'

'Gorgeous heifers. Just two. High-yielding girls. They come in to be milked rolling full. Udders rocking with cream.' He looked at Norman's mother most particularly pleasantly as he said it. She snapped her beads between the first two fingers of her right hand and said, 'Perhaps for Norman's sake, I'll say yes. He never gets all that goodness.'

'I am sure that's not so. I've particularly noticed you and young Norman here. You take care to feed him wholesome, and you must have eaten wholesome, to have kept yourself so.'

Not vain about how she looked any more, Peggy was easy to flatter about her son. The move from vanity about one's own looks to those of one's children is biological, the first burning out and the second kindling with the first birth. Although Norman was by now a full-grown young man, his mother took the credit for his shining health just as though she still soaked his rusk for him each morning.

'I'm Ernest Cargill. Proprietor here. And at the garages on the road out of town. By the Maiden Hotel, where I also preside.' He made himself sound like an enormous hen, crouching low over his eggs.

'Interested in motors?' Ernest Cargill asked Norman.

'I hope to be a piano tuner. I'm apprenticed.'

'There's one thing you need for that job, son,' said Ernest Cargill, dishing out another sod of trifle.

'What's that, Mr Cargill?' Peggy asked.

'Ernest, Ernest. Everybody does. Everybody nice as you.'

Does he mean to insult her, Norman wondered, but his mother was moving around in her chair in a pleased way and he could tell her mind was not on his father's evening meal as it regularly was at this time.

'What do you need to be a piano tuner, Mr Cargill?' asked Norman.

'I should have thought you'd know that.' Mr Cargill spoke in a dismissive voice. The change was as between an open and a closed door into a welcoming shop, overspilling bags and colour one moment, the bell and the shutters the next.

Peggy was quick to notice affront to her son and picked in her bag for her purse. Cargill saw that he had lost some purchase over her although he could not place the cause.

'Real solid-gold copper-bottomed talent. That's what you need. And I'll undertake that's what you've got.' He stretched back on the wooden chair that was like a school chair, and rolled his body at Peggy and Norman. It was perfectly egg-shaped, the little shoulders giving on to a dome of stomach and curving down to the start of the insectlike legs, the long fly of the trousers threateningly flat.

For two weeks after that, Norman did not collect his mother after work. He had not yet met Denise, but he liked the piano tuner to whom he was apprenticed, and went back some evenings to have dinner with him and his wife. They had two rolls for the pianola that had been made from the actual playing of Rachmaninov.

'We've no pianola, maybe, but the potential to hear that great player himself. You can look at those holes and just tell. Hearing it might be a disappointment. The piano would not be anything like the one he played. This way though, I see the intervals,' said the piano tuner. 'That's how it is on paper. The holes don't hold like the notes you hear. There's a space around them.'

Ernest Cargill began to call round at the haberdasher's. He bought bits of ribbon and yards of elastic, explaining that these were for tying mirrors in the cages of his budgerigars and holding the night-cosies close around the cages. He did not say who sewed him the elasticated cosies, or if he made them himself. One day, he bought two and a half yards of fawn wool, and asked for it to be wrapped, together with as many balls of white angora as would make a short-sleeved jumper. The soft balls and the folded cloth were left at the door for Peggy that night as she left the shop, wrapped in stout brown paper and tied with the kind of string that is reluctant to repeat its knotting in reverse.

Since she was a good housewife however, Norman's mother slowly unpicked the string. Stan watched, not interested but offended at this unusual turn to his evening. The room was as it had been always in Norman's life, a green kitchen up to waist height, cream up the rest of the walls, pipes under the sink coughing, the pulley of washing hauled up to the ceiling.

Peggy rolled the string into a tidy loop, waisted it with its end, and set it aside. She opened the parcel's brown paper like a book and lifted up the kittenish angora, ball after ball. Each one she carried to the work bag that hung off the back of the chair she used, and stowed it. She behaved as though she were being lent these balls of wool just to look after for a time, for someone else.

Stan said, 'Does this mean I'm to starve?'

Peggy said, and Norman recognised that she was now able to give because she had been given to, 'I'll do rich pastry with onion gravy over beef mince and the pie and cream to follow.'

Then her son knew that she had not been buying the cream that had recently appeared in their lives.

His father, he saw, was directly pleased about the dinner to come, too tired to consider its actual source. His mother wrapped the skirt length up in the brown paper. She put it away with the winter blankets in the wooden box on the stair.

As he watched the angora jumper take shape between his mother's softly probing, softly conversing, knitting needles, Norman saw the new way she would be seen by Mr Cargill take shape in the white wool. She would be a woman fed with cream and dressed in wool – fed and dressed by him. He wondered if she knew how plain a small eventual surrender appeared to her son, or if she knew of it herself.

His father continued apparently unaware. This pleased Norman, for he did not think that any surrender to Mr Cargill by his mother need be definitive. He could imagine her accepting something quite innocent in the way of an offer – a trip to the pictures, a walk – and how surprised she would be and bothered by the spelling out of the unsaid. At that stage, Norman believed, he could still stave off Mr Cargill, perhaps with some offputting filial behaviour. Then it would be only a matter of weeks until Mr Cargill became another of the quiet jokes linking mother and son in a way that did not prejudice the father but gave them patience with him.

Peggy and Mr Cargill married on Norman's twenty-eighth birthday. Although angora does not take dye and the jumper was not new, Peggy wore it, under a remodelled suit made of pre-war cloth. The furry wool over his mother's breast took Norman's attention. He thought of Mr Cargill's head there, the airy animality of the wool in his nostrils. He wondered whether it had been his mother's decision to wear the jumper, which might indicate an erotic bond between bride and groom, or Mr Cargill's, which would just go to show he was a mean old brute.

Peggy was fifty that year, her new husband – Ernest – sixty-eight years old.

'Lovely thing is, I'm retired. Or semi,' Mr Cargill would say. 'Semi meaning I still have to do as she says.' At this he would indicate Peggy as though she had unfulfillable private whims.

Stan dealt with it in silence. How it took him was in one fell swoop. From being a taciturn fit man in early middle age, he adopted the manner and appearance of a broken grandfather.

His pipe, that had been the fruity conclusion of each day, became his mouthpiece. He hid inside its smoke. Norman had the idea that once his father had sent out enough smoke he just absented himself, so that you might have been able to pass a hand clean through the wad of pipe smoke filling the kitchen chair on top of an old pair of corduroy legs. The beige tartan slippers that had only come out when Stan was ill were all he wore indoors now. He took to talking at night, outside, among the overblown cabbages and dithering moths. He would dig for hours, without energy or purpose, turning over the soil as though looking for something very small he had lost.

Stan's ears and cheeks grew whiskery, his veins purple. He ate little, removing his teeth for longer periods of time each day until he put them in only for visitors. His eyes hardened to a babyish unadapting blue. He seemed to be concentrating on missing all he could, as if the implications of anything might be too great to support. He felt the furniture as he progressed through his small house, touching it with hands that were always on the verge of trembling. The tone of the furniture in the house loosened. Two window sashes frayed away. The casement window in the eaves was opened minutely further each night by the ivy's furtive persistent growing.

Although Stan was ten years younger than Mr Cargill, it did not seem so in the first years of Peggy's new marriage. It was as though she had carried an indulgence from time away from the house where Norman grew up and into the detached brick house she now shared with Ernest Cargill. Norman feared that there was something in marriage – and by this time he *had* met Denise – that filled a man with a temporary defiance of time, a fullness as brute but as desirable as whatever it is that makes an apple an apple, a pear a pear. Norman too, never having experienced this fullness, began to fear its loss. Before sleep, he plotted its attainment.

Resistant to finding himself one day deserted or widowed, Norman at this time resisted marriage.

He was visiting his father, sanding the back of a rough-running drawer, when there was a knocking at the back door.

Stan pushed himself up out of his chair and moved towards it, hollow-legged and slow, the slippers shuffling on the red oilcloth floor. The smoke sat where he had left it, over the chair.

It was Ernest Cargill, less weighty, less red, than he had looked before his marriage that had lifted time from him.

'Sit down,' he said to Stan.

'It's my house,' said Stan.

'You'll need to sit down.'

'I know what I need.'

'You'll need to get your father a hot drink,' said his stepfather to Norman.

'It's his house,' said Norman. There was a panting heart somewhere in the room, a hot unsaid phrase. As the youngest man of the three, linked through his mother to both the others, Norman listened to the silence and weighed it.

'Go on, Dad,' he said, 'sit down.'

'That's right. That's it,' said Ernest Cargill.

Norman looked at his stepfather, not a man to come to a back door, nor one to show consideration for his wife's first husband and his needs. All this talk of needing suggested that the chair, the hot drink were wanted to stem a need for more than merely rest or refreshment.

When he had the two stubbornly silent old men – for they seemed to have come closer in years by this contact with one another – sat down with cups of tea, Norman asked Mr Cargill, 'Was it fatal?'

He did not understand where this question had come from and worried as he spoke that he might not make himself clear.

'I mean to say: is my mother going to live? Or are we beyond that?'

Stan looked as though the idea of her death were not so far from the fact of her departure. He did not seem shaken, nor satisfied, but shrunk and cold. The latent trembling of his shiny-skinned hands ticked into action, that was all. He could only run down from here.

Mr Cargill stepped towards Stanley and shook him warmly by the beating hand, as though catching a bird.

'*You* will understand what a blow this is to me, Stan,' he said. 'Only you, very likely. Since it could have been you she was married to.'

'It was,' said Stan.

Norman made the second cups of tea he could see were in order.

Four years later, he was still making cups of tea for the two old men, washing, cooking and cleaning for them, collecting their bandages, powders and pills. For his father had been made old by the same clot in Peggy's brain that had widowed Mr Cargill when she fell down over the counter at the haberdasher's, setting off a long hoop of curtain tape that bowled smoothly across the floor, havered and fell flat, dry as a spent coin.

It was not until he had nursed first his father and then the less destructible Mr Cargill until there was no more to be done that young Norman, born in 1921, was able to marry Denise and move into their first home together, the retirement apartment at the conjunction of one busy and one quiet road, where they lived with abandoned youthful carelessness within their love, even if it seemed to one passing that they were an old couple content to sit knitting and smoking under the gaze of a cat with a rhythmic tail and a clock that would not tell much more time.

Pass the Parcel

A year younger than the century, I tell the nurses, and watch the expressions form up on their blank young faces. Once, being a year younger than the century meant that I was thirteen, but now it means that I am some age for which I am accounted wonderful and at which no friend remains to me. I have tried to make friends with new people, but their destination is not the same as mine. They will come to rest in another time, when I will have become part of the past, a kind of compost for their own flowering. It doesn't do to look too closely at the components of the compost, but once it has reduced to a fine-textured lumpless loam it will serve its purpose well enough. At the time, of course, we did not know what we were throwing upon the compost heap. Along with the old ways, constricting corsetry and weak emperors, we chucked a multitude of living bones. Those many wars were open-mouthed for food, and liked it fresh. The bodies that did come home had often left their minds behind for good.

We can't seem to pass it on, the awful truth we know. It's a parcel we can't pass, tired and messy now, with out-of-date stamps and string too knotted to be worth saving. It's been redirected so often there's not much room for more words on the wrapping, but it always comes back to the sender. No one wants it. It's not a nice present, the past that is mine.

Here's where the difference is, as I see it, between being me and being the next-door old woman, lying in the bed light and grey as driftwood; it seems to me that her wits have stolen away from her, so she is no longer holding the parcel. She is living, I perceive, in the now, like a baby. Not that I envy her. She is like a baby in other ways, and must be moved and swabbed and powdered in a manner I hope she does not mind. I would mind.

I don't like people up close to me; I should hate them near me in that way. Having things done for me is my idea of hell. It is this streak that has kept me going; I've derived my energy from it. It kept up my appearance too, at least fifteen years longer than my poor child's looks lasted. Her softness bloated her and blurred her features, while I have kept myself down to the bone with willpower, discipline, self-restraint. I have not been one to take sugar. You could not show me the occasion on which I have lost command, and so it is here in hospital although I am a year younger than the century, and have hair the colour of old thin polished forks, done like a child's in an Alice band and hanging down my aching back. Here I wear clothes I know are not my own. They come from a room full of uncreasable garments chosen by the dead.

I shall not have a deathbed; it will be a chair. I shall meet death awake and sitting up, though I shall not rise to greet it. It will have come to relieve me of the parcel, which grows heavier in ways I do not care for, while the parts of the parcel that might once have appealed to me, the coloured and scented bows that held my life in shape like good sheets in a linen press, and the folded tissue of memories, seem to have gone to dust.

This had not been my understanding. The old people whom I knew when I was young remembered not the great impersonal events but the vinegar-and-fruitcake taste of farthing toffee, or the stripes on a spinning top. I have been awaiting these sweet visitations from my early life. But I find that those things I remember are facts, not feelings or sensations. What I recall is old news: wars and bombs, death plural or unnatural, great shiftings of boundaries and skies full of killing rain. The shinier events of the time in which I lived, the sort of events that are recorded in magazines rather than newsprint, have fallen away.

Remembering is accounted an indulgence. Old folk are meant to smile over their memories, turning the pages like a tired mother with her mid-morning coloured paper, in the certainty of small reliable gratifications well earned. If I ever possessed such memories, they have been collected by some operative keen to reduce clutter in the minds of old women. I am left with the dingy impacted weight of a million stored newspapers. As they rot down, they become drier and more acid, the events they record more monumental, arbitrary and heartless. I search my memory for scraps of colour. I enter more rooms stacked with towers of newspaper, great autumnal heaps of events – but bled of the colour of autumn. The rooms frequently display one wall blown off and wallpaper indecently open to the sky. I find no human traces, no boot or bowl or knife. Were I to find such a thing, what would I do? Put it away, certainly, for I have always insisted upon everything in its own place. I am the tidiest person I have ever known; I say it in all modesty. I could reduce the Milky Way to order, given time.

I know I had some moments that must have meant something, that you might expect to have left something of themselves behind; I had a husband and a daughter, after all. Of him I recall his motorcycle sidecar and his hard collars for the office, his household accounting and his succumbing, moribund, to televised boxing, and later to golf. I never loved him as I loved the parquet floor, that made under my houseworking feet a rewarding bony sound of business and direction. But I should never have had that floor without him; perhaps my cool heart has been my salvation.

The daughter was a disappointment. It was fortunate I did not fall for her at once, as I saw other mothers fall for their new babies, or I might have been downcast when things fell out badly. I had the satisfaction of knowing I had tried with her; it was not I but she who failed. Still it is strange that I have no sweet memories of her; children are said to be sweet, after all, and she was once a child, though all I recall of it is the struggling, to get her out of me, and, once she was out, to keep her within the necessary boundaries. She has failed me in that too. She offers no sweet memories, even though she is dead.

It was like her to die, just when the children of our acquaintances were giving them grandchildren. She was too selfish for that. If any man would have had her, to marry that is, which I doubt. There was one she wanted, but we could not have him. My husband had not worked himself to the bone for that, to see his only descendant marry a nobody without prospects and more airs than common sense. He had paint on his twills when he visited, and he encouraged her to cut off her hair. I made her go back and have it made into a switch, naturally. I told her, 'With your face you will find you need all the hair you can get.' She had the features of a horse without the domestic skills. Her hair was her one attribute, and my God how we worked over it, my husband and I. He would skelp her with the brush if ever she mentioned getting it cut, and I would give it a hundred strokes at night with the same brush to keep it shiny from the roots to the bitter end. I had her stand up for this after the hair grew past her sit-upon.

She had dirty gypsy ways and vandalised the frocks I bought her. There was a mother-of-pearl gown, tight at the waist, with runs of buttons all down the forearm, and pixie detailing. She dyed it. Black, so it shimmered like curtains caught in a house-fire. I said to her, 'What did you think you were doing?' and she said, 'Dyeing.'

She never fitted in with us and the reason is we were too soft. We were generous. I turned out her room for her every day till she died. She would never have had to work, unless she insisted on remaining unmarried. She was not feminine, that was the trouble. She had no idea of how to make the best of herself. It is doubtful that she ever asked herself what it was a man wanted, although I had told her enough times.

I could not have had the progeny of that whore in my house. She took it with her when she went, which was not as stupid as she usually contrived to be. She wasn't far gone, but it would have showed soon and her father would have killed her. She took that off his hands and did the job herself. The boy moved away from here and is no doubt a big noise in the world of paint, up in London. A huge mouth he had, always laughing; he was polite in that way they are when they think they know more than you. His father, unlike my husband, had not made a tidy fortune with his own hands. You could tell that right away.

Of course she had messed it up, but with her gone we returned to the old life. I threw her pyjama-case monkey out, and the shelf of books. I changed the candlewick in her room to a fresh willow green on both the beds. I had told her she could have a friend to stay every year round her birthday, but she said, 'No thank you.' It was as though she didn't think I'd make her precious friend welcome. Now we know *what* we know, perhaps it's as well we didn't have the birthday visitor. We were not good enough for our daughter, that was it. She wanted messy people, used to bounty, loiterers and loungers taking their blessings for granted. You could tell that boy came from money, he always wore the same old clothes.

No, she was not a feminine creature, my daughter. Her great feet and hands and the way she talked right the way around a thing as though she was eating it, these told against her, and the glasses she needed from the reading she insisted she enjoyed, just to make us feel inferior for having done real work. She had no friends round our home, everyone in the road saw the difficulties we had with her, and the way she took it out of us, smoking cigarettes in the street with no hat on and wearing outfits you would not be seen dead in. I sometimes wondered why we raked the gravel and swept up the leaves when she would be coming home from school to mess them up again. It was worse than a dog, but with none of the gratitude.

It doesn't take genius to see the woman in the next bed has been without the advantages that have made my life what it is. She lies there with only the Complan in the beaker to look forward to. Her nightdresses are shocking, bright robes with no shape and ridiculous pictures on them of bears in space rockets, or dancing carrots in the arms of manly leeks. Her slippers are big furry cows' faces, with a pink curly tongue poking out of the front of each one, and rolling eyes – the scared-soppy eyes of creatures in cartoons. Not feminine. No self-respect. She can't wear the slippers, but she has them. Now, what is the point of that, to have something you do not need? All around her bed is clutter, most of it useless. There are chocolate bars in disorderly piles, and other confectionery including special-occasion boxes with large bows on them. There are always flowers, invariably in want of rearrangement. The magazines look no better than they ought, with 'true love' stories printed so large on the pages you could not help reading the words from here where I sit, even if you were not forced to listen while one of the interminable daughters or grandchildren reads to the old object in the bed. They turn her and stroke her and dust off the biscuit crumbs they have made on her as they shout and munch and giggle and coo around the bed. They talk to her all the time. It's pointless, naturally. I could tell them that. They make a great operation of drawing the curtains round her bed – it's a cot really – and changing her nightgown for another unsuitable creation. They hold her hands and kiss them, not on the back as foreign men do in the films, but on the knuckles, sometimes once for each knuckle. Well, it's not my way. The overuse of kissing has not escaped my notice as a general trend. It has at least doubled, and that is among the merely acquainted.

What need has she in the next bed for privacy? She surely has no pride. She knows nothing of her present circumstances. All that old woman can have left to her is her memories, and a soft shapeless little bundle they must compose.

We've open visiting hours here. All day they are at it, the family of the dying old woman, as though they can introduce themselves to death when it comes and make it part of the family.

I shall be alone when we meet, up and dressed, like the bride of the century, than which I am younger by a year. I shall give back the parcel that I have to pass. It is not light at all. How ever I carried it I do not know. And I did so alone. I have never had that much use for other people.

Around the bed of the old woman who does not move sit the members of her family, in dark coats and with bare heads. Some of them have handkerchiefs that are white like letters. The narrow bed is heaped with boxes, wrapped in glowing paper tied with ribbons that seem to shimmer. Light is coming from them in this meanly lit room. There is a warmth like sunlight, not like fire. I cannot tell you where it comes from.

We have open visiting hours here and I see that I have a visitor. We have not met before, but I feel that I know him at once. So distinguished a person cannot have come for her before me. I am scented and ready. My back is straight. I have something to hand over to him.

With the excellent manners you might expect from him, I see that my visitor is stopping awhile by the bed next to mine. Let him come to me soon. The weight of this parcel is killing me.

Tact comes easily to him, that much is clear. He has seated himself discreetly among those who surround the bed and is taking the hands of the old woman in his. The four hands lie still, in a clasp as loose and strong as a heavy chain, among the heaped parcels, which seem, like the light thrown by coloured glass on pale stone, to be fading as the room grows darker. Can it be that the visitor has forgotten me?

'We have open visiting hours here,' I remind him. But he does not look up.

Here comes the tea woman with her heavy trolley. The large kettle on it is a two-hander, but even with two hands it is hard to control. She pours the tea into the mugs without stopping between each one, like a gardener watering well-rooted bulbs in pots from a watering can without a rose. The upper tray of the trolley is awash with tea. No one has thought to ask me whether in fact I do take milk, so I receive it.

Something appears to be bringing the old woman in the next bed to life.

The tea woman puts the mug of tea upon my table with care. It is considerate of her to avoid slopping it. She is very deaf. Too late, I see her putting sugar in my drink. I look up to remonstrate with her, but she is saying something.

'Sweets for the sweet,' she says.

Change of Use

In the pantry at the back of the long house, Mary shifted back a little on the edge of the stone sink, as she had done since these Thursday rituals began. She wanted to balance so she could drift off into her own thoughts without falling in or letting Mr Charteris know that she was not fully with him as he pushed away at her with his hands wringing one another on the rattling taps behind her back. She had given him green beans for lunch for a change, instead of peas with the Thursday shepherd's pie. She could smell the blackberry and apple she was making for his dinner cooking away under its crumble in the low oven.

'Tell me your name again, my dear,' said Mr Charteris.

'Dorothy,' said Mary, to liven things up.

Overwhelmed by this unanticipated new companion, Mr Charteris shook sadly as though to rid himself of dust, buttoned, sighed, pushed Mary aside like a curtain and washed his hands under taps that quivered as the water promised to arrive, held off and then gushed out, hot and chalky, through the aged piping into the sink where tonight's potatoes eyed him smugly from the colander.

He dried his hands while Mary set the kettle to boil. Upstairs the house slept, as it would for another twenty-five minutes.

He felt astonishingly well, astonishingly.

He smelt the tea as she spooned it from the red-and-gold caddy, saw her skin it seemed to him glow with the new life Thursdays must bring her, felt the sunshine as it came in slabs through the barred deep windows of the back of the house that looked on to lawn and shrubs and finally thicket, copse and wood. No one knew the house as he did. He had been a boy here and would die here. Each room held its story for him.

Mr Charteris sat down and rested his forearms on the kitchen table.

Mary brought him a tray of old silver, some cloths and the tin of polish.

'The lid's hard,' said Mr Charteris. 'Got stuck. When it dries this stuff's like glue.'

'I'm sure you can do it,' said Mary, pouring water on to the tea leaves from the heavy kettle off the stove. She kicked herself for not having tested the lid of the polish tin. This part was as important for him as what had gone before. She was sure that these Thursdays didn't take life from him but put it back. Maybe the care she was offering him was not orthodox, but it was natural.

'There. Done it. Nothing like experience,' said Mr Charteris.

She hoped he wouldn't look too closely at the silver on the tray. Not much of it matched and not all of it was silver. She'd brought some deliberately for him from other places she worked at.

'This tea's just the thing,' said Mr Charteris. 'Polishing dries out the tubes.'

She looked over at him from the lower oven where she was testing the crumble with a spoon. Her overall was getting tight. She shut the heavy door and bathed in the heat of butter and sugar burning together. It all made her hungry, she couldn't help it. She was hungry all the time now.

'Yes, and that is thirsty work too,' said Mr Charteris, supposing he should now pat Mary's bottom to go with the words, but not bothering to get up and go over to her actually to do this, because now came the reliable pleasure of his afternoon, the creaming and dipping and rubbing and the revelation of the silver. The distinction between his younger days and these later years was this for him: then he had been blind to the beauty of habit; now it was a luxury, a conscious indulgence as irresistible as yawning, stretching, surrendering to sleep.

Habit had become his bride, his chosen ravishment, his companion elect. It was simply that his wish to share his habit with just one other person at a time was not encouraged by the new masters here.

Mary was wondering how to keep the room empty for long enough to let Mr Charteris be through with his polishing. She relied upon the herd instinct, the set of rules that kept the rest of the residents of the house hung about their routine like a beard of bees.

He was holding up each knife to the light, checking each fork for speckles of erosion, the bruise of tarnish. To the left of the tray on the silver cloth he set the cleaned utensils, to the right lay the unpolished. The whole collection shone about as much as a dish of sardines and vinegar on toast. Still it made him so glad that she guessed he saw a shine not visible to her.

She heard the stomp and waltz of the polishing machine start up on the ballroom floor above. Along the kitchen ceiling ran wiring and pipes that made abrupt changes of direction. From hooks along the wall hung clutches of keys. A plastic fire extinguisher in a glass case sat above its predecessor, a heavy metal torpedo that said on its side 'Last Date of Service: June 1956'.

She heard a rustle in the pantry.

In there, the baleful wedges of wholesale cheese lay plastic-sealed and piled on the slate shelf. Mary reached in her hand behind one and pulled out the humane mousetrap. The creature inside flustered between its perspex chambers.

How humane was it to take the humane mousetrap to the outhouse where the cats had their hideout? She carried the fretful snack and tipped it out in front of the cat she considered to be the idlest. That way, it was fairer.

Two slow frivolous bats of its paw later, the cat was happily prolonging this small local torment.

From the back door, the kitchen looked as it could have almost any Thursday afternoon of the century as Mr Charteris had by now often described it to her.

Mr Charteris polished away, his apron black, his extensible cuff-restrainers glistening, the cup of tea neglected. His hair was white as salt, his face of a kind that is no longer trained into being – unremarkable features withheld by years of emulative mimicry into an expression of checked emotion and impersonal superiority. But his eyes were a disturbingly self-willed brown, where one might have expected self-effacing blue.

Looking out from the other kitchen door facing the gates at the front of the house and up the outer stairway to the terrace, Mary saw today's afternoon beginning. Two of the older ladies were wheeled out, a sunshade set above them, a tea tray brought. No bell had woken the after-lunch sleepers, but the windows began to show movement behind themselves; a few blinds were raised. In the main rooms, between the grave, flattened, central columns of the pediment, there was the sound of dance music, a raised voice, an insistent hard tapping.

Among the trees on the lawn, figures dressed just like Mary moved between chairs and benches, recliners covered with rugs where still bodies lay, stirring them, sometimes with a word, sometimes a touch. They seemed to be competing with one another to awaken a sleeper. Over some of the bodies, the overalled men and women shrugged vehemently, like cricketers loosening up. It was as though there were two teams, one ghoulishly dedicated to fun and activity, the other to repose. In the wide green of the afternoon, somnolence had the worst of it for the time being but could well show form later. The classical enclosure of the park suggested an eventual triumph of sleep.

The gates in front of the house's wide face implied a fixed modesty that must prevail in the end. The house would shut itself away, a fading beauty needing sleep in order to reawaken refreshed.

Driving the laundry van in at the gates, Francis Mullard changed down at the turning off the main road, felt the cattle grid under the wheels, slowed again on turning into the asphalted back drive, and wondered if the grid kept the old folks in, too. In the back of the van the sheets were cold and heavy inside the hampers. The van had been parked in the underground car-park of the laundry, where it never got warm, even in a summer like this one.

Francis's own grandmother was living at home with them at present. Her very active ways had knocked them for six at first, but now they were used to her walking miles in the night over their heads and bringing alarmed or desperate or boring strangers back to the house from her random samplings of different places and acts of worship.

Gran had forced Francis and Pat to get out much more.

They could not endure her pity at the start of their rare coincidental weekends off, when they were prepared to settle in to two days of doing nothing much, and she ran them through her commitments. She was a freelance indexer of historical works, and a self-appointed tidier of graves and churches, so the kitchen and living room were convenient spaces for setting out the details of a reign, a battle, a marriage or a plot.

The rubbish bin and waste-paper baskets overflowed with the things Francis's grandmother had found unfitting in church or cemetery, gloves or cans or inspirational paperbacks, silver-paper horseshoes and ballpoint pens.

'Don't put down that pot!' Gran shrieked to Pat, as he tried to fetch Francis's tea in the morning. 'You could unsettle the Anabaptists!'

While they were out at work, Pat at the restaurant and Francis driving the laundry around, Gran covered any space there was with 3 x 5" index cards and blue post-its. Both Francis and Pat worked shifts, so they never knew if the other had even attempted to release some space from the formation of battle at Oudenarde, the machinations of the Cabal or Ironbridge Telford's gazetted surviving works. When they got in they either fetched something to eat and took it up to bed, or rushed out, feeling illicit and safe. Very rarely, they shared a precarious feast with Francis's grandmother.

In a way, Gran had brought back the cramped romantic first days of their love, when they had nothing to hide because no one would have believed even if they'd written it out loud all over the bathroom mirror. They were such good friends, friends from their perambulators, more like brothers. This was the line still adopted by Francis's mother, Kay, who hoovered between the feet of her husband as he sat in his chair, and always baked double to freeze half in case of sudden guests.

It was fortunate that Francis had always loved Pat, since there'd been no sudden guest, ever, within a cherry's spit of their house.

Sometimes at night Pat would make a meal for Francis and Gran, picking his way between the bits of information on paper and the birds' nests of ecclesiastical leavings. He would recreate what he had served in the restaurant earlier. Although he wasn't yet a chef, he had the curiosity and steady hands for it; he worked so hard it was really only a matter of time before he got the promotion. He was at the stage now when you did the one thing over and over till you could do it in your sleep – if you got any, that was. It seemed oddly miniature to him to concoct meals just for Francis and his grandmother, an eccentric hobby nothing much to do with work. Himself, he ate through the pores all day and could barely stand food at the end of it. He ate smoke and drank water. When he saw Francis's thickening waist, he was proud of it.

'I made that,' he'd say to Gran, who would reply, 'Much to be proud of there,' and join Pat outside the lean-to for a cig after whatever rich meal the boy had made.

All very comfortable, until just recently, when Kay had started on about the calls she was getting from dissatisfied authors.

'They say Mother's having them on. Either that, or she's losing her accuracy,' she said to Pat, whom she'd rung at the restaurant, sure of getting a better hearing than she would from her own son. 'You can't do work for other people and be inaccurate. They plain don't like it. It shows them up.'

'Perhaps she means to,' said Pat, which was no more than what he thought.

'She's always been scrupulous about her research. She even stores her thoughts alphabetically. If you ask about the car you don't have to wait as long as if you ask her about Francis. And if I ask about you there's a slightly longer wait while she locates P.'

'She's maybe tired of sorting other people's words.'

'If you like it, it's not the sort of thing you go off,' said Kay. 'I should know, I've never cared a fig for it and still don't.'

Since she was not Pat's mother, he was not as irked by her angle as Francis would have been.

He approached Francis.

'Do you think your grandmother's losing it?' he asked.

'Nope. She may have a project on, though.' Francis had walked back from the depot where he had left the van. He was determined to do something about it before he had to change his waist size for good. He'd give Pat a surprise.

'Try one of these. Red pepper straws. A bit of Gruyère and several dozen eggs.' Pat had made them specially, but pretended he'd brought them from work. Gran was upstairs working on an overcrowded letter 'V' in a work on the history of lenses and their effect on art history, whose author was at that moment enjoying some of Pat's cheese straws brought home by his wife in her handbag, after a business lunch.

'What type of project?' asked Pat.

'I think she's trying to get sent to a home.'

'No one does that. It's lonely, and it costs all you've got, no matter how much you've got. The body only gives out when it's cried all it can and spent all there is.'

'*You* say that,' said Francis, kissing him. 'But I think she's being tactful. That's why my mother's so tactless she could perform amputations with *her* afterthoughts. Because her mother's so tactful she makes everyone believe she's the one at fault, not them.'

'But no one wants to go into a home. Have you seen inside one? Home is what they're not. They can't call them what they are. Asylum is a lovely word in every way compared with what they are.'

'Maybe she's got some idea of going to a place where she can think it all out and then just lie down and float off. *I* don't know.'

'Bed's that place,' said Pat, who hated being alone and could not sort through his memories for very long without meeting Francis there, and fearing the day when they would not be within reach of one another.

'And move! And bend! And stretch!' sang the voice at the centre of the house, unsexed as a parrot. Mary walked up the right flank of the outside staircase up to the façade and looked in through the ballroom window.

Accompanied by a piano, the old men and women in nightwear or loose combinations of cotton followed the gestures of the strong fit body, wielding a smart black cane, that called to them. In their movements they gave hints of what they saw, like quiet flightless birds. They did not dance or exercise so much as talk with their hands, their necks, their knees, remembering longer, more abandoned, gestures they had once made.

The room smelled of powder and pads, and the unkind reek of setting lotion. The hairdresser had been that morning to see to the hair of the women. His visit was less to do with appearance than appearances. The old men hid in the smoking room when the hairdresser came, in order to set up their own evil pong.

It was while the perms and sets and demiwaves were taking shape on a Thursday that Mary was able to join Mr Charteris in the pantry.

He had won her with his golden tongue.

'You're new,' he said. 'I always show the new maids the ropes.'

She knew better than to correct his words. A number of them, being old, spoke like old people couldn't help but do. She'd a lot of time for old people. She'd worked in several homes before, though none as exclusive – meaning expensive – as this. Some of them paid their own bills, others got paid for by children, not without a grumble at the end of the month.

Mr Charteris had arrangements, and that was all Mary had heard, though she had heard one old trout call him a 'scholarship boy' and then whinny with the pleasure being unpleasant gives to those who do not fight it.

Mr Charteris continued: 'Any difficulties at all with the other girls, come straight to me. Don't waste your time going to Mrs How's Yer Father or troubling old Oojamaflip.' He twisted the stud under his bow tie and then levelled off its ends. 'There's nothing I can't tell you about the house. Nothing at all. Man and boy I've been here, starting in the carpenter's yard on crack-backed chairs and coming right through till I got where I am now.'

Mary was unsure what a person might want to know about a house, and where exactly Mr Charteris had got to.

'God, it must be old if *you've* been here all along,' she said, and was delighted when he laughed. He had assertive teeth, every one his own.

'I followed on after only five others like myself. That's not many butlers over the two-seventy-odd years. Not that the earlier ones could rightly be called butlers.'

Mary, who understood from the television that butlers were men who stood still, sneered, and talked posh, asked, 'The work can't have been hard, though?'

Mr Charteris considered the mornings of his life when he, at much the age of this girl, had collaborated in the daily launch of the house, cleaned, polished, dazzling, rebegun, all on the sweat of eight men and sixteen girls, repeating with their bodies actions of the most tedious and exhausting kind in order to give a context to the ease of others, like men blowing bottles from the burning roots of their lungs just to hold scent that would waft off an earlobe unnoticed in the breeze.

'I've had a woman in every room of the house,' said Mr Charteris to Mary.

He revisited the house in the way he preferred in his mind, through the oxters and ribbons and stays and mouthings of the Roses, Daisys, Rubys, Violets, Marias and Elizas who had been drawn by him into each room's mystery, so that he understood the attic through Hetty's red hair and startling milky snores, the music room through the stifled tears and later laughter of Lavender as he lowered the music stool slowly beneath her by swivelling the mahogany discs at either side within her skirts, the ballroom by the chilly biting of Daphne as they pushed together inside the curtains, the kitchen through the blissful humming of Euphemia's skin under his mouth, and later through the regrettable harrying of his own late wife.

'Every room?' said Mary, not interested, nor paying attention, really, not having listened, as people often do not to the old. She just couldn't help, being a trained geriatric nurse, running with the feeble thread. When she found it attached to a cunning rope she was caught by her own decency, the first snare.

Knowing well the sunshine it is to be needed, even by someone who means little, and sensing his distinct, perhaps unrepeatable, advantage, Mr Charteris said to Mary, relying on her tenderness and on his own undimmed brown eyes, 'Every room, my dear, except the pantry.'

These afternoons, the little treats of food given privately, the counterfeit tasks undertaken by Mr Charteris in the aftermath of his making good that late omission, went on beyond the one time it would in principle have taken. Who could say whether Mary had not learned from the old man, just before he sank, the radiant satisfaction of domestic habit, that it was not she who escaped from regulation and certainty into the life of the back of the house, into invented duties and words that were as plain and mysterious as the low windows giving out on to the deeps of the park where no one went any more, or not so that it was known?

The back stairs of the house were cool even in this heat. The service lift creaked on its cables down past the stone stairs to Francis, where he stood with the laundry hamper poised on its mobile ramp, ready to load. He pushed the creaking thing in to the lift, and pulled on the cables, calling upwards, 'All yours, Mary.'

He heard her tug and brake on the cables, and ran up the stone stairs to her, ready to pull out the hamper and help her roll it to the laundry room on the pallet on casters that stood ready in the top corridor. The floors were timber, not lino, up here.

'Come and help me sort it if you can spare the time,' said Mary. 'It's beautiful work.'

He supposed at first that she spoke that way on account of having a vocation, as he supposed a nurse must.

But the work *was* beautiful today in the laundry room, its high brief windows letting light in from both sides of the roof, the shelves and wooden floor smelling of dry lavender and lavender wax. Mary and Francis pulled out sleeve after heavy sleeve of laundered white sheet.

'We could do the laundry here if it was brought up to date. There's the room, but no machines. They'd cost. But Lord knows what you cost.'

'It's not rightly me. I drive the van. They wash the sheets.'

'You know what I mean.'

'You look well today, Mary,' said Francis, certain he would not be misunderstood. 'You always look well. It must be encouraging for the residents.'

'Thanks,' said Mary. 'All I am is alive.'

Outside two pigeons skirmished in a lead gutter, the green and pink off their breasts firing through the old glass, their exalted cooing boastful.

'I've a grandmother living at home with me and my friend at the moment. She works with papers. Lately there have been complaints that she's losing her grip. I don't think she is. I think she's being tactful.'

'Tactful?' Mary pushed a pile of sheets to the back of a shelf. It moved with a toppling weight over the papered shelf and then settled against the white wall. 'Who to?'

'In case my friend and I want a bit of space.'

'Do you now?'

'Well, we wouldn't mind *space*. She covers everything with bits of paper. And she brings home worshippers of whatever denomination has irritated her recently.'

'Irritated her?'

'By keeping a messy churchyard. Or, if she can get in, an untidy church. They tend to be rural. She reaches those by bus.'

'She brings them home?'

'Yes, you know. After she's tidied up the place of worship, she attends a service or two and then lures them home. They sit and talk. She draws them out. They frequently return. We've made a number of friends.'

'So she is active and sociable?'

Francis did not like the sound of those words. They described human traits with a functional tongue.

'I love her. When I say we could do with a bit more space, that's all I mean. She takes up a certain amount of room. I want her with us, unless she wants to be away herself. How do I find out what she wants? I don't believe her work *is* slipping. I don't see it. I've only my mother's word for it. Chuck me those draw sheets and I'll go up the steps.'

'You want to know what she wants?'

'I want to know what she wants.'

'Bring her here to look. It's one of the best. The place is beautiful. She could fill her whole room – they get a room to themselves, you know – with pieces of paper. She could have visitors. At least between certain hours. Not in the evening. They get a bath when they want, as long as it's twice a week and they don't use bath oil. That ups the fractures and *that* looks bad. They don't have shepherd's pie every single day. Sister doesn't always open their letters. The toilets have emergency bells that get an annual service. There's a weekly hairdresser. There are socials.'

'It sounds great,' said Francis, his heart flat.

'Yes,' said Mary, 'and it's not free either.'

Francis's grandmother replaced the telephone. She enjoyed the fact that her daughter Kay did not recognise her when she called up in the voice of a learned and exasperated historian or an angry man of letters who had made allowances for an old woman long enough.

Indexing had at last lost its charm for Lavender Maclehose. She had it in mind to get away, and to use the part of her savings she had not earmarked for these two dear good boys.

There was the funeral account tidied up, with the undertaker at last convinced about her plan of having confetti and mimosa – whatever the time of year – and making sure that six dozen pink roses were left behind in the vestry for the cleaner.

'I'm home,' called her grandson. 'Do you fancy a cig while I cut a lettuce?'

'Delicious,' said his grandmother, hoping it would do for whatever he had said. So much of her time now was spent day-dreaming. She had it planned. It would be soon. Her knowledge of rural buses would help.

It was still light in the small garden. Francis cut a pale crinkled lettuce. It left a woody boss, weeping milk. He lit his grandmother's cigarette and looked at the gardens beyond, the wigwams of runner beans with their red flowers, the tipsy roses and tired children refusing to leave their darkening climbing frames.

'Don't ever think you must leave unless it's what you want,' he said to his grandmother. 'We've all the room in the world here for you, you know that. Pretend I haven't said this.'

Pat had brought the perfect dinner for the three of them off the last shift. They sat in the silvery narrow garden. There was cold soup made out of herbs and cream, a cheese the size of a flat iron, and two slices of a kind of berry cake. They burned a khaki candle to keep off the gnats. It was an old citronella candle from the ironmongery where Francis had once worked. They had enough nails for life.

Lavender had taken care not to tidy up in any depth before she ran away. She said goodnight to Pat and to Francis in her usual brusque fashion, even remembering to cross the bedroom floor again and again as she did most nights.

When she was sure they were asleep, she took her grip and left the two letters on the kitchen counter, beside the kettle. One for her daughter, one for the two men.

She closed the door with a dog-owner's stealth.

The street was drenched with dew and lamplight as she walked down it and out towards the bypass.

It was too early for milkfloats, too late for country buses. She walked more quickly than she had for years. With no one to watch her, she was again young as she made her way to the road that led to the house she had known before Kay was born, the house where she had worked so hard she vowed to work with her brain only, ever after, so that she had worked nights to become a housekeeper of books, a spring-cleaner of the alphabet.

She was on her way back to the house that she had come to miss as you miss the use of your young body, the house she was ready to reinhabit at the end. She dreamed as she made her way along the awakening road of working again at the dusting and ceaseless polishing of wood, the testing of the fine furniture to see it was all in working order so that others might use it, others who did not know that on the piano stool where sat little Miss Veronica there had only that morning been a spin and a flurry at the heart of a whirl of petticoats scented with nothing more rare than lavender wax.

ACKNOWLEDGEMENTS

The following stories first appeared elsewhere:

'Shredding the Icebergs', *New Scottish Writing*, Ed. Harry Ritchie (Bloomsbury, 1996)
'Carla's Face', *Flamingo Scottish Short Stories* (Flamingo, 1995)
'The Only Only', *New Writing 3*, Eds. Andrew Motion and Candice Rodd (Minerva in association with the British Council, 1994)
'Those American Thoughts', *New Scottish Writing 1997* (Flamingo, 1997)
'On the Shingle', *20 Under 35*, Ed. Peter Straus (Sceptre, 1988)
'Wally Dugs', *The Devil and Dr Tuberose: Scottish Short Stories, 1991* (HarperCollins, 1991)
'Homesickness', *Storia 4 Green* (Pandora, 1990)
'The Buttercoat', *Independent on Sunday* (June 1997)
'A Revolution in China', *New Writing 5*, Eds. Christopher Hope and Peter Porter (Vintage in association with the British Council, 1996)
'Sweetie Rationing', *Soho Square 2*, Ed. Ian Hamilton (Bloomsbury, 1989)
'A Jeely Piece', *Looking for the Spark* (HarperCollins, 1994)
'Seven Magpies', *New Writing 4*, Eds. A. S. Byatt and Alan Hollinghurst (Vintage in association with the British Council, 1995)
'Strawberries', *A Roomful of Birds: Scottish Short Stories 1990* (Collins, 1990)
'White Goods', *Observer* (6 August 1989)
'Advent Windows', *City Limits* (15–29 December 1988)
'On the Seventh Day of Christmas', *Observer* (1 January 1995)

'Being a People Person', *Revenge*, Ed. Kate Saunders (Virago, 1990)
'With Every Tick of the Heart', *The Catch*, Ed. Peter Ayrton (Serpent's Tail, 1997)
'Pass the Parcel', *Femmes de Sícle*, Ed. Joan Smith (Chatto & Windus, 1992)
'Change of Use', A Bloomsbury Quid (Bloomsbury, 1996)

A NOTE ON THE TYPE

The text of this book is set Adobe Garamond. It is one of several versions of Garamond based on the designs of Claude Garamond. It is thought that Garamond based his font on Bembo, cut in 1495 by Francesco Griffo in collaboration with the Italian printer Aldus Manutius. Garamond types were first used in books printed in Paris around 1532. Many of the present-day versions of this type are based on the *Typi Academiae* of Jean Jannon cut in Sedan in 1615.

Claude Garamond was born in Paris in 1480. He learned how to cut type from his father and by the age of fifteen he was able to fashion steel punches the size of a pica with great precision. At the age of sixty he was commissioned by King Francis I to design a Greek alphabet, for this he was given the honourable title of royal type founder. He died in 1561.

ALSO AVAILABLE BY CANDIA McWILLIAM

A CASE OF KNIVES

Shortlisted for the Whitbread Best First Novel Prize
Winner of the Betty Trask Award

Lucas Salik is a heart surgeon, renowned for performing bold experiments on other people's hearts. Ostensibly chilly, he harbours a secret obsession for his reckless and charismatic friend Hal. When Hal announces his intention to find a wife, Lucas is forced to carry out his most complex operation yet: to engineer the marriage, setting it on a perilous path to failure. But just as things appear to be working out, Lucas starts receiving ominous letters that threaten to jeopardize his intentions, his career – and his life.

*

'A novel of formidable accomplishment'
SUNDAY TIMES

'Elegant and really quite savage ... I welcome this natural successor to Iris Murdoch'
PUNCH

'Poised, startling and innovative, *A Case of Knives* marks the debut of an astonishingly accomplished new writer'
ANITA BROOKNER

'A humane and impressive first novel, unusual in its choice of canvas and challenging in its technique'
TATLER

A LITTLE STRANGER

Daisy needs to hire a new nanny for her son; the efficient and capable Margaret Pride appears to be the perfect candidate. But as Daisy becomes increasingly removed from family life and the nanny becomes more prominent, Daisy begins to notice oddities in Margaret's behaviour and realises that not everything is as it seems.

Masterfully constructed and crackling with tension, *A Little Stranger* reveals that self-deception can be just as dangerous as the deceit of others.

*

'Compelling and unsettling'
GUARDIAN

'Obsession and corruption are the novel's themes ... Candia McWilliam has lost none of the orchidaceous flamboyance that distinguished her first novel'
SHENA MACKAY, SUNDAY TIMES

'There is no doubt about the strength and originality of this talent'
SPECTATOR

*

DEBATABLE LAND

Winner of the Guardian Fiction Prize

Set on a sailing boat as it travels from Tahiti to New Zealand, *Debatable Land* is a story of memory, childhood and longing. On board *Ardent Spirit* are the painter Alec Dundas, escaping a failed relationship; Logan Urquhart, the restless skipper; his troubled second wife Elspeth, who fears Logan is slipping away from her; Nick and Sandro, two marine nomads; and Gabriel, an attractive young woman who captivates the men.

As the ship sails from island to island, the inner dramas of these six disparate individuals spill over into their relationships with one another. But when a storm arrives, they are wrenched from the personal and forced to face the present danger.

*

'McWilliam is an astonishing wordmaster who time and again dazzles the reader'

PENELOPE FITZGERALD, TLS

'Full of startling insight ... just the sort of companion one would want to take on a long journey'

JUSTINE PICARDIE, INDEPENDENT ON SUNDAY

'A very distinguished examination into stability and instability, pattern and memory, and the drifting terror of our lives'

GUARDIAN

*